CW00859757

DARK
STRIKE

SHADOW AND LIGHT
BOOK SEVEN

KIM RICHARDSON

FABLEPRINT

This book is a work of fiction. Any references to
historical events, real people, or real locales are used
fictitiously. Other names, characters, places, and
incidents are the product of the author's imagination, and
any resemblance to actual events or locales or persons,
living or dead, is entirely coincidental.

FABLEPRINT

Dark Strike, Shadow and Light, Book Seven
Copyright © 2020 by Kim Richardson
All rights reserved, including the right of reproduction
in whole or in any form.
Cover by Kim Richardson
Text in this book was set in Garamond.
Printed in the United States of America
Summary: As Rowyn continues trying to make sense of
the changing events and relationships in her life, she
discovers the truth behind Lucian's plans, plans that
could tear the world apart.?
[1. Supernatural—Fiction. 2. Demonology—Fiction.
3. Magic—Fiction].
ISBN-13: 9798650629443

BOOKS BY KIM RICHARDSON

SHADOW AND LIGHT
Dark Hunt
Dark Bound
Dark Rise
Dark Gift
Dark Curse
Dark Angel
Dark Strike

THE DARK FILES
Spells & Ashes
Charms & Demons
Hexes & Flames
Curses & Blood

SOUL GUARDIANS SERIES
Marked
Elemental
Horizon
Netherworld
Seirs
Mortal
Reapers
Seals

THE HORIZON CHRONICLES
The Soul Thief
The Helm of Darkness
The City of Flame and Shadow
The Lord of Darkness

DIVIDED REALMS
Steel Maiden
Witch Queen
Blood Magic

MYSTICS SERIES

The Seventh Sense
The Alpha Nation
The Nexus

DARK
STRIKE

SHADOW AND LIGHT
BOOK SEVEN

KIM RICHARDSON

CHAPTER

1

"Look! A gray hair! A *friggin'* gray hair!" yowled Tyrius, his right paw in the air with what I suspected was a hair pinched between his toes. He stilled, his blue eyes wide, and then keeled over on the kitchen counter on his back, his legs splayed and twitching like a dying beetle. "My kids are going to be the death of me. I just know it. I feel it in my bones."

I rolled my eyes and tore open the box with the word KITCHEN written on it in blocky letters. I reached in and grabbed the first glass, unwrapped the newspaper and tossed the paper on the floor before placing the glass on the kitchen cabinet's first shelf. "That's not a gray hair. That's a white one, silly. In case you've forgotten... you're *covered* in beige and white hair." I grabbed another glass from the box.

"You're overreacting a little. Don't you think? They're just kids. Kids are supposed to drive their parents crazy. Everyone knows that."

Two months had passed since Kora had given birth to four beautiful baby baals, all white, two with Tyrius's blue eyes and the other two with their mother's yellow eyes. I'd seen my share of kittens before, but these were spectacular, with wide, intelligent baal eyes and a giant dose of cuteness.

My grandmother had been beside herself with glee that she could provide a home for this new family. She spoiled them rotten, with freshly cooked meals every day and "Raw meat Fridays."

Tyrius rolled back and sat, his tail curled around his feet. "That's just it. They're not kids anymore. I can do kids. I can tolerate all the sticky paws and drool—even on occasion some furballs. Kids are cute. They're happy to see you. They're all smiles and want cuddles." The cat narrowed his eyes. "But these ones... they're teenagers. They don't listen. They're defiant. They talk back. They think they know everything."

I laughed. "I was just like that once." I thought about it. "Still am."

"Ha. Ha." Tyrius's tail twitched behind him. "They're a bunch of little devils."

"They *are* a bunch of little devils. Demons. Devils. Same difference."

Tyrius's eyebrows dropped over his eyes and his ears lowered. "You're not exactly being a supportive best friend. What happened to 'I'll always have your back, Tyrius' or 'I'm on your side, Tyrius'?"

I let out a long sigh. "It'll be fine. It's just a phase. All teenagers are supposed to drive their parents crazy. It's in their DNA. They'll grow out of it."

"Not soon enough." The cat picked at the nail of his front paw. "Wait till you have your own kids. You'll see. The talking back is especially brutal."

"Well, it's way too early to have *that* conversation with Gareth." I wouldn't want to scare away the elf with baby talk. "Besides, I'm not sure kids are in my foreseeable future. Plus, in my line of work, it's probably a bad idea to even think of starting a family. I wouldn't want my kids to be orphaned before they turn two." If I ever did decide to have a family of my own, I would without a doubt quit the Hunting business at least until they were young adults.

"Speaking of procreation." Tyrius spat out his nail. "Where's that elf of yours? Still selling his drugs over in New Jersey?"

"Herbal medicine," I corrected.

"Tomato. Tomahto."

I pushed the tall glass to the back of the shelf. Twilight Natural Medicine was Gareth's shop that sold medicinal herbs in Hoboken, New Jersey, to anyone who needed it—half-breeds and humans. "He's still debating whether or not to keep his store open in New Jersey or close it and open a new one here in Thornville."

"Well, it would make more sense since you live here now."

I smiled and glanced around the small galley kitchen made up of white shaker cabinets and subway tiles. "It would."

Gareth and I had decided to find a place of our own and move in together. It was the logical next step in our relationship, and we were practically inseparable. It made sense to find a place we both liked to start our lives together.

With my grandmother not getting any younger, I wanted to find a place near her. Turned out, the house across the street from hers was up for rent and I jumped on it as soon as I saw the owner hammering in a FOR RENT sign on the front lawn. In fact, I had run out of my gran's house, yelling, "Don't do it!" and "I'm here!" all the while swinging my arms at the old man, frightening him half to death.

I would have been frightened of me too.

The poor old man, Mr. Wallace, now my landlord, had slipped on the grass and fallen back on his behind, dragging the sign down with him. *Oops.* I'd helped him up, of course. We'd signed the papers that afternoon. That was a week ago.

The fact that it was a rental was even better. Not having to deal with taxes or a hefty down payment, which I didn't have, was a blessing. Renting, for now, was just what I needed.

The house was a small, light blue two-story American Foursquare with white trim and a large front porch. Red, orange, and pink petunias draped from the flower boxes below the front windows, and mature lilac trees flanked the house on both sides.

4

Even though they weren't in bloom anymore, their vibrant green leaves were a lovely contrast with the blue of the house. I would have signed on the dotted line just for the lilacs.

The house had three bedrooms, two of which became our separate offices, and just one bathroom upstairs. It had been renovated over the years, always keeping to its true architecture, and it was a lovely home.

Gareth, bless that sexy elf, didn't mind being so far from his shop and told me he'd be happy with whatever I chose. Good thing he didn't know I'd signed the papers *before* I called him to tell him about the place. *Oopsy.*

And the bonus? The elf cooked *and* cleaned. I'm not lying. Men like that were practically extinct. He was a keeper. I was a very lucky gal.

His father's face, with his perpetual frown, flashed in my mind's eye. Gareth's father was the warden of Imadell, the elven city. I wondered what he'd think of his son, a High-born elf, living with the likes of me, an angel-born with archdemon essence in her veins who was still working out where she belonged. He'd hate it—that was a fact—and the thought brought a smile to my face.

I was no longer Unmarked, an angel-born without the mark of archangels. The proof was that glorious P-shaped birthmark on my neck, which I couldn't stop staring at without grinning like an idiot. I was officially marked and blessed by the archangel's sigil, just like all angel-borns and just like my parents.

Though the archangel Raphael had done it, she'd given me the archangel Michael's sigil, same as Layla's.

Now, with the added protection of the sigil, Layla and I would no longer be subject to demons, greater demons, or even archdemons, like the king of all douches—Lucian. He nor any other archdemon bastard could infuse us with his power anymore. The only reason Layla and I had his essence, why we were Unmarked in the first place, was to help him steal the Holy Grail. Yeah, it didn't turn out as he'd planned. Suck it, Lucian.

Granted, we still had his archdemon essence in us, but it didn't make us bad, not really. Not unless we wanted to be bad. However, it did make us stronger, more resilient to demonic energies. And maybe a little badass too.

Layla and I were both part of the angel-born army. We'd been signed up as Operatives, kind of like a special police unit for the angel-born, with a regular salary. It wasn't a nine-to-five job. It was more of a twenty-four-hour job with a case-by-case approach. The assignments were given to us by our boss, the Head of House Michael.

The first few weeks on the job had been especially busy. Following Lucian's douche move, thousands of demons had escaped through his Hellmouth, and we'd worked around the clock to track down and vanquish them all. My Hunter skills had really come in handy. The other angel-born Operatives had been a little standoffish at first, and I was grateful to have Layla with me so I didn't feel so awkward.

But I'd earned my place there. I'd literally *died* for it. And if the other angel-borns had a problem with me or Layla, they could go screw themselves. Because I wasn't leaving.

Things improved after the third week. Most probably because I'd tracked and killed two hundred and fifty-six demons on my own. Color me impressed. The respect started coming in after that, which was just fine by me.

I folded the now-empty box, placed it on top of the pile of empty cardboard boxes, and moved on to the next one filled with plates.

"Is that more of Gareth's stuff?" the baal lowered himself on the counter, stretching his long, elegant limbs as he lay down. He looked like one of those cat statues in ancient Egypt.

"Yes," I answered. "I never had much of anything."

"I know."

"And most of what I had was destroyed by those werewolves."

"Along with Father Thomas's kitchen."

"Along with Father Thomas's kitchen."

"Well," said the cat. "Now with your new job, you can afford to buy new stuff if you want. But it looks like you won't need to. The elf has enough kitchen supplies to open a restaurant."

I turned to look at the mountain of unopened boxes with the word PULLOMANCY written in bold. "That's what he cooks his elf magic with. He asked me not to touch them until he gets home."

The cat tipped his head. "So… are you going to open them?"

I grinned. "What do I look like? Of course I am." It wouldn't hurt to take a little peek. The elf's magic intrigued me. Now that we lived together, I'd get a real sense of how he *cooked* his magic. He *was* going to teach me. There was no getting out of that one.

Tyrius stopped cleaning his side in mid-lick. "What's that sloppy smile about? If you're thinking about ways to boink the elf on the kitchen counter, I'm going to hurl."

I shook my head. "Don't be gross. I'm just happy. Okay? Can't I be happy for once? I finally have a great guy in my life and a real job. I'm renting this fantastic house. What more can a gal want?" A bigger closet? To eat cheesecake every day without adding any extra pounds? A girl could still dream.

"I'm not used to that expression of 'smiling' on your face is all." Tyrius continued to clean himself. "And you're doing it *a lot* lately."

"So?"

"I'm used to the killer frown or the crazy eyes. You know the ones. This here… it's like a new Rowyn."

"And what?" I pressed my hands on my hips. "You don't like this new Rowyn?"

It was his turn to roll his eyes at me. "I'm just *saying*… if you'll let me. I'm just getting to know the new Rowyn. It's going to take me some time is all."

"Hmmm."

"I mean… you did *die* and returned as a sparkling extraterrestrial. It was a *Twilight* moment without the vampires. That has to mess with one's mind a little."

I dipped my head. "There is that."

Tyrius scratched behind his ear and shook his head. "You were a freaking meat suit, Rowyn. We spent years making fun of them. I even kept a 'Best Of' list."

"I know. I was there." And it was an experience I would never forget. Especially the getting stabbed part, then the dying, and finally the ending up in Horizon, chatting with an oracle. It had been a mind-blowing experience, yes. But it had also been awesome.

The Siamese cat cocked his head. "You think they'll come calling on you again for your services?"

"The angel legion?" I laughed again, reaching down and grabbing a plate from the box. "I think I've died enough times this year. Once was enough. Thank you very much."

A knock came from the front door.

Tyrius jumped to his feet, his ears swiveling around the top of his head. "Demon balls," he cursed. "The celestial cavalry is back!"

The plate slipped from my fingers, but I caught it before it smashed to pieces on the floor. "No. It can't be." Could it?

"It's your day off. Right?" asked the cat. "So, it's not the angel-born needing you to polish their egos. This smells like the big kahunas. Halos anonymous."

I licked my lips, frowning. "They never used the front door before. They've always just *showed* up." And never once invited. Okay, I'll admit angels weren't my favorite celestial beings before. But now that I'd lived in their skin—literally—I'd never feel the same way again. I might even feel a bit of respect, on a good day.

So, why would they show up now?

The baal sniffed the air. "I'm not smelling any celestial farts. But it doesn't mean it's not them. Imodium does exist in Horizon."

I set the plate down on the counter. My heart thumped in my chest as I made my way through the small hallway that opened up to the living room on my left, passed the staircase on the right that led to the second floor, and moved to the front door. I could make out a shadow on the front porch of someone wearing dark clothing, but the privacy glass kept me from seeing who it was.

Something brushed against my leg and rushed past me. "Tyrius. Don't do anything stupid." I glared down at the cat. "Even if it *is* angels. Got it?"

The cat sat next to the door sill and looked up at me. "But stupid is so much more fun!"

Great. "I mean it, Tyrius. Anything stupid, anything at all, and I'm sending you home. To be with your kids."

The cat's mouth fell open. "You wouldn't."

"Don't test me, kitty. I'm getting my crazy eyes again." I took a deep breath and pulled open the front door.

"Father Thomas?" I stared at the priest. He wore his usual dark ensemble of black slacks and a black shirt, the white square of his clerical collar stark against the deep tones. He stood a few inches taller than me with a drool-worthy, athletic physique, and though I'd never actually known his age, I pegged him to be somewhere in his early thirties.

"How's it hanging, Padre?" said Tyrius, and for a moment I thought I heard him purr.

My eyes never left the priest. Something was wrong. His usual handsome features were twisted in fear, showing lines of pain around his eyes and mouth. He looked like he'd seen a ghost. Or something worse. The priest wasn't the type to scare easily.

Father Thomas was a modern-day Templar Knight, a band of priests who waged a secret war against the church's enemies—demons, half-breeds, and other supernatural baddies that posed a threat to the church—which the church hid from the public. They called themselves the Knights of Heaven, and they were a team specially appointed by the church to investigate all the "unusual crimes" that happened in the city and the surrounding areas, specifically New York City.

"What's happened?" I questioned with dread settling in the pit of my gut.

His dark brown eyes flashed with a broken spirit that made my heart clench. "A priest," he said, his voice haggard like I'd never heard before. He sighed and added, "A member of the Knights of Heaven has been murdered."

Oh crap.

CHAPTER

2

St. Joseph's Church, Father Thomas's assigned parish church, was Thornville's oldest catholic church, dating back to the seventeenth century. An architectural stone beauty, it boasted expansive stained-glass windows and gargoyles perched high atop the towers. The gargoyles were my favorite. Some part of me wished they could break free from their stone confinements and come alive, and then we could become friends. Yes. I was a little mad that way. But they were so cute with their claws and teeth and tails and wings. They reminded me of Tyrius, only bigger and without the fur.

One thing was for sure. I'd always enjoyed my visits. Until now.

I stood in one of the many separate offices that branched off from the church's main building at the back and a level up from the main floor. Chairs and side tables were strewn all over the place, discarded and broken and tumbled. Papers littered the floor and books lay in piles at the foot of a tall bookcase as though an earthquake had shaken them all off. An assortment of swords and daggers that could skewer an elephant decorated the wall on the left and gleamed in the morning sun.

Hello, pretties. They were practically begging to be handled, preferably by my calloused, not-so-ladylike hands.

Yes, these priests *loved* their swords. I did too. And I'd kill for a collection like that.

Below a window framed with heavy gold and red drapes sat a wooden desk, fitting the rest of the eighteenth-century-style wooden chairs that were all smashed.

I'd been in Father Thomas's office before, and this one was nearly identical. Except for the fact that it looked like it'd been hit by a hurricane—and the dead priest.

The body lay in the middle of the room, facing up, atop an exquisite burgundy and blue Persian rug that stretched the length of the room. I guessed he was in his mid to late forties with light-colored hair and a short, trim beard. His eyes were closed, and his face was cemented in fear or pain. It was hard to tell. Perhaps both. But I did know whatever had killed him either hurt like hell or scared him to death.

He wore the same black ensemble, snug around a muscled and fit physique, just like Father Thomas. He had no injuries, no wounds, no bruises, and no blood on his body. Not even a scratch. I saw nothing to indicate how he died. But there was no denying this man was indeed very *dead*.

My stomach rolled at the stench of rotten flesh, and I covered my mouth and nose with my hand until my stomach settled. Spewing up my gran's buttermilk pancake breakfast wouldn't do anyone any good. Especially since those were some damn good pancakes.

The choking sewer-smell and sickly sweetness that rose from the body indicated an advanced stage of decomposition. But that wasn't the case. Or at least, that's not what it looked like.

Guessing by the pasty, graying of his skin, the pale lips, the blue fingertips, the body was still in the "fresh stage" of death. In other words, it shouldn't be smelling like maggots were having a meat fest in the priest's innards. Not for another couple of days.

It wasn't bloated, and there wasn't any spillage from the nose or mouth. It was as though it had all the smells of a week-old corpse but none of the physical appearance that should go along with it.

In my line of work, I'd seen my share of dead bodies—some with their skin shredded into ribbons, some with their heads cut right off, and some burned until you couldn't tell if the victim was human or animal. Others were left in pieces, which took a really long time to bag when their parts were scattered all over the city. And yet this one… something was off with this one.

This man did not die of natural causes like a heart attack or a stroke. Something supernatural had killed him.

The priest was one of the elite Knights of Heaven, which meant he was a trained warrior, a killer. He was a slayer with a clerical collar, not the type of man who could be easily apprehended or killed. Think ninja samurai priests and you'd be right.

My eyes went back to the collection of swords and daggers mounted on the wall. Not because they were pretty—okay, *maybe* a little because they were pretty—but because they would have been my first choice if something or someone had tried to kill me. But each iron hook still held its weapon. Not a single one was missing. He didn't even use them. Or he didn't have time to.

Whoever or whatever killed him had been a strong sonofabitch.

Father Thomas turned to me and said, "I wanted your opinion before I call the coroner. They'll think he had a heart attack or a stroke."

I shook my head. "This was no heart attack." There was nothing natural about this death.

"Smells weird," said Tyrius as he moved carefully around the body, stopping and sniffing along the way like a trained police detection dog. A crystal hung from a pink ribbon wrapped around his neck like a makeshift collar. It was a charmed pendant I'd made for him months ago. The spell disguised Tyrius's demon energy from the church and made him appear as a regular cat, hiding his true form and allowing him entrance to the church.

I lowered my hand. "Weird as in... he's decomposing weird?" I asked the cat.

Tyrius sneezed, shook his head, and sat back. "Well, he doesn't smell like roses. I mean, yes, the dude smells like he's been dipping in New York City's sewer system on a hot summer day. But there's something else. Something that shouldn't be. Something... different."

"Like what?" I'd learned long ago to always listen to the baal demon's gut. If Tyrius said something was odd about the stinky rotting corpse's smell, I knew it was in my best interest to listen.

"Mmm." Tyrius leaned his forehead toward the priest's head and took another sniff. "Not sure. I mean... I know I've smelled this before. I know I have... I just... damn it. I can't remember."

"It's all right. Take your time, Tyrius." I felt Father Thomas's eyes on me. I knew we didn't have that much time before the coroner came and the other members of the church started to wander in.

"A demon killed him," said Father Thomas, his voice trembling slightly. "There's no other explanation."

There could be hundreds of other explanations. "That's what we're trying to determine. We don't want to be too hasty and miss something important." Now that I was representing the angel-borns, I didn't want to screw this up.

The priest frowned at me. "What else could do that to a man? Look at him. There's not a scratch on him. Father Martin was one of our best knights. He's killed many demons. Many. I don't understand how this could have happened. How the demon entered the church."

"It wouldn't be the first time a demon sneaked its way inside hallowed ground," I told him.

Tyrius's ears swirled in my direction. "If you're referring to *this* demon, I can assure you, no sneaking was involved. How could I with this pink ribbon wrapped around my neck? I look like a mashed-up version of an Easter Bunny."

The uneasy feeling in my gut tripled. A Greater demon or even an archdemon could have easily broken the hallowed ground wards to kill the priest. Lucian, the king of cosmic douches, came to mind. Granted he wouldn't do anything unless there was something in it for him. That went for all archdemons. The question was why? What did they gain by the priest's death?

"I need another go." Tyrius went back to sniffing along the dead priest's body.

"Who found him?" I asked Father Thomas, discomfort still gnawing at my belly.

The priest clenched his jaw, his eyes brimming with tears. "I did. This morning. I wanted to ask Father Martin's advice about a case I've been working on." His eyes moved back to the body and then flicked away like he was having a hard time believing what he was seeing. He wasn't ready to accept it. Or it was just too painful.

I knew the brotherhood was tight, and I felt sorry for Father Thomas. If I did hugs, I would have hugged him.

"When was the last time you saw him alive?"

"Last night. Around ten p.m." Father Thomas rubbed his face with his shaking hands. "He was here. Alive before I left. He was alive, Rowyn."

I looked around the room at the papers scattered on the floor and books. "So, he was killed sometime between ten at night and eight this morning."

The priest nodded. "Yes."

"Do you know what he was working on?"

The priest shrugged. "Demonic cases? That's what he always worked on—the bulk of his cases. He had an affinity for it."

I moved around the room, careful not to step on any of the books or papers on the floor. I glanced at the old books with leather bindings. *A Priest's Guide to Exorcism, Know Your Demon, How to Banish the Supernatural, Demonology 101 Volume 8*. Well, at least he was consistent. The Knights of Heaven were notorious for their skills in successful exorcisms. Though their numbers were few, they were the best. And now there was one less.

I spun on the spot, taking in the dilapidated state of the room. "His office is totaled. They were looking for something."

"Or that's what they want you to think," commented Tyrius and then he dipped his head and smelled the dead priest's fingers. He jumped back and made a face. "Damn, that's ripe."

Still, in my experience, demons didn't care to stage a crime scene. They came for the kill. For the human soul. They rarely cared about anything else. Unless this was personal and the demon in question had had it in for the priest.

I stepped forward and stared down at the body. "If a demon did kill him, I'm going to need a list of demons Father Martin has recently banished—no, make that *all* the demons he's banished in his lifetime." I knew demons, and they absolutely held grudges. The priest had made many enemies over the years, and if a demon had the chance for payback, I was certain they'd come here to kill the priest.

Father Thomas arched an eyebrow. His dark eyes flickered between me and the dead priest, and pensive lines appeared on his face. "We catalog all exorcised demons and banishments. I can get you all that information later today."

"Good." It was a start.

"It's a long list," said the priest. "Father Martin traveled all over the world, banishing as many demons as he could."

"I understand," I told him. "But it's our best chance at finding which demon did this. Once we know who, we can make the necessary preparations." Like, kill the bastard once and for all.

An energized buzz of voices arose as priests began circulating the hallways.

Father Thomas moved quickly to shut the door.

"Who's going to do the church's investigation?" I asked him, wondering why he didn't want the others to see.

The priest locked the door. "The church will decide. But I'm going to ask to lead the investigation. I still want you to investigate it, Rowyn. You have access to records we don't. And your Hunter skills will be invaluable here. I'll make sure to send your invoice to the church." A shadow crossed his face. He gave the chamber a somewhat disbelieving stare and then shook his head. "This is really bad for the brotherhood. The church has its own set of rules. We can't bend them. I need you on this, Rowyn."

"You've got me. Don't worry." I knew exactly what he wanted from me. He wanted someone who didn't care about *bending* the rules. Me.

But I had the feeling he didn't just want me to bend them. He wanted me to *break* them. I could do that.

Father Thomas's face twitched, and I knew he was struggling with his internal emotions, like all men, because of the "real men don't cry" bullshit. I'd never seen Father Thomas so rattled before, and I didn't like it.

I took a deep breath—as much as I could without inhaling too much of that rotten stench—and knelt next to the body. First I checked his wrists, and then I pulled his collar down and checked the skin around his neck.

"What are you looking for?" Father Thomas leaned over me.

"Sometimes demons leave their mark. A branding, if you will, their killing pattern. They want to take credit for the killing. They want you to know, like a serial killer taunting the detective. Demons and serial killers are very much alike. They're narcissistic. And dicks."

"I can get you some gloves," offered the priest, making Tyrius snort.

I glared at the cat, who pretended to be interested in the dead priest's hair. "No thank you." I gave Father Thomas a tight smile. "The latex would suppress the demonic energies. I need to feel the skin to get a sense of the supernatural auras."

I continued to search around the dead priest's body, checking his ankles, his legs, all the usual spots where demons left their marks. The skin was ice-cold like it had been in a freezer, which was another indication of a supernatural death, but I wasn't getting any kind of the familiar demonic energies. It was as though they were gone. Lifted. But if the priest had been killed only a few hours ago, there should still be residual energies on the body and in the air.

Yet, something else was present.

A sensation I'd never felt before. It was faint. It wasn't cold or warm, it was just... different. But one thing I knew for sure, it was definitely powerful.

My heart sped up a little at the sheer feeling of something new, something dark.

I crab-crawled back toward the head next to Tyrius and checked behind the dead priest's left ear.

"Are you feeling any demonic energies?" asked the priest after a moment.

I settled on my knees, reached over, and turned the head gently to the side to check behind the right ear. "I should… but I'm not getting the usual demonic vibes."

"Me either," said Tyrius. "Totally vibeless. Like there's something blocking out all traces of demon energies on the body."

"I take it that's not normal?" asked Father Thomas as he crossed his arms over his chest.

I sighed and leaned back on my knees. "In my line of work, anything's possible." I checked the dead priest's hairline. "But I'm definitely sensing something."

The priest uncrossed his arms and stepped forward. "What?"

"Like I said," commented Tyrius. "Something's here. I know I've felt it before. I just… can't remember *where* or *what* it is."

I stared at the dead priest's face. His lips were parted, almost like he was trying to tell me something.

"What are you thinking, Rowyn?" Tyrius sat next to the head, his blue eyes gleaming.

The answers were here. I knew they were. And I was going to find them.

I reached over, carefully placed my fingers over the dead priest's right eyelid, and pried it open.

I sucked in a breath through my teeth.

His eye was yellow. The iris, pupil, and sclera were yellow, like he was suffering from a bad case of jaundice.

There was only one reason why the eyes turned yellow.

"His soul was taken," I said after a moment.

I heard Father Thomas gasp. Not only did the demon kill Father Martin, but it had taken the priest's soul. I was used to demons devouring the souls of humans. But there was something profoundly wrong and sacrilegious about taking a priest's soul.

"It's worse than that," said Tyrius.

My heart thrashed against my chest. "Worse than taking the soul of a priest? That's at the top of my 'really wrong' list."

The cat's eyes were wide with concern. "Remember when I said I had felt this before? This *feeling* I'm getting from the body that I couldn't quite put my finger on?"

"Yeah."

"I remember now."

I swallowed hard, not liking the rising tension in his voice. "Tell me, Tyrius. What?"

"A demon didn't kill the priest." The cat waited until he seemed satisfied that he had my full attention and said, "A necromancer did."

Well, crap.

CHAPTER

3

A goddamn necromancer was in my city and had killed a priest. And I knew next to nothing about them. Well, apart from the universally common knowledge of the rising of the dead and all that.

I was clueless. And I hated it.

Clueless did not bode well inside me. As an experienced Hunter, it was my job to know everything there was to know about every supernatural baddie, including necromancers. But the truth was, I'd never encountered one. Ever. Worse, the angel-born Elder Codex database—a computerized program like an encyclopedia for the supernatural—barely had any information about them either. If the angel-born had something on the necromancers, it would be in there.

I was practically blue in the face as Daniel, the angel-born techie who worked the program and served as the expert of the archives, had laughed when I'd called and asked him about necromancers.

"Wait? You're serious?" he'd said after a long moment of silence while I imagined kicking him in the face.

Still being new on the job, I'd bitten my tongue before I'd made the irreversible mistake and cursed him out. So, I opted for my second choice. "You're lucky I'm on the phone and not standing next to you right now. 'Cause I'd kick the smile off your face." You little shit.

That had sobered him right up.

After that, he'd told me basically what I'd already known. Necromancers were humans who practiced a form of magic, Death magic—that was the only new part. Necromancy was a practice of magic involving communication with the dead by either summoning their spirits as apparitions or raising them bodily to bring them back from the dead or to use them as a weapon.

"That's it?" I'd asked Daniel. "That's all there is? Are you kidding me?"

"Sorry, Rowyn, but that's all I've got," he'd answered.

"I could have Googled that."

"Yup. You could have."

"And you call yourselves the experts." I'd hung after that, no point in continuing to attack Daniel. It wasn't his fault the angel-borns did a piss-poor job of collecting more data on necromancers.

I was expecting a lot more from the angel-borns, maybe something that would help me figure out why a necromancer killed a priest and took his soul. From what I understood, necromancers were master puppeteers. They loved to reanimate the dead and use them as weapons. But Father Martin's body had not been animated, not from what I gathered at the scene. No. The necromancer had killed him and left. But why? Why would he or she (because Daniel had also just told me some necromancers were female) kill a priest? What did the person gain from the priest's death?

I needed some answers. Father Thomas needed some answers. He'd been so good to me over the years, and I owed him. Hell, I owed him a new kitchen and then some. I owed him to track down the SOB who'd killed his friend, and then, well, we'd have a little dance of death.

While I was at it, I'd also filed a case number with the angel-born Council regarding the priest's death, thus informing them of the situation and details while naming myself the sole proprietor of the case. No other angel-borns were on it—not yet anyway. My personal connection to Father Thomas made this case personal to me. If the necromancer wasn't afraid to kill one priest, who's to say he or she wouldn't kill another. I wasn't about to let anything happen to Father Thomas. Hell no.

My phone beeped with a text message. I reached over the piles of papers, bills, and books that littered my desk and grabbed it. It was Gareth. I'd texted him the moment Tyrius and I had left the church, getting him up to speed on the necromancer situation and hoping he could shed a little light on this case.

Gareth: *I don't know much about necromancers. I know just as much as you do. They like to play with the dead. I'll call my brother and see if he knows anything. I'm closing up early. Be there soon.*

Me: *You better bring that tight elf ass home.*

Gareth: *Yes, ma'am.*

I laughed and put my phone back on the piles of papers. The thought of his large, manly hands on my body sent a thrill of delicious pricks over my skin. *Focus, Rowyn.*

Right. The naughty thoughts of what I wanted to do to the elf would have to wait.

Moving on…

I pulled my laptop closer, opened Google and typed "necromancers and priests" in the search bar. I scrolled down the usual hits, looking for something that would catch my attention. But after an hour of going over the same bits of information, that necromancers practiced magic involving the dead, I wasn't any closer at finding anything that would help my case.

I rubbed my eyes, feeling the burn from staring at the screen for so long and forgetting to blink.

"Rowyn?" I heard Tyrius's voice coming from downstairs.

"Up here!" I called back.

A few moments later the Siamese cat padded into my office. "Anything?" he leaped up expertly on my desk and walked over to my laptop.

"It's basically the same stuff written by different people." I sighed through my nose. "How are Kora and the kids?"

The cat raised a brow. "Kaia tried to burn Krystal's tail with a match. And Titus thought it would be fun to lock Tyson in the broom closet for two hours."

I let out a snort. "At least they're having fun."

"You call that fun?" asked the cat, exasperated. "It's like a war zone over there. Kora's yelling and throwing things. Gran's shouting and then drinking. You try having your dinner while everyone's throwing around insults."

I reached over and scratched under his chin. "You came over here for some quiet time. Didn't you?"

Tyrius looked a little guilty. "No. I came over because we have a case to work on."

I blinked. "Right." Part of me knew he came here to get some peace, but I knew he also wanted to help me with the new case. God knew I needed help.

"What about the angel-borns?" inquired the cat. "They've got tons of info on all things supernatural."

I shook my head. "Nah. That was a bust. They don't know any more than we do. I did put in a request for further information, if it becomes available, but basically, they've got nothing."

"Sorry, Rowyn. I wish I knew more about these necromancers, but Death magic is rare. I thought it was abolished centuries ago, to be honest. I mean, who wants to play around with the dead? All those maggots and stringy, rotten flesh? It's really disgusting."

I leaned back in my chair. "Yeah, well, there are lots of freaks in the world. Necromancers are just another breed." Another breed I was going to kill.

The baal lay down over my electrical bill and stretched. "Why do you suppose they killed the priest?" He stared at my pen next to him and knocked it down with a swipe of his paw. *Cats. Always knocking things down. What's up with that?*

I reached down and picked up my pen. Twirling it between my fingers, I said, "Why do people commit murder? What's the driving force behind any killing? All murders and killings are motivated by something. Right? Usually it's financial greed, sexual lust, or the pursuit of power."

"You can rule out the sex part," said the cat. "Unless the priest had something going on the side."

I shook my head. "There was nothing sexual about this killing. We would have seen it otherwise. So, that leaves greed and power."

Tyrius flicked his tail. "We all know the church is swimming in cash. And the priest's office was trashed. Maybe they *were* looking for something."

I put the pen to my lips. "Yeah. I thought about that."

"Like what?" asked Tyrius as he casually knocked my yellow Post-it notepad to the floor.

"No idea. I'll have to ask Father Thomas." I reached down, grabbed my Post-it pad and wrote the question on it.

"If you want my opinion," said the cat, "my guess would be power. It's always about power. Especially with magic. You can never have enough of it. These necromancers are no different."

Tyrius did have a point. "Death magic," I muttered. Something occurred to me. "What about the witches? You think they would know more about the necromancers? They practice magic too. Maybe they're like their long-lost cousins or something."

Tyrius snorted and tapped my liquid paper bottle to the floor. "No way. I've lived with my share of witches over the centuries, White and Dark, good and bad. But never, and I mean *never*, would any witch want to be mixed in with *that* lot. I mean, you've got your White and Dark magic, your elemental magic, even blood magic. But nothing compares to Death magic. We're talking about using the loss of life for magic—like the dead are battery-charged. It's twisted. It's sick. Witches don't play with Death magic."

I pursed my lips together. "Maybe some do."

The cat's jaw fell open. "Don't you dare go see that old hag Evanora. I forbid it! You hear me! She put a collar on me and tried to bleed you to death!"

It was my turn to laugh. "I remember." But she had also saved my life. "I was thinking of asking Gareth to pay her a visit. She *loves* the elf. If anyone can make her talk, he's the guy. And if she knows anything about Death magic, it's worth a try."

Tyrius mumbled something under his breath. "Okay. Good. That's good."

My head throbbed with a sudden headache, which I recognized as my body trying to tell me to hydrate. "I need some water." I'd been sitting at that desk for so long even my butt ached, and the right side was practically numb.

I pushed my chair back, slipped my phone into my pocket, and headed down the stairs to the kitchen, rubbing my numb ass with Tyrius padding next to me.

"Okay, so we know a necromancer killed a priest." I opened the fridge, grabbed my Brita water pitcher, and filled my glass. "So, where do we find them? Any ideas?"

Tyrius leaped on the kitchen counter and sat. "At a cemetery maybe? If I worked with the dead, that's where I'd be."

I swallowed some water. "Maybe. But if that's true, I would have seen one by now." Cemeteries were like my playgrounds. I was in a cemetery at least once every two weeks, killing a ghoul who was feasting on the flesh of a newly buried body. It was easy money. "But maybe you're right. We can start here in Thornville's cemetery and ask around. See if anyone saw anything or if any of the gravesites have been disturbed."

"It would go faster if the elf was here," commented the cat. "How long till Gareth gets here?"

I took another gulp of water. "Not for another two hours. Depending on traffic." The thought of the elf had my stomach in butterflies. The fact that we'd been together officially for over four months and he still did that to me was a very good sign.

My phone beeped with another text message, and I pulled it out. "Father Thomas wants to see me right away." I looked up and met the cat's blue gaze. "Says he's got something from the necromancers."

Tyrius arched a brow. "Hopefully it's not contagious."

I slipped my phone back into my pocket. "This is good. Who knows? Maybe we'll have this case solved by the end of the day."

"Ha," laughed the cat, his tail lashing out behind him. "That'll be the day. After what I've seen, these necromancers are brutal. Savages. What we need is a team."

I cocked a brow. "And where do you think we'll find this team?"

The front door burst open.

Layla stood in the threshold wearing a pink and black leather striped body-hugging ensemble, a bustier that pushed her breasts up to her neck, and a wicked gleam in her eyes. Her long dark hair was pulled back in a French braid, and knee-high boots with six-inch heels gave her more height. She looked like an S&M Amazon warrior princess all packaged together.

A black leather whip hung in her hand. And with a powerful thrust, she let the whip rip with a resounding crack.

"I'm ready to whip me some necromancers," she said, beaming.

I laughed. She was the best little sister *ever.*

CHAPTER
4

"Looks like she thought you said you were hunting a *nympho* and not a necro," commented Tyrius, a smile in his voice.

Yes, my little sis was an extrovert, a little flamboyant most of the time, and liked to dress seductively. But that was who she was, and I wouldn't want it any other way. She'd earned the right to wear whatever she wanted. And if you had a problem with it, well, that was *your* problem because she looked fantastic.

My heart clenched at the memory of seeing her on the ground with her blood pooled around her. Layla had accepted Lucian's gift, his darkness, and he'd tricked her into thinking he'd make her all-powerful, when in fact he'd planned to sacrifice her life to complete the ritual he needed to open the Hellmouth.

I'd nearly lost her.

Layla and I both worked for the angel-born Council now, which was why I'd texted her earlier. If I needed someone else working with me on this case, I was choosing Layla. Not because she was my sister—well, okay, maybe a little bit—but because she could kick some serious ass. And, let's face it, she was fun.

Why kick butt while sporting a sour expression when you could laugh your head off the entire time?

My boots clunked on the paved walkway that led to the church's side entrance under an arched oak door framed by lilac trees. "Is Danto working at the club?" The two were usually inseparable, practically sewed at the hip since the very first day they met. Danto owned the V-Lounge, a vampire club in New York City, which also doubled as his place of business.

Layla looked at me intently and said, "He's stuck working out some vampire territorial problems. All I know is they want to merge the New Jersey Court with New York's, and that's got the vampires all riled up."

I frowned at her. "Is it serious?"

Layla's full lips spread into a wide smile. "Nothing he can't handle."

She was right about that. Danto could handle himself and then some. As the Head vampire in New

York City Court, he'd certainly seen his share of rowdy vamps.

"Tyrius. You wearing your crystal?" I'd left so quickly I'd forgotten to check if the cat had the charmed collar on.

The cat's nails bit into the flesh of my shoulder. "If you mean this gaudy, pink, Hello Kitty choker that's giving me torticollis? Then yes. Yes, I am."

A smile tugged at the corners of my lips. "Good." I raised my fist, knocked and pushed open the door, not waiting for Father Thomas or any other priest. Maybe I'd grown bold in my years of working for the church. Or maybe I just didn't give a rat's ass what they thought about me.

I held the door open for Layla, and then the two of us moved inside the church and through a small lobby with wood paneling and antique rugs.

The whole place was sparkling clean, and the air smelled of wood and musty carpets. A distant murmur of voices drifted out as I walked up the flight of stairs and made for Father Martin's private office. The voices grew louder, and they were coming from the dead priest's office. The bursts in sudden pitch told me it was a heated argument, but I couldn't make out what was being said.

"They're fighting?" Tyrius's breath was warm against my cheek as I neared the office. He shifted on my shoulder until he found a comfortable spot. "Priests fight? What the hell do priests fight about? Who's got the bigger clerical collar?"

"Hush, you," I whispered. "Don't forget who's paying us extra for this job."

"Okay, okay. Don't kill the kitty," grumbled Tyrius, making Layla laugh.

I walked into the office just as the volume of voices had reached a dangerous height.

Father Martin's office was exactly like I'd left it, except eight priests were now assembled in it and his body was gone.

A collective silence filtered through the room as the priests all turned and stared at us. Their expressions ranged from shock and disappointment to outrage and anger.

I could deal with the usual sneers and glares of haughty disdain, but I was not prepared for what happened next.

In a blur of black cloth and silver blades, four priests crossed the room faster than I thought humans could move. I blinked at the four sharp swords pointed at my throat.

Impressive. If I wasn't already convinced the moment I moved they'd cut me, I would have clapped.

Tyrius whistled. "I thought the Knights of Heaven were on our side."

I felt Layla brush my shoulder and saw a wink of a silver blade in her hand as she pointed it at the nearest priest's groin. "You touch my sister, and I'm going to castrate you, priest. And it's going to hurt like a bitch."

"Take it easy, Layla." But she had it right. I ground my teeth in frustration. "Uh—Father Thomas?" I called over the priests' heads. "I think you need to call off your dogs." *Before Layla and I cut them into pretty priest fillets.*

At that, all the priests' eyes hardened. Either they didn't like the dog comment, or they could read my mind. Tyrius's nails bit down harder into my flesh.

"Father Thomas asked me to come here," I told the four priests, keeping the conversation going as my heart thrashed in my chest. "I didn't come here to fight. But if you cut me with your pretty swords, I *will* defend myself. I don't care that you're men of the cloth. I will kill you. Don't think I won't."

The priest with short red hair snarled. "Abominations can't enter the church. They will be *removed*."

I raised my brow. "Abominations? Really? Is this how it's going to be? Name-calling?" Growing up as an Unmarked within the angel-born community, I had a master's degree in name-calling. I'd heard them all. Granted, I had thought with my new sigil, my archangel brand, that having the blood of an archdemon running in my veins wouldn't matter anymore. Guess I was wrong.

Waves of heat rushed to my face. "You're starting to piss me off, Red," I told him. "All of you. Out of my way before I make tiny priest cubes with your clerical flesh."

Layla giggled. "Dibs on the bald one," she said, and I heard the excitement in her voice. She was almost shaking with it. She wanted to fight. "He looks like a bleeder."

I laughed. God, I loved that girl.

Red's mouth twisted, baring his teeth to the gums. "You're just a woman."

Oh, he went there. Did he? Okay then. "Well. I'd rather be a woman than a man with the church's collar wrapped tightly around his neck."

Tyrius snickered. "You can't even fart without asking for permission."

I leaned forward until I felt the tip of his sword pierce the skin on my neck. "I've killed bigger, stronger men than you with my eyes closed."

"And with her hands tied behind her back," cheered my furry friend. "And hopping on one leg."

"Oh—wait!" called Layla, and she pushed up her bustier making the girls lift a little higher. "Okay. I'm ready now," she added with a smile.

"Enough." Father Thomas appeared behind the line of attack priests. He put his hand on one of the priests' shoulders, but he was looking at me with a kind of "stop it, Rowyn" expression. "Let them through. I've asked them to come."

Tyrius straightened on my shoulder. "You heard el padre. Vámonos, estúpidos."

For a second, I didn't think the armed priests would listen, but then as one they stepped back and sheathed their swords around their waists, under their long, black jackets. Red took his sweet time, all the while giving me looks.

I batted my eyelashes at him. "Watch out, Red. If you keep staring at me like that, I'm going to think you want to sleep with me." Oops. I couldn't help myself.

Red's face went three shades redder and he turned around, speaking in hushed tones with the bald priest Layla had called dibs on.

After making sure the priests weren't going to pull their weapons on us again, I sheathed my soul blades around my waist and stepped into the room.

I flicked my eyes between the priests. "Looks like we missed the party," I said to no one in particular. "Care to share?"

One of the priests, a big fellow who'd stayed behind with Father Thomas and who could have easily passed for a werewolf, scowled deeply, making his already small eyes smaller. "What are they doing here?" he growled at Father Thomas who'd been flipping the pages of a notepad in his hands.

"I asked Rowyn for help," answered Father Thomas, giving a slight nod of his head in my general direction.

"This is the church's business. You don't have the right to get *them* involved."

I glowered at his use of the word *them*, like we were diseased and highly contagious. Part of me wanted to leave and let the church deal with their own problems. That was until I spotted Layla sashaying her way around the cluster of priests, licking her lips seductively as she circled them. The priests looked like they were in hell.

Okay. I'll stay for a bit.

"We're going to need her help, Father Peter," continued Father Thomas, and he snapped the notepad shut, his brow furrowed. "I've already cleared this with the church."

"That's a demon on her shoulder," said Father Peter. "You know the church's views on that. How could you let that happen? How could you let that abomination enter our sacred church?"

Oh. Crap. So, that's why they were all looking at Tyrius with fury in their eyes and why their hands suddenly got twitchy for the weapons on the walls. It had a bit to do with me and Layla, but the real issue was Tyrius. No matter how cute and cuddly he looked, he was still a demon.

Damn them. They had no idea how wrong they were. Ignorant. I was glad Father Thomas wasn't like them.

Tyrius let out a growl. "Buddy, I hate coming here just as much as you hate me being here," spat the cat, and I reached up and scratched his head for comfort.

Father Peter's expression twisted in revulsion, his eyes on Father Thomas. "The church would *never* permit you to engage with the hypocrites and the sinners. You're putting the church in danger by allowing demons in."

Anger hit me like a red wave. I really didn't like that priest. "If I wanted to let demons in, trust me, I could have easily conjured a few in here. Your church isn't as strongly protected as you might think."

Okay. Not the right thing to say, but he was asking for it.

Father Thomas gave me an exasperated look before turning his attention back to the priest. "I think Father Martin would want us to do whatever it took to find his killers. Don't you think? If that means hiring extra hands to do it, that's exactly what I'm going to do."

Ah-ha. Father Thomas the rebel. I had the feeling he hadn't asked the church for permission to involve us, or rather, involve Tyrius. Naughty, naughty. I liked him even more.

"Looks to me like Father Thomas is the odd one out," said Tyrius.

"Looks that way." Yup, he sure looked like the church's black sheep.

I bit down a laugh as Layla bent over to adjust her boots, knocking into one of the priests with her round butt. She was having way too much fun.

"Layla, stop scaring the priests," I teased.

She straightened and pushed up her bustier with both hands. "I think they're afraid of my breasts. But it might be my vagina."

Father Peter glowered at me, all sour and dour. "I think I'll have words with Cardinal Vannelli," he told Father Thomas. "You'll be looking for a new parish when this is over."

Father Thomas's face darkened but he said nothing as the other priest stormed past him and out the door. After a moment, all the other priests upped and left with Layla blowing kisses after them.

I walked over and stood next to Father Thomas. "I'm sorry. I didn't know the welcome committee would be so unwelcoming."

Father Thomas drew in a slow breath. "This is not your fault, Rowyn. I asked you to come."

"But you didn't check with the church first. And now they're pissed at you." The last thing I wanted was for the priest to lose his position because of me. This was not how you paid back a priest for bailing you out of tight situations over the years.

"I found something," he answered, totally not answering. He flipped open the notepad he'd been holding the entire time. "Here." He pointed his finger on the page. "It says—"

"Temple," I read, seeing it written in bold letters in the margin and circled a few times.

Layla appeared at the priest's side, practically leaning on him. "What else does it say?"

"I've been reading his notes," informed Father Thomas. "He was investigating the necromancers. I don't know how he figured it out. There are six of these notepads. I haven't had time to go through all of them yet. Not with all that's been going on here. I had to make arrangements to have his body transported to the morgue." He stared at the ground, his dark eyes pensive and sad.

Tyrius leaned forward on my shoulder. "Don't worry, Padre. We've got you."

Father Thomas fell quiet and then moved toward the desk where five more of the similar notepads were spread out. "He was definitely working on something.

I don't think any of the other priests knew. Some of the records here date back a few months."

I followed the priest to the desk with Layla right next to me. "He must have found something important enough to have these necromancers want to kill him." Enough for a necromancer to come to the church, kill the priest, and take his soul.

Father Thomas nodded. "Yes. I believe that's true."

"Yeah, but what?" asked Tyrius and then he leaped off my shoulder and landed on the desk.

Layla opened one of the notepads, her fingers flipping through the pages. "Maybe it's written in the rest of the notes."

"I think it has something to do with this." Father Thomas showed me the notepad again.

Two words were circled on the page. "*The Passage?*" I read out loud. "What do you think it means?"

The priest pressed his lips tightly together. "I'm not sure. Some ritual, perhaps? If he had confided in me," said the priest. "I could have helped him. Maybe this," he raised his arms, gesturing around the room, "might never have happened."

"Don't do that to yourself," I told him, speaking from experience. "It'll just make you feel worse, and it won't bring him back. He chose *not* to tell you. He had his reasons. Maybe because he knew it would put your life in danger. Obviously, he was close to discovering something about the necromancers. I don't think just knowing about them was enough to get himself killed. He was onto them."

Tyrius sniffed one of the notepads and then looked up at me. "About what? What can a priest do to a bloody necromancer? Exorcise him?"

Good question. "I don't know yet. But with some time, I can figure it out." I looked at Father Thomas. "Do any of the other priests know anything? Because if they do, their life might be in danger."

The priest shook his head. "No. I don't think Father Martin shared his investigation with anyone else. I asked the priests, and they seemed just as shocked as I was at these findings."

Layla pulled herself up on the desk and sat with her legs swinging. "Unless they lied to ya."

Father Thomas cut her a glance but said nothing. He clenched his jaw, his thoughts racing behind his dark eyes. Interesting. Looked like some tension was brewing among the Knights of Heaven. If I were to guess, it looked like they didn't trust Father Thomas. Maybe to the point they'd keep valuable information from him.

I wasn't stupid enough to think that if I asked Father Peter, he would willingly give me some intel on whatever Father Martin was working on. If he knew something and didn't tell Father Thomas, no amount of begging would get me those answers.

"Maybe he confronted the necromancers with something," commented Tyrius as he began to sniff the next notepad. "A dirty necromancer secret got him killed."

"Possibly." I picked up one of the notepads and flipped through it. Every line was jammed with the priest's handwriting. I had to read the first sentence three times before it made any sense. It would take days to go through it all.

I placed the notepad back on the desk. "Well, it won't do any good to speculate who knows what and who told whom without any real evidence or a motive." I met the priest's gaze. "So, this temple. Any ideas where it is?"

"Yes." Father Thomas flipped the pages of the notepad in his hand. After a moment he pointed to the middle of a page. "In Fairview. He speaks of a building on the outskirts of the cemetery."

"That's got to be it. We should check it out." My insides jumped in excitement. Good. We were getting somewhere.

Layla jumped off the desk and landed with her arms straight in the air above her head like a gymnast. "I knew this was going to be an awesome day."

"I'll keep reading these," said the priest, his shoulders tightening with added tension. "They should keep me busy for at least a day or two."

"Let me know if you find anything," I said, feeling the thrill of the hunt stirring in me. "What do you want me to do if we find a necromancer?" I knew what I'd prefer to do, but this was the church's—or rather, Father Thomas's—business, and since he was paying me for Hunting the necromancer down, he was the boss.

The priest's expression was locked into something just shy of a grimace, and his dark eyes burned with pent-up aggression. He looked like he wanted a fight and would gladly jump on the first opportunity to get into one as his eyes moved to the rack of weapons on the wall.

He said nothing for a long time. "Bring him here."

I gave a nod, not bothering to mention that the necromancer could also be female. Some of the nastiest villains I'd faced in my lifetime were females. "You've got it," I said, feeling marginally better now that we had somewhere to go. The idea of smacking around a few necromancers made me all giddy inside.

I rubbed my hands together and smiled at Tyrius and Layla. "Looks like we're going to crash a temple."

CHAPTER

5

Fairview was the next town adjacent to Thornville. Though I'd been there before, I didn't know it well enough to ignore my loyal GPS. With the three of us in my Subaru, and Tyrius riding shotgun on Layla's lap, by the time we arrived at the local cemetery, it was half-past seven at night. The dark skies blanketed the surrounding cemetery in long, moving shadows, adding another level of creepiness to the eerie cemetery.

I slowed down when I hit Old Wellington Drive and drove past the cemetery until the headstones ended where a line of tall trees emerged. The graveyard backed up to a dense forest of vast oaks and ancient pines. Through the trees was a clearing, and in the middle sat a single building.

"That's got to be it," said Layla, having spotted the building. She shivered and looked over at me, beaming. "I've been dying to try out Danto's new gift." She tapped the whip at her waist and giggled. *Interesting gift.*

Tyrius coughed out a laugh. "I've gotta see this."

I parked my subbie at the curb, and we all clambered out.

The building didn't look like a temple or a church. It had a flat roof and no windows from what I could see. It looked like a giant, rectangular cement block with nothing spectacular or indicative that a group of Death magic practitioners congregated there. If I didn't know where to look, I would have driven right past it.

Knee-high grasses and weeds swayed in a breeze. An old, overgrown and crumbling brick walkway led from the street to the temple, and it didn't make me feel any better.

"That's a necromancer temple?" asked Tyrius incredulously as he came around and stood next to me. "Where's all the death memorabilia and heads on spikes? Looks more like a prison."

"It kinda does." Come to think of it, it did look like a prison. I could even make out a chain-link fence surrounding the building. We might have to cut our way in.

I moved to the back of my Subaru, popped the trunk, and grabbed a rusty set of bolt cutters.

The cat snorted. "You look like you've broken out of prison before. Care to share?"

"Gareth gave me these," I said, and the thought of the elf brought a smile on my face. "Thought I could use some tools. You know, just in case." I grabbed a large black duffel bag stuffed with some more of Gareth's old tools and showed the cat.

"A girl can never be too prepared." I dropped the bag as I shut the trunk and locked the car.

After I checked my weapons belt, I turned to face Tyrius and Layla. "Do we need a plan before we go in there, or do we just wing it?"

Tyrius shrugged. "My mind went blank at the mention of wings… big, fat, juicy, barbecue chicken wings. Why are we here again?"

"I was thinking," I started again. "Before we go in there, we have to have some sort of plan. We can't just go in and take them over with our killer looks." I wondered if Layla's tight clothes might work in our favor if they were indeed all male. But then again, so were the priests, and they had all looked mildly embarrassed at the sexuality that oozed from her.

Layla planted her feet, her hands on her hips. "We do what we always do. We go in. We kill. We get out. Easy peasy."

I grinned. I was so proud of her. "Usually, I would have to agree with you."

"But these turds are humans," commented Tyrius. "You can't just go in there and blast them to pieces."

"Why not?" laughed Layla. "I'm really, really good at it."

I gave her a weak smile. "Well, for one, Father Thomas needs to question them. So, we need to bring one back—preferably the one who killed the priest—still in one piece and alive. I don't want a necromancer bleeding out in my car. And Tyrius is right. We're not allowed to kill humans without a legitimate reason."

Layla gave me a pout. "Even if they're really, really bad?"

"Yes."

Her pout deepened. "But we have proof that necromancers killed the priest. You said so yourself. The yellow eyes?"

"Yes, I did. And you're right. But we don't know how many are in there or if they're all involved."

Tyrius hissed. "I bet they are. Necromancers are tight, from what I remember. You hurt one of them, and they all come after you like a plague."

"Maybe. But we need to be smart. No killing—"

"But some hurting, right?" asked Layla, and she made a show of pulling out her new whip.

"Yeah, I guess a tiny bit of hurting should be fine."

Layla let out a squeak, an ecstatic and entirely creepy expression of joy lighting her face and a strange, almost homicidal gleam in her eye. Oh, boy.

"Onward!" Tyrius jumped up and stood with his right leg pointing and his tail out straight behind him like a pointer dog.

I tried not to laugh as I followed the Siamese cat down the path. He seemed more interested in leaving his scent every few feet than getting us to the building.

We hit the fence, and the gate was unlocked. So I yanked the gate door open and tossed the cutters to the ground. I'd pick them up on our way out. We slipped through the gate and continued on the path.

When we were about twenty feet from the building, I felt it.

A rush of energy swept through and around us, cold and foul and thick. My insides twisted with sudden nausea, causing my skin to riddle in goosebumps. Dark, dangerous magic churned, drawing my attention to the temple's facade. This was the same cold energy I'd felt next to the dead priest— a kind of magic that destroys, rots, and corrupts.

"You feel that?" asked Layla. Her back stiffened in trepidation, and from the worry etched on her face, I knew she was thinking of Lucian and what he'd done to her.

"Yeah." I didn't stop walking and kept an even pace as I made it to the front of the building. Or was it the side? It was just a wall of cement. Weird.

I walked over to the left side of the building. It was the same. No windows. No doors.

"Maybe this is the back of the temple?" offered the cat.

"Let's go around the other way." I marched through the tall grasses until I hit the end of the building, which was maybe a hundred feet and turned. The rest of the temple was an even cement wall.

"What the hell is this?" I growled. Frustrated, I ran the length of the back of the building and then jogged the entire right side, seeing no windows, no doors, and no point of entry. Nothing. It was as though someone had poured a giant concrete box.

"How are we supposed to get in if there's no door?" Layla had lost some of her sass and her expression was tight.

"There's got to be a way in. If the necromancers can get in, so can we." I pressed my hand on the cement wall and then wished I hadn't.

I hissed in pain and yanked it back.

"You okay?" Layla grabbed my hand and examined it. "It's not burned. You're not burned."

I pulled my hand away. "I'm fine. It was like... like the wall bit me." Now I'd never imagined speaking those words. This was a strange night.

"It's a glamour," informed the cat, and I noticed he was keeping his distance. "A powerful one. I can't even see through it. I think only the necromancers can."

"Great." I rubbed my hand on my jeans, feeling as though I should wipe off whatever had bitten me.

Tyrius looked up at me. "Maybe we should call Gareth."

"You think he could help?"

The cat tipped his head. "His magic is different. It's worth a shot."

He was right. I pulled out my phone and called the elf. "He's not answering." I slipped my phone back in my pocket. "We'll have to figure out how to get in without him."

Tyrius put a paw on my leg and gave me a level look. "Rowyn. I don't know how else we *can* get in without some sort of magic. Maybe we should call it a night and try again tomorrow."

"No." We'd come all this way, and I wasn't ready to give up when Father Thomas needed my help. "There's got to be a way—"

"Someone's coming," hissed Tyrius, the fur on his back standing up and his blue eyes flashing with blue demonic energy.

Layla and I both dropped to the ground. Crouching, I whipped my head around toward where Tyrius was staring, my heart thrashing in my chest. Through the tall grasses, I saw a figure marching up the same walkway we'd just used.

I pointed to the bushes behind us. "There. Hide!"

The three of us crouched-ran to the nearest brush. Well, just me and Layla, which is a lot harder than it looks when you're not used to running on all fours. Using the thick brush as a cover, I raised my head. The figure hadn't broken its pace. Male, from the sheer size of the shoulders, he wore a heavy black cloak and cowl that hid any possible details of appearance—how original—with a swirly symbol etched on the front that was impossible to decipher in the folds of the cloth.

"You think he saw us?" asked Tyrius, lying next to me with his fur tickling my cheek.

"We'll soon find out." But I didn't think so. He wasn't looking in our direction.

"Let's get him," said Layla, the smile returning to her face and her eyes wide with excitement.

"Are you crazy, woman?" hissed Tyrius. "That's a necromancer right there."

Layla raised a skeptical brow. "Rowyn and I can take care of a little human."

"A little human who can do Death magic? You have no idea what he's capable of. You want to take that chance?"

"Yes." Layla glowered at the cat, looking like she'd want nothing else but to use her whip on him. Great. This was just what I needed.

"He has a point," I said, keeping my voice low and my eyes on the necromancer. "They don't draw their magic from demons, like witches. You and I have more resilience when it comes to witch magic. This is different. They're different." I had no idea what to expect, but I wasn't leaving without at least some answers or a necromancer in my grip. I wasn't about to let them hurt Father Thomas.

I watched as the necromancer turned from the front and moved to the right side of the building until his back was to us. He raised his hands, and though I couldn't see his face, I heard the whispers of a chant. A wild, whirling wind rose around the necromancer, catching his robe and billowing it around him. The air had the sudden stink of sulfur and rot.

"Something's happening," I whispered, not daring to blink to not miss anything.

The wall facing the necromancer shifted and rippled, as though it were made of water. And there, standing before the necromancer was a simple black door.

Layla shifted next to me. "Come on, Rowyn. There's just the one. We're not going to get another chance." Her eyes gleamed. "I'll distract him while you knock him out from the back."

"No."

"Why not?" she questioned. I heard the frustration in her voice as the necromancer pulled open the temple's door, his frame backlit by the yellow light that spilled out.

I let out a steady breath, feeling bold and a little crazy. "I want to know what's inside," I answered, making Tyrius curse. The necromancer slipped through the opening and disappeared behind the door.

Adrenaline rushed into my body. "Quick, before the door disappears!" I urged, and I shot forward through the tall grasses toward the temple's door.

CHAPTER
6

I'd never actually been in a temple. Scratch that—I'd never actually been in a *necromancer* temple. So, of course, I had imagined all manner of zombies and other dead things crawling around inside. I hadn't expected it to be empty and cold.

The cold hit me like a sledgehammer, and it was suddenly all I could do just to keep from shrieking in surprise and discomfort. It was worse than stepping into a morgue, which I'd done multiple times. It was walking into a freezer and staying there for over an hour. Yeah, friggin' cold.

These bastards were humans, so how could they stand it?

We found ourselves in a hallway consisting of the same cement that made up the exterior. Flaming torches lined the walls, giving us enough light to see our surroundings. Despite the numerous blazing torches, their fire didn't seem to ease the coldness of this place. I let out a breath and was even more surprised it didn't come out in swirls of white mist.

Apart from the freaking cold, the scent of death was all around us, a giant dose of it as though somewhere inside this temple were thousands of rotting corpses. Nice.

With my heart in my throat I eased the door closed, feeling a slight roll of magic over my skin. I listened for any sudden movements as well as the tread of the necromancer we'd followed in. Nothing. I couldn't hear a thing apart from my heart thrashing in my ears. And nothing but shadow was visible at the end of the hallway. That necromancer was long gone. But I was going to find him.

"Demon balls. It's like a friggin' freezer in here," grumbled the cat. "I can't feel my ears. I think my ears fell off."

"It's not so bad." Yeah it was, and it was an effort to keep my teeth from chattering. I looked over to Layla whose shoulders were bare because of her bustier. At least I was wearing a shirt over a cami. However, Layla didn't seem bothered by the cold. She wasn't shivering in the least. The woman was too hot-blooded.

"Makes you wonder if these guys are actually human. Doesn't it?" said the cat, his voice echoing

59

softly. "Humans are not resistant to cold. Their bodies aren't made that way. And that dude who went in wasn't exactly dressed for his tour in the Arctic."

"That's true." His cloak was heavy, but he'd need something warmer if he stayed inside the temple for longer than five minutes. So, what did that make them? Half-humans? Something else?

"You think they're demons?" Layla yanked out her soul blade, and I noticed she'd fastened her whip on her waist. You could whip a demon, but you needed a blade to kill it.

I shook my head. "I'm not sure. We won't know until we face one." I took a breath. "But we better start moving if we don't want to end up like angel-born popsicles."

Tyrius snorted. "Where to?" asked the cat, and I noticed his fur had puffed up around him. It looked like it had magically thickened, as though he'd magicked himself a thicker coat.

I pulled out a soul blade and glanced down the hallway. "Follow the smell."

"I never thought I'd hear you say that," muttered the cat, a hint of a smile in his voice as he bounded forward with Layla following closely behind him.

Okay, so I didn't have much of a plan once we got inside. I still wanted to question these necromancers and find the bastard who'd offed the priest. Yet, I knew just being inside the temple was a breakthrough. We needed information. I wanted to see with my own eyes what these necromancers were about. Maybe this house tour would help us figure out what they were up to because the bad guys were always working out plans.

As we moved deeper into the temple, there were no other doors or hallways. Just one straight hall led us to a set of stairs that gave way to a lower level ending in shadow. The temple had a prison vibe, and I couldn't wait to get the hell out.

Tyrius froze. "You hear that?"

I halted next to Layla and listened. "Voices," I answered, hearing the faint but undeniable drift of voices. Though too far to make out what they were saying, I definitely heard more than one.

"Let's go." After a glance over my shoulder, and seeing no necromancer about to jump us, I gave Tyrius a thumbs up and we all climbed down the stairs.

With every step, the voices grew louder, my heart thumping to match. Darkness grew, and I flattened myself on the wall, using the shadows to conceal myself as much as possible.

When we reached the bottom, we found ourselves passing into an open space beyond, like an atrium, at least two hundred feet long and about a hundred feet wide. Stone walls about twenty feet high lined the long sides of the rectangle while the far end boasted a dais. Pillars rose from the bottom, supporting the uneven walls of the cavern amid mounds of collapsed earth and beams that looked like they'd been added in way before the temple was built. The temperature had dropped another five or ten degrees. The voices were louder, but they were mumbled, and I couldn't figure out what they were saying. The scent of rot and the feel of death were overwhelming. Dread knotted my gut, but we'd made it this far. I was not going back without something.

I motioned to Tyrius and Layla to follow as I ducked and crawled behind one of the pillars and glanced down for a better look.

The ground was a mix of hard-packed earth and winding roots. Ringed around a black marble altar were twelve black-robed figures. Necromancers.

Their cowls were drawn back, and I could finally look into the face of a necromancer. The faces were gaunt and thin, like they hadn't had a good meal in years. The group was of indeterminable ages and sexes. I'd been right. Women were here too, but that didn't have my tension rising. What was resting on the altar made my heart pound.

A young woman, by the looks of her, lay on her back, her naked body stark against the dim light. I couldn't see any bonds around her wrists or ankles, but it didn't mean she wasn't tied down. They could be using their Death magic to keep her there. She blinked, looking up at the earth ceiling. She was alive.

Tyrius climbed up on my shoulder. "Demon balls," cursed the cat, his voice low enough for only Layla and me to hear. "They're going to sacrifice a virgin."

Thick incense wafted up from flaming braziers around the circle, giving the cold air a sharp scent of sulfur mixed with some other foul smell I couldn't place.

"I've seen this movie," I whispered. It was like I'd just stepped into the *Indiana Jones and the Temple of Doom* movie to the scene where Indy, Willie, and Shorty had stumbled upon the Thuggees who were sacrificing human lives to the goddess Kali. The movie was a classic and one of my favs, but *this* was real life.

One of the male necromancers' voices rose in pitch to something audible.

"We offer you this sacrifice, Master," expressed the necromancer. "An offering to the new enlightenment that will begin." The bones of his face were sharp and gaunt, and the light of the braziers reflected off his bald head. I pegged him for their leader. He might look old at first glance, even frail from his thin hands, but I didn't get that impression. He stood straight and tall. His voice rippled with vigor and command, and he stood like a man who owned the room—a man with all the power and strength.

Maybe *he* had killed Father Martin.

Layla brushed up against me, her eyes on the woman below. "We have to save her." Her dark eyes were full of fury as they moved around the necromancers, narrowing further into sharp little chips of ice.

I squeezed her arm gently. "We will but not yet." Yes, that's exactly what I was thinking too. But I needed more. Just a little more.

"We offer you this life," continued the necromancer, his voice a slow chant whose words twisted and writhed through him. "Let it stop the flow of life into death. To commence the flow of death. Let The Passage begin."

"So shall it be," chorused the other necromancers together, making my flesh rise in goosebumps.

"What the hell have they been smoking?" murmured Tyrius.

I had to agree. What was this nonsense? Though drivel it might be, I still wanted to hear more about "The Passage." Father Martin had written it in one of those journals. I had a feeling it had something to do with the priest's death.

The necromancer leader broke the circle and moved toward the altar. When he raised his hands, a dark dagger hung in the right one. Damn. He was going to kill her, like, right now.

"They must have drugged her." Tyrius's voice drifted into my ear. "Look. She's not even resisting. Probably so out of it she has no idea they're about to slice her open and offer her innards to this master of theirs."

"In death, we shall rise," chanted the necromancer leader.

Great. Not more of this end-of-the-world crap.

"Blood will be spilled. Death will be eternal, and balance will be restored," continued the necromancer, his chant flowing smoothly from his mouth in an unbroken stream.

"So shall it be," repeated the other necromancers in unison. *Once was creepy enough, thank you very much.*

The necromancer leader then placed the dagger in the woman's hands, surprising the hell out of me.

"Umm. I might be way off in my sacrificial wisdom and all," commented the cat. "But… the virgin doesn't usually have a dagger. Right?"

"Right." What was going on? I'd heard the necromancer leader. He'd said they were about to sacrifice her, her life. If *he* wasn't going to kill her, what was the dagger for?

The air grew tight and heavy with sudden energy, a power that was gaining momentum and growing into a feral, raging current. Shadows rose from the ground near the altar like specters, faceless, and hovering, and I counted ten. I had never seen shadows like that before. They gave me the heebie-jeebies.

"What *are* those?" whispered Layla, and I heard the rising tension in her voice.

I shook my head, unable to look away. "No idea." But I had a feeling that whatever *they* were, they were here to kill that woman.

"Rowyn," urged Tyrius, his nails biting into the skin around my shoulders.

"I know." I looked around for a staircase or something that would lead us to the lower level, and the only one I could see was straight across from us. It would work.

"This way," I pointed and spun around.

By the time I'd felt the presence behind us, it was already too late.

CHAPTER
7

A necromancer stood facing us. A male. And an ugly one at that.

For a second I thought I was staring at a ghoul. His face was pale, almost paperwhite. His eyes were sunken, making his cheekbones stand out like he'd never had any flesh there to fill them out. Ever. The skin on his face was wrinkled, as if he'd spent most of his life out in the sun without getting a tan, which would totally suck. He had no hair on his head, no eyebrows, and no eyelashes. He stood about six-two, thin, and again, I wasn't fooled by no meat on his bones. These guys practiced Death magic, whatever that was. I had a feeling I was about to get my introductory course.

Excellent.

The necromancer's dark gray lips twisted into a sneer. Pale eyes watched us, the same way a kid might ogle a candy store. My warning flags went up.

"Blithering, necromancer balls!" cried Tyrius. "I never even felt him coming."

With Tyrius still on my shoulder, I stood up slowly and took a step away from Layla to give us both ample room to fight this ugly sonofabitch. He was just the one, after all, and I felt a little foolish and bold. I was more than a bit pissed off that these guys had killed a priest.

I gave him a toothy grin. "I'm really diggin' the Voldemort vibe."

The necromancer's face didn't even twitch. He didn't even blink.

"I don't think he knows who Voldemort is," the cat said to my ear, making Layla laugh.

I shrugged. "His loss."

When I looked over my shoulder, all the necromancers were looking straight up at us. Awesome. At least they'd stopped whatever ritual they were performing. I still needed to save the woman.

Those creepy shadows were gone too. That was a win for us.

I looked back at the necromancer and noticed the red symbol on his black robe. He was the one we'd followed in. He must have seen us, which meant he let us follow him. He *let* us inside. I was starting to feel like the idiot who'd led her friends into a trap.

He watched me and then moved his gaze over to Layla, sizing her up. A slow and creepy smile spread over his face.

"Two little mouses caught in a trap," he said, his voice surprisingly normal and almost dull. Yeah. It was a trap. *Rowyn, you idiot.*

"Who you calling a mouse, freak," growled Tyrius, his fur bristling around him. "And it's *mice*, not *mouses*, you illiterate douche."

The necromancer's nostrils flared like he was taking in Tyrius's scent. "A witch demon. We have uses for you."

Fury surged and I lifted my soul blade. "You come near my friend, necromancer, and I'll shove your intestines down your throat. Yeah. That's right. I know what you are."

When the necromancer smiled again, he showed me his yellow, rotten teeth. "Blood will be spilled. Death will be eternal, and balance will be restored. So shall it be."

"So shall I kick your bony ass," I said to him, and Layla clapped her hands together. *Love her.*

The necromancer stood there smiling. He looked way too confident with us being three against one. I didn't like it.

"He doesn't have a weapon. Look at his hands," muttered the cat.

I didn't want to. The dude's hands were skeletal with dirt-packed yellow nails like he'd been gardening. Only these guys didn't marvel in produce. They marveled in the dead.

He was cocky to be without a visible weapon. It could only mean one thing.

He was about to pull some of his Death magic.

I pointed my blade at the necromancer. "You can stand there and keep smiling if you want, but we're going to go down there and get that woman. And then we're all walking out of this hellhole."

The necromancer never stopped grinning, and I finally understood why.

The shuffling of many feet sounded behind me.

I spun around, my soul blade gripped in my hand.

As the wall of lumbering people neared us, I counted about a dozen. Empty, staring eyes in sunken, deathly, mindless faces. The chanting of the necromancers had been replaced by the grinding of dead joints and the padding of dead feet. They had vague human forms, echoes of who they once were with gaping mouths, guttural wet cries, and unintelligent moans. Bones clicked through necrotic flesh as they advanced, leaving a trail of dirt, maggots, old blood, and mud in their wake. Nice.

Worse, they looked juicy and fresh... like they were still decomposing, as though they'd only just clambered out of their graves.

Necromancers' puppets. The necromancers had risen the dead.

Tyrius adjusted his weight on my shoulder. "Zombies."

"No shit." It explained the pungent smell of rot in this place. It made me wonder if the zombies had been here the whole time.

There was a loud crack of a whip, and I turned to see Layla's eyes bright, looking positively excited at the prospect of killing some zombies.

"A hundred bucks goes to the one who kills the most zombies," she announced, a soul blade in her left hand while her whip hung in the other.

I smiled at her. "You're on, sis." My smile widened at the frown on the necromancer's face.

"Kill them," commanded the necromancer.

And then, as one, the animated dead things rushed forward.

CHAPTER

8

I didn't have my zombie 101 manual with me, not that I had one, and not that it would have come in handy at the moment. We all saw the movies. No one started reading manuals when a herd of zombies was after them. That would be dumb.

So, how do you kill zombies? By cutting off their heads or sticking your blade into their brains. Yeah, Hollywood had it right. Without the use of their brains, they were just a rotten meat suit. The necromancers needed the dead things to have brains to control them. No brain. No control. No problem.

Tyrius leaped off my shoulders. "Come on, you bursting blisters! You maggot-infested puppets!"

The baal demon planted his feet, and his body shimmered with an internal light as he readied himself to Hulk-out and change into his alter ego—a magnificent black panther.

I looked over my shoulder at the necromancer as I pointed my blade at him. "This is just a temporary setback," I warned him. "I'll be seeing you soon, Morty." I had to give him a name. I needed to know what to call him before I killed the skinny SOB.

The necromancer just stood there, his expression blank. These guys were weird.

A loud growl shook the temple, and I spun around. Where a Siamese had stood seconds ago was a three-hundred-pound black panther. Now that was a *big* kitty.

"Mine!" cried Layla as she vaulted at the nearest zombie, a dark-skinned male, with her weapons high and a mad look in her eyes.

It was really hard to take her seriously when she looked like that.

The herd broke away into a loose fighting formation, and some shifted toward me, reeking of undead and hungry for blood.

Okie dokie.

As they neared, I felt a cold, evil magic cling to them, fueling their rage. The necromancer magic. Their Death magic.

A female zombie with half her scalp missing charged me. I ducked and rolled. My blade slid into the flesh of its gut. A dark blood gushed out from its from front, and the sudden spilling of rotten innards plopped to the floor with a sickening suction sound.

"Okay. *That* was gross."

Never stopping, I jammed my blade through its ear and pushed into its brain. I yanked out my blade just as another zombie lunged at me.

I rocked back and then swung my soul blade across the zombie's throat, putting all my weight into it.

The zombie's head vanished, replaced by a spray of ugly, rotten gore hitting me in the face and all over my front. Great. The zombie's body thrashed for a second and then fell drunkenly to one side, collapsing into stillness.

I wiped some of the zombie blood from my eyes. "Can't say I've missed this."

"Two!" came Layla's happy cry and I caught a glimpse of a zombie's head slip to the ground as she yanked back her whip, managing to slice the dead thing's head right off as though she'd used a sword. That was one sharp whip.

I heard a growl to my left and whirled around.

Tyrius, the black panther, leaped into the air and tackled a zombie that had flung itself at me. He met it with an ugly sound of impact. The panther and the animated corpse dropped to the floor. The zombie rolled up on its feet and charged at Tyrius, but the panther lunged and got his massive teeth into the corpse's neck. He shook his head violently while the zombie stumbled and reeled under the ferocity of the attack. With his powerful jaws, Tyrius clamped down on the thing's neck. In a horrifying snap, the head popped off and rolled to the ground in a spray of blood. Tyrius let go of the body and then he lifted a great paw and slammed it down on the head, crushing it.

Attaboy.

A moan brought me around. Another zombie bypassed the herd and reached out for me, its horrid mouth gaping open.

I sidestepped, lunged, and grazed its chest with my soul blade. I missed. The zombie spun around, and I winced as it scratched my throat with its decomposed, gnarled nails. Yikes.

I leaped back. "I'm not sure if I should be impressed that you managed to miss that or disgusted at the way you smell like you're sweating feces."

"Uhhggghhh," groaned the zombie as it shuffled forward.

"Uhhggghhh," I mocked and rammed my soul blade into its throat, severing the arteries and slicing through the bones of its neck. The zombie's mouth gaped open, spewing dark blood. I jerked my blade back and shoved it into its frontal lobe.

I kicked it in the stomach and the zombie dropped to the floor.

"Five!" I heard Layla's excited shout over the groans and moans of the remaining zombies. Dark blood spotted her face and chest, staining her pretty outfit. She caught me looking and grinned. She even took the time to give me a little wave.

The woman was mad.

Two zombies rushed me at once. No rest for the wicked.

I plunged my blade right into the nearest zombie's open mouth, sliding smoothly between its upper palate and up into its brain. I yanked my blade back just as the other zombie hit me.

I staggered to the side but kept my blade swinging. I sliced into the gut of the other zombie with a wet sucking noise, giving me a show of its intestines as they slipped through the cut like giant spaghetti noodles. Nice.

I barely had time to brandish my blade again as the undead came at me, hissing and snarling like a wild beast. The undead thing flailed around wildly, striking with heavy sweeps of its arms. I spun and sidestepped, coming up around it from the back, as I plunged my blade into the back of its head.

I jerked my blade back when the zombie sagged to the floor.

Panting, I took a moment to look around. Tyrius was sitting on the ground, washing himself with a pile of zombies at his feet. The zombies' faces had been crushed and torn until they were no longer recognizable as something that had once been human.

All the zombies, or rather, what was left of them, lay in crumbled piles on the ground. They weren't even twitching. The herd was finished.

"You owe me a hundred bucks," said Layla, her eyes gleaming with a feverish glee and her chin dripping with blood that wasn't hers.

The hall was drenched in blood, and so was I. The other thing I noticed was that Morty was gone. No big surprise there.

I heard something metal hitting a hard surface and rushed to the edge of the cavern's walkway to glance down. The woman was on the ground next to the altar, the dark dagger still in her hand.

Shit. I didn't know if those things would come back and kill her. I'd missed my chance at a wringing a necromancer's neck, but I wasn't about to let an innocent die.

I looked at Layla and Tyrius. "Come on. She needs our help," I urged and then took off running along to the walkway. I made it to the other side and leaped down the staircase two at a time.

When I got to the altar, the woman was on her feet with the dagger pointed at her chest.

"Whoa, there," I said, slowing to a stop. I sheathed my blade and raised my hands. "It's all over now. You're safe. Just… take it easy. Okay? Give me the knife." If I was cold in this place with clothes on, this woman would be a human popsicle if we didn't get her out of here soon. First, I needed to get that sharp knife away from her.

Tear-filled eyes looked at me. "You *ruined* everything!" spat the woman, her back stiff and her eyes angry.

Okay. I was *not* expecting that. A thank you, maybe? "Excuse me?" She was obviously delusional. "I just saved your life. Clearly, you're on some heavy drugs and have no idea what you're saying." I didn't want to have to argue with a naked, heavily drugged woman. Yet her eyes were clear and sharp.

Layla came around to my left side. "What's going on?" she asked just as Tyrius appeared on my other side.

"I'm not sure," I told her. At the sight of the black panther, the woman's eyes widened, and she took a step back, the dagger shaking precariously close to her middle.

I put my hand up and gestured at the panther. "Tyrius. Stay right there. Okay, kitty?" I didn't want to freak the woman out more than she already was. God knew what drugs they'd given her. The panther tipped his head in response and stayed where he was.

"Listen," I said, turning back to the woman. Looking at her more closely, she was a bit older than me, maybe thirty, with brown curly hair and large hazel eyes. "Just give me the knife, okay? It's all over," I said again. "They can't hurt you anymore."

The woman let out a laugh. "Hurt me?" Her face was set in a wide and manic smile. "You should have minded your own business, you stupid bitch." She pushed the tip of the knife against her chest. "I'm offering myself to Death," said the woman importantly, like I was supposed to know what that meant.

Layla snickered as she sheathed her soul blade and whip at her waist. "The crazy naked lady is all yours."

I frowned at the woman. "Enough with the stupid pills, lady." I held out my hand. "Now, be a good girl and give me the goddamn knife."

The woman held up her head in defiance. "Blood will be spilled. Death will be eternal, and balance will be restored. So shall it be."

"Give me the knife," I ordered again, my patience running out.

"Blood will be spilled."

Okay. I'd had enough with the crazy talk. So, I did what I had to.

I slapped her. Hard.

The woman's head snapped back to the side and she stumbled. She turned back to face me and said, "I *am* going to die. It's what I was born to do. You can't stop me."

"Watch me." I slapped her again and shook her for good measure. "Snap out of it! Are you crazy? You don't want to die for these Voldemort wannabes. You want to live. Living is good."

The woman laughed even though two large handprints marred her face. Mine. Were my hands that large? "My life belongs to Death," she said, importantly. "Who are you to take it from him?"

"Rowyn Sinclair," I informed her and slapped her again.

This time the woman stumbled back, and when she looked up at me again, her eyes burned with fury. But then her face went calm, and her hands twisted on the blade's handle, preparing to stab herself.

She was going to do it. I believed it. I also didn't have time for this crap.

I made a fist, leaped forward, and punched her hard on her right temple.

Her eyes rolled into the back of her head and she went limp, crumbling to the ground as the dagger slipped from her hand.

I reached down and picked up the blade. As soon as my skin made contact with the metal, I felt it. The blade sang with a cold, buzzing power, reminiscent of the necromancer's energy. It didn't feel vile or ominous in my hand, just… different. It was pretty to look at. And the more I stared at it, the more I realized it wasn't forged from metal but of a gleaming black stone that looked a lot like glass. Very, very pretty. And now it was mine.

I looked at the unconscious woman on the ground and said, "So shall it be, you crazy bitch."

CHAPTER
9

By the time we made it back to the church, it was close to midnight. We'd wrapped up the crazy woman in a spare blanket I had in the back of my Subaru and laid her across the back seats.

The plan had been to grab a necromancer—which didn't happen—so the next best thing was the naked crazy woman who'd wanted to sacrifice herself to Death, which didn't settle well with me.

I didn't want her to know where I lived, so the only other logical place was the church. I'd already called the priest and told him what happened in great detail. When I was done, he'd suggested we bring her to the church, which was fine by me. Father

Thomas's church was also a sanctuary for all things supernatural, so it made sense to take her there.

I drove up the church's parking lot and killed the engine. A man with a dark fedora and a long black trench coat leaned against the lamppost, his hands jammed in his coat pockets.

"Look, the elf's here," said Tyrius, his paws on the dashboard. The kitty had changed back to his Siamese self so we could all fit in the car. Then he'd curled into a ball on Layla's lap and slept the whole way to recharge. His Hulk-out had drained him.

I opened my door and Tyrius jumped out before running over to the elf. "Dude, you just missed the zombie fight of the year!"

"Zombie fight?" Gareth came over to the car as Layla and I clambered out. He eyed me, his eyes rolling up my jeans to my splattered top and face. The light cast a shadow over the elf's face, making him mysterious and uber-sexy. His dark brown hair peeked under his hat, which hid those cute pointy ears. I wanted to nibble them.

Concern creased his features.

"Don't worry," I said. "Not my blood." I gave him a smile. "Long story." I opened the back passenger door. "Can you help me with this woman? She doesn't look it, but she's a heavy one."

"Don't forget crazy," reminded Layla as she crossed her arms. "She was about to kill herself if Rowyn hadn't stopped her. Total nutjob."

Gareth leaned inside the car. "What did you do to her?" he asked as he pulled away.

I shrugged. "I might have *accidentally* knocked her out."

The elf squinted at me. "You accidentally knocked her out?"

"That's right. I tripped and then I accidentally made a fist and accidentally hit her on the head."

Tyrius snorted. "Good one."

"Thank you." I took a bow.

Gareth raised a skeptical brow and then reached in, carefully pulled the woman closer, and lifted her in his arms. Her head lolled back against his big, strong arms. I was totally turned on at how strong he was but also a little jealous I wasn't the one in his arms. It looked comfy.

I frowned. "You're making it look way too easy." It had taken Layla and me lots of cursing and sweating and yanking just to get her up the stairs and out of the temple. It didn't help that she'd been naked the whole time.

"Just get the door." Gareth strolled towards the church's side door as though he wasn't carrying the weight of another human being in his arms.

"I'll get the door," said Layla as she jogged ahead of the elf with a spring that shouldn't be possible in those six-inch heels.

"Come on, lazy butt," prompted Tyrius as he padded forward to catch up with Gareth.

When I got to the door, Father Thomas was already there holding it open for the elf.

"Hurry," urged the priest as he cast his gaze around the neighborhood, though I didn't know who would be up at this hour and watching the church.

The priest did a double-take at the state of me, not Layla because she'd managed to mysteriously wipe off the blood from her face and clothes during the car ride over here. Me, well, I looked like an extra in a b-rated zombie movie—the first ones to die, you know the ones.

"You should see the other guy," I said, smiling and hoping to lift the mood. He didn't smile back. Now I felt like an idiot. It's not like I had time for a change of clothes and a shower. I would have to smell like zombie guts. Yay me.

Feeling a little self-conscious, I wiped my boots on the grass. It was the best I could do.

We all went inside, and Father Thomas led us to the back and up to the level where the offices were. The priest was practically running, and I was very curious when he ushered us inside his office, shut the door, and locked it behind him.

"Put her here." Father Thomas pulled out one of his upholstered chairs with a chunky cushion in brown leather. His expression was grim.

Gareth did as the priest instructed and laid the unconscious woman in the chair, careful not to pull on the blanket that hid her nakedness. We all crowded around her as her head continued to loll to the side. She was still very unconscious. I must have hit her harder than I'd thought. Double whoops.

The elf reached out and squeezed my hand. I squeezed back.

"I'm going to need to ask her some questions," said the priest. His expression was tight, and he kept curling and uncurling his fingers. I'd never seen him so agitated. He'd always been cool and collected, and if I were to guess, he looked a little freaked out. I didn't like it.

"No problem." Before I could stop her, Layla smacked the woman across the face, grabbed her shoulders and shook her hard. "Wake up! Wake up or I'm going to smack you again."

It did the trick.

The woman's eyes fluttered open though her gaze was distant and unfocused. She blinked a few times and when her eyes settled on me, she frowned.

I smiled at her. "There you are. Did you have a nice nap?"

The woman glowered at me and then looked around the room. "Where am I?"

"Somewhere safe," said Father Thomas. He grabbed an identical chair, placed it in front of her, and sat down. He leaned forward on the edge. "What's your name?"

The woman shifted in her chair and gave a short laugh. "You're going to be sorry." Her eyes moved around us. "You're all dead. They'll be coming for you now. You just wait."

"That's nice." I moved until I was right above her and leaned over. "How about you answer the nice priest before I play not-so-nice on your face?"

"Yeah," said Layla as she blew a large pink bubble. The bubble burst. "What she said."

"I've got to see this." Tyrius chortled and leaped upon Father Thomas's desk for a better view.

"I'm not telling you anything." The woman's smile was twisted, but her eyes were clear and bright. "You'll just have to kill me."

"Right. And finish the job for you? Not going to happen." I knew her death meant something—a spell or some ritual—but I wasn't sure what. Either way, I wasn't about to help it along either. I crossed my arms. "Gareth. If you please."

Layla took a step back as the elf pulled out his right hand from inside his jacket. Light pink dust spilled from his closed fist.

The woman's eyes widened at the sight of the elf dust. "What is that?"

"Truth dust," answered the elf.

"Stay away from me." She leaned back in her chair, looking like she was getting ready to bolt. Which was a stupid idea because I *would* stop her.

That defiance I'd seen earlier in her was replaced by fear. She inched forward in the chair.

With a flick of his wrist, Gareth flung the dust over the woman.

Pink settled on her like a burst of faerie dust. The woman flailed her arms in the air and around her face in an attempt to escape the dust. Too late.

She coughed. And coughed again. Then she settled back in her chair with her eyes closed and her face scrunched up. When she opened her eyes again, her expression was blank and her eyes were distant like she was in a hypnotic state, staring at something that wasn't there.

"What's your name," repeated Father Thomas after Gareth had given him an encouraging nod.

The woman stirred like she was trying to recall something. "Cynthia."

"It's nice to meet you, Cynthia," said Father Thomas, his voice controlled, though his shoulders were tight with tension. "Can you tell me what you were doing in the necromancer temple tonight?"

"I was offering myself to Death," said Cynthia, her voice calm and collected like she was commenting on Father Thomas's pretty furnishings.

But the fact she had offered herself freely as a sacrifice wasn't what had my blood pressure rising. The way she referred to death, as though *death* was a thing or a person, was very disturbing.

The priest edged forward. "Why? Why would you do that, Cynthia? Every life is precious. Every life has a purpose."

Cynthia blinked. "My life has a purpose. To offer it to Death. It's why I was born."

Yikes. I shared a sidelong glance with Gareth. His quizzical brow told me he was just as in the dark as I was.

Father Thomas took a deep breath. "Can you tell me what would have happened if you had offered your life tonight?"

Cynthia took a few slow blinks. "Let it stop the flow of life into death. To commence the flow of death. Let The Passage begin," she said in a monotone voice. "Let it commence in the flow of the river, of life and death. Blood will be spilled. Death will be eternal, and balance will be restored. So shall it be."

"Again with the crazy talk," muttered Tyrius. "She's missing some seriously big screws in that seriously empty head."

The priest studied her face, and I could tell he felt sorry for her.

I leaned closer. "Ask her what 'The Passage' means."

"Cynthia," said Father Thomas, "can you tell me about this passage? What is it exactly? What does it mean?"

Cynthia stared blankly at the priest. "I'm not supposed to tell."

The priest looked up at Gareth. "Is your dust still working?"

"Yes." Gareth bent over and took a closer look at Cynthia. "I gave her a large dose. She should be very willing to answer your questions. It could be just a repressed emotion. Or that they've put a blockage on that part of her. But that's really hard to do."

"Ask her again," I urged, hoping a little more encouragement would loosen her tongue. We hadn't fought a herd of decomposing corpses for nothing.

The priest turned and faced the woman. "Cynthia. I'm your friend. Friends tell each other everything. Don't they?" he said with a huge, sincere smile. He reached out and grabbed her hands in his. "I'm your friend, Cynthia. And you are my friend. So, you see… you can tell me."

Nice. Looked like the priest had had some practice with this before.

"Yes," said Cynthia. "You are my friend."

I nearly let out a laugh when I caught Layla staring at the priest as though she'd never seen him before.

Father Thomas hesitated. "That's great, Cynthia. You're doing great. Now. Tell me about The Passage. What does it mean?"

Cynthia's lips parted and she said, "The Passage will begin when all life ceases to exist. Life will pass into death. Then there will be balance."

I shook my head. "I still don't get it."

"Me neither." Tyrius stretched on the desk. "I'm hungry. You got anything to eat in this joint?" Tyrius opened his mouth again but shut it at the glare on my face.

Father Thomas looked up at me. "It must be just the journey in which all lives must pass when they die. Which is what most religions believe. The travel from life into death."

"Hmmm. Maybe." I wasn't so sure. I was more inclined to think it was more ominous than that. We were talking about necromancers, a group of psycho humans that animated the flesh of the dead.

The priest turned his attention back on the woman. "Cynthia, who said you weren't supposed to tell?"

Cynthia swallowed and said, "The High necromancer. Lord Krull."

I frowned. *Lord Krull.* I'd never heard the name. But then again, I didn't know much when it came to necromancers.

"Is he the one in charge of the others? Is he the one who asked you to sacrifice yourself?" asked Father Thomas.

Cynthia nodded. "Yes."

I moved to stand just above Cynthia. "Is the High necromancer the one you referred to earlier as Death?" I figured it would be easier if I asked her directly.

"No," answered the woman, and I felt a chill roll up my spine and settle around my neck.

"Is Death a person?" I tried again. Maybe he was above this High necromancer, the one who called the shots.

Cynthia shook her head slowly with her brows wrinkled. "No."

I looked to the priest, who was frowning, before turning back to Cynthia. "What *is* Death?"

Cynthia stilled and then blinked. "Death is the Master. Death is everything."

"Great." I rubbed my eyes with my hands. I knew something was there, either something she couldn't tell us because she didn't know or something she didn't understand.

"Cynthia." Father Thomas squeezed her hands. "Why did the necromancers kill Father Martin? Did he know something about them? A secret, perhaps?"

"I don't know," said the woman, and a frown creased her features.

Gareth cut me a glance, his eyebrows low and skeptical, and I gave him a shrug. I knew what he was thinking, that maybe this was a giant waste of time. Perhaps I should have listened to Layla and grabbed the necromancer instead.

"She's not exactly helping us." Layla rested the palms of her hands on the desk. "Maybe we should have left her there."

Part of me agreed with her. But the other part still needed questions answered.

I knelt next to Cynthia and touched her arm, imitating the priest's gentle manner. "Cynthia. Do you know what the necromancers want? What they want most of all?"

The woman smiled for the first time. "Yes."

Good. We were getting somewhere.

Father Thomas snapped his attention to me and then gestured for me to continue with my line of questioning.

"That's great, Cynthia," I soothed, trying to smooth my features in what I hoped was a friendly look. "Can you tell me what that is? I think I've forgotten." Tyrius shot me a look and I shrugged. I had to try something.

"To fulfill the prophecy," the woman replied.

I moaned through clenched teeth. You'd think I'd be happy with that answer. But I wasn't. Anything to do with prophecies usually resulted in lots of lost lives and one or two idiots who believed they were the "chosen ones." The night was just getting better and better.

I licked my lips. "Cynthia. What *is* the prophecy?"

The woman's hazel eyes met mine and she said, "The Death Walker will break down the wall between life and death. Then the dead shall rise."

Awesome.

CHAPTER

10

The following morning we raided the necromancer temple. And when I say "we," I mean, me, Tyrius, Layla, Gareth, Father Thomas, and ten of his Knights of Heaven. I hadn't expected to find the necromancers there, and I'd told Father Thomas as much. But he was acting on the church's orders, and they wanted to bring down these false worshipers.

Just as I had expected, the necromancers were gone. We'd spent two hours going through all the rooms and the underground tunnels Tyrius had discovered through a hidden passageway, finding only what was left of the zombies we'd obliterated, some rats and spiders, and lots and lots of flies. Gross.

The necromancers had taken all the evidence. There were no papers, no books, no ritual cups or even a single candle left. They'd wiped the place clean. Gareth was going around sprinkling his elf dust on banisters and doorknobs looking for prints. If one of these necromancers had been arrested before, he or she would be in either system—human or the angel-born. But so far his efforts had been futile. Nothing. The necromancers had been meticulous and organized. It told me this wasn't the first time they'd left in a hurry.

The Knights of Heaven insisted on taking pictures and cataloging everything. Layla and I did the same, partly because we didn't want to look like we weren't helping, but we also needed to document the case file I'd opened.

"I've finished doing my rounds," came Tyrius's voice.

I looked away from the altar I'd been investigating, which was the only evidence the necromancers didn't take with them. Probably because it weighed a few hundred pounds.

"Your rounds?" I asked.

The Siamese cat pranced towards me, tail in the air, and leaped upon the altar. "That's right. I've marked every doorway, every corner, every nook and cranny of this disgusting place with my scent."

I raised a skeptical brow. "Tyrius. Did you pee on the necromancers' stuff?"

He beamed. "You bet I did. Twice."

I let out a laugh, which awarded me some pretty nasty looks from a few of the priests who were investigating some of the runes and sigil markings on the ground. I had already taken pictures of those, and I'd look into them later. No need to get too close to the priests who had drawn swords on me. I wouldn't forget that.

The cat licked his paw and proceeded to rub his face. "I don't think the priests like us very much."

"We have that in common," I said, my gaze moving toward them.

Father Peter's face was screwed up in a permanent frown whenever I was around. He stood next to Father Thomas and away from the other priests in some heated discussion, if I were to guess by the hard expression on Father Thomas's face.

"I don't care what they think. I care what Father Thomas thinks." Father Thomas was my friend and ally. I'd do just about anything for him. Father Peter? Well, he could kiss my you-know-what.

"You think Cynthia will be all right?" Tyrius's voice was pitched low. "I mean… I know she's pretty messed up, but maybe with some counseling she could turn out okay."

I looked at the cat and pocketed my phone. "I don't know. She seemed pretty brainwashed. Someone with such a strong conviction without the help of drugs or magic says to me that she was indoctrinated at a very young age. Possibly her entire life. But with Father Thomas looking out for her, I'd say she has a pretty good chance of getting better." I hoped.

Father Thomas had informed me that he and the church would look after Cynthia. He said he would give her the best treatment out there, whatever that meant. I didn't trust the other Knights of Heaven, but I trusted Father Thomas. I knew he would do the best he could to help that poor woman—though part of me thought it was already too late for that.

The cat sat on the altar and cocked his head. "Well, at least it wasn't a total bust. She did tell us the name of the High necromancer and this supposed prophecy they believe in. Better than nothin'."

"True." I sighed and looked over at Gareth, who was now sprinkling some gold dust on the ground near the cluster of priests with a strange smile on his face. He caught me staring and winked. Naughty elf. He was just doing that to get a rise out of them. I could just kiss him right now.

"Well. It's definitely not as cold as before," noted the cat. "Why do you think that is?"

"I think it's a direct link to their magic." I wasn't positive, but it made sense. "Now that they're gone and took most of their magical supplies, or whatever they use to conjure their Death magic, the temple's temperature is back to normal." I could still sense some residual magic but just barely. The necromancers were long gone.

"Where do you think they went?"

"No idea." My gaze moved back to Father Thomas who'd darkened two shades since a few moments ago and looked like he was about to rip off Father Peter's clerical collar. "Maybe that's worth another chat with Cynthia. We could ask her."

"Guys!" Layla came rushing down the steps, which she managed to make look effortless and sexy. The priests all turned her way. She glanced at them when she hit the bottom and blew them kisses and finger waves.

"What?" I asked, seeing Gareth making his way toward us.

Layla's face was flushed when she reached me. "Outside. I found something really weird."

"Weirder than this place?"

"Oh yeah." Layla's eyes tightened at the edges. "But you need to come look."

The elf came up to us. "What is it?" He stood with his hands in his pockets, studying Layla with calm, intelligent eyes.

"There's a trail in the woods," said Layla. "The trees are marked with strange symbols and some have these scary amulets hanging from their branches."

"Where does the path lead?" asked Gareth.

Layla shook her head. "I don't know. I didn't make it that far."

"It's a start." I looked to Tyrius and Gareth. "Let's check it out."

The four of us left the temple and headed outside. I was glad for the fresh air. Anything was better than that rotten, stale air in the temple.

"Where, Layla?" I asked, making my way through the tall grass.

"Here." Layla rushed to the first line of trees directly behind the temple. "In here. This way," she urged, and we all filed in behind her.

As soon as we broke through the first line of trees, I saw the path. It was rough, and anyone could have missed it if they weren't looking, but it was definitely a path. There were flat stones here and there, but it was mostly hardpacked dirt. The path took us under a long line of birch and ash trees, the branches reaching low and tugging on my hair in places. After two minutes, the path became more obvious, clearly laid out as a route and not some wildlife path.

The deeper we went, the darker it got, and it felt more like it was late in the evening instead of barely eleven a.m. The air was cooler, and I noticed I couldn't hear any chirps from the birds or cries from angry squirrels telling us off for being in their territory. I always knew to trust animals. If they didn't come to this part of the woods, it could only mean they were afraid of it. Evil lurked here.

I pushed some branches out of my face and kept on the bit of path I could see as Layla led us on. She'd replaced her pink and black outfit for an all-black one that was leather, though it looked painted on, like a one-piece leather jumpsuit. She had on the same stiletto boots yet hadn't tripped once. The woman was a walking, high-heeled miracle.

The air intensified with a sudden raging, cold energy like I had sensed back at the temple. All my warning flags were sailing in a thunderstorm.

"There," said Layla pointing at something hanging from a branch.

I moved next to her and peered closer. A stick figure hung from a thin strand of rope. The figure was made of rope and bones, really tiny bones, and contorted to make it look like a person. Its limbs were twisted and it had a knot of rope as a head with no features. Tiny runes were painted on it in brown that looked disturbingly like dried blood.

"Creepy," I said, staring at the strange voodoo doll-like bone figurine. I didn't peg necromancers to practice voodoo or anything similar, but then again, I still knew next to nothing about them.

Gareth brushed up against my shoulder. "Looks like voodoo magic."

My eyes met the elf's. "You think the necromancers are dabbling in voodoo?"

The elf shrugged. "I don't know, but you don't put it on display like that just for the birds."

"If you find that creepy... you're gonna love this."

I turned at the level of alarm in Tyrius's voice and jerked my gaze at what the cat was pointing to.

"Damn." An entire section of the trees was covered in those creepy dolls, like ornaments in a nightmarish version of a decorated Christmas tree. What was worse than creepy? Sinister. There was something sinister about these ornaments. I yanked out my phone and snapped a few pictures to show Father Thomas later. He would want to know about these.

"Told you it was weird." Layla moved to a nearby tree, her hand extended like she wanted to touch one.

My breath caught. "Don't touch it!" I cried and grabbed her hand back. "Could be cursed or something."

Tyrius sneezed and shook his head. "Yeah. Could turn you into a necromancer puppet."

The thought of my sister ending up as one of those zombies had bile rising in my throat. That was never going to happen. Never.

"Maybe they're a warning?" said the cat. "To scare the wandering mindless human away?"

"Well, whatever they are, they're freaky. Let's keep going." I yanked out my soul blade and trudged forward. Now I was leading the group. If something evil was out there, I wanted to be the first thing it saw before I cut off its head.

After five minutes of lumbering through the trees and bushes on a trail that was barely there, Layla stopped and whirled around. "This is as far as I went."

I turned on the spot, seeing only more trees and more of those creepy necromancer bone and rope dolls.

Tyrius brushed up against my leg. "Where to? You want to go back?"

"No. Let's keep going," I told them. "You don't decorate a path like this if it doesn't lead to somewhere."

"True," answered the cat. "Come on, y'all. Let's follow the creepy voodoo doll road!" Tyrius padded forward like a bloodhound on a scent.

I followed the cat with Layla right behind me and Gareth taking up the back. I had no idea where we were going or what we could expect when we reached the end if there was an end. We weren't exactly prepared for a hike in the woods either. The last thing I needed was for us to get lost.

The deeper we went, the more ominous the forest felt. It was almost like it had eyes, like it was watching us and didn't like what it saw. Without the natural sounds of animals and insects, it was as though the forest was holding its breath in anticipation of what it was about to do next.

Light rose around us. The density of the forest thinned, and we stepped into a clearing of tall grasses.

In the middle of the clearing was a barn made of old weatherworn wood with two large hay doors at the front and no windows. It was the ideal place to hide something, far away from prying eyes. Maybe a weapon.

"What are you thinking?" Tyrius's blue eyes glistened up at me.

"The necromancers are hiding something. We need to see what's in there."

"Rowyn, wait!" shouted Gareth, but I was already sprinting across the field.

The image of Father Thomas dead on the floor fueled me with a surge of adrenaline. I would *not* let that happen. Whatever weapon was in there, I was going to destroy it. You could bet your necromancer ass I would.

I rushed through the tall grass, happy to be out of the dense forest, with a breeze rustling through my hair.

My heart was slamming against my chest when I reached the barn. The hay doors were locked with a simple iron latch. Angling my soul blade still in my right hand, I placed my hands on the latch. But a strong hand jerked me away.

"What's the matter with you?" Gareth's face was twisted in anger and fear. "We don't know what's in there."

My anger bubbled up but died at the real fear I saw in his eyes. Fear for me.

"I know… I just… okay, yeah, not smart." He had me there.

Tyrius bounded into view. "You are one crazy-ass woman!" cried the cat. "One second I step into a wall of grass and the next you're gone. Don't do that again. You scared the crap out of me."

"Sorry."

Layla's face was flushed when she reached us, which made her even more beautiful. "I think I might have to get new boots—"

A sound of shuffling and scraping came from inside the barn. Something was in there.

The four of us jumped back and then stilled in unison.

I strained my ears, trying to get a sense of what was in there. Could be farm animals. Goats? Maybe even sheep?

"It's not barn animals," said the cat, reading my thoughts with his nose in the air, his nostrils flaring.

Layla pointed her blade at the barn doors. "You think they're zombies in there?"

Good point. I looked at Gareth, my heart clenching at the memory of the pain I saw there. "If I were them," I said, my voice low. "It's as good a place as any to hide them."

Tyrius took another sniff. "I'm not getting the deluxe rotten flesh smell of the day," said the cat. "But it doesn't mean it's not them."

At that moment, a familiar conjoined moaning sifted from inside the barn.

Zombies.

I shifted my weight. "You heard that? We can't leave a barn full of zombies."

"No, we can't." Gareth moved to the hay doors and put his hand on the latch. "Get ready."

Together, Layla and I took up defensive stances while Tyrius crouched next to Gareth.

"Now!" With a quick upward motion, Gareth lifted the latch, pulled open the barn doors, and stepped back.

I rushed forward, ready to slice me up some animated corpses—and froze.

Trouble was, these were not zombies.

A cluster of people stood together in the barn, maybe forty or more. Some turned at the sound of the barn doors opening, and some were staring into space, looking the other way. A few were off to the sides, their heads resting on the walls of the barn.

I stared, unable to move for a moment, a sickly little feeling of dread rolling through me.

Those who faced me stared with distant and dull expressions, as though the person they'd once been had been erased. They watched me with the same eyes as Father Martin's—the same yellow eyes.

Their souls had been taken.

CHAPTER
11

"**D**emon balls," cursed the cat, the fur on his back rising. "They've got no souls. They've got no friggin' souls, Rowyn!"

They've got no souls, I repeated in my head, trying to make sense of what I was seeing.

I swept my gaze around the barn. Every one of those people I looked at had yellow eyes. I swallowed hard, a feeling of nausea settling in my gut.

All these people, these innocent human beings, had all been robbed of what made them, them—their spirit, their individuality, their souls.

A mix of anger and fear rushed through my core. "But… how is this possible? How is it that they're still alive?"

The image of the dead priest leaped into the forefront of my thoughts. I didn't know a person could live without a soul. I'd always thought once the soul was removed, it was a death sentence. The body and the soul went together. The body was like a machine, and the soul was the power that operated it. The battery. Without the power, the machine was useless.

But these people were alive. I could see their chests rising and falling with every breath. This couldn't be real… could it? How could they be standing here alive but without a soul? It didn't make sense.

"I wouldn't call this alive." Gareth moved inside the barn, his face grim and full of horror as he inspected a thirty-year-old man without getting too close or touching him.

Layla peered inside. "It's like they're sleeping."

"Or in a coma," said the cat. He sniffed the leg of a young blonde woman. "One thing's for sure. They have the reek of necromancy all over them."

I took a deep breath and tried to get my heart rate under control. I couldn't let either fear or anger do my thinking for me.

I moved past Layla and stepped into the barn, making my way toward an elderly woman who reminded me of my gran. I snapped my fingers in her face. She didn't even flinch. Or blink. It was like I wasn't even there. It was almost as though she was blind but wasn't. "Maybe this is something else. A spell? A curse?"

"It's a curse all right," spat the baal demon. "A necromancer curse that took these people's souls, that's what. They've been robbed of their humanity. They're just empty shells now, vessels."

I watched as the old woman walked away from me, her yellow eyes distant and her face blank. "But how, Tyrius? You know as well as I do no one can live without their soul. Once a soul is removed, they're dead. The body dies. It withers away to nothing. But this... these people are *alive*."

The cat turned his blue eyes on me. "I don't know what to tell you. It's like they're in a perpetual sleepwalking state or something." The cat bounced off and ran around the barn, stopping and sniffing everyone one at a time.

"And they're just..." I looked around the barn at all the people. They were all different in sizes, genders, and ethnicities. Nothing was remotely similar about these people apart from they were all human. "They're just standing here. The door's open. But none of them even glanced at the opening. Not one made to leave." I didn't want to say it, but I did. "It's like they're waiting."

"Waiting for what?" Gareth looked at me.

"I don't know, but it can't be good."

Tyrius padded back. "Well, they're all human. I'm not getting any half-breed or angel-born vibes. So we know the necromancers are only using humans."

"For the moment." I didn't think they'd stop at humans for whatever they were doing. Because, why stop there?

"Why are they keeping them here like this?" Layla sheathed her blade. Growing anger made her voice clearer and sharper, if not louder. "It's sick."

"It is that," agreed the cat as he sat on the barn floor and wrapped his tail around his feet. "It's giving me the chills." He shivered like he was trying to shake off some water from his fur.

I let out a long sigh through my nose. "I don't know why or how the necromancers took their souls and left them alive," I said, still not understanding how this was even possible, though it was staring at me in the face. "But they put them in here for a reason. To hide them."

Tyrius flicked his tail. "And then they left in a hurry, so they left these poor bastards behind?"

A thought occurred to me. "If they kept them alive and hid them, it means they're important. Important enough to keep them away from everyone. Which means…" A smile twisted on my face. "They'll be back. The necromancers will come back here for them."

Tyrius's ears swiveled over his head. "Are you thinking what I'm thinking."

My smile widened. "Ambush."

"Now you're talking my language," said the cat.

"We're going to wait for them," I said, seeing it clearly in my head. "And when they show up… we'll take them down." Or kill them. I didn't care. I wanted them to die after seeing this. This was sick, perverse. No one should be allowed to treat people this way. No one.

I sensed movement behind me, and I turned to find a young boy of about ten shuffling his way toward me. I sucked in a breath through my teeth.

"Oh, no."

The little boy wandered closer, maybe driven by the sound of my voice. His eyes were yellow, just like all the others, and his face was pale and distant, making my heart clench. He stopped when he was about five feet away from me and teetered for a moment. Then he turned around and stared up at the ceiling or at something only he could see.

I felt my eyes burn as my anger bubbled to the surface again. "We can't let them get away with this. This isn't right."

I felt a hand on my lower back. "They won't," said Gareth as he moved next to me, and I let the warmth of his hand soothe me for a moment. "They're going to pay for this. I swear it."

I turned at the pure venom in the tone of his voice. His face was a dark cast, and I could see the fury that burned behind his eyes.

"At least they're not attacking us." Tyrius got up and moved to smell the young boy. "At least they're not zombies."

But I wasn't sure what was worse. Being an animated dead thing or a comatose living thing. This was so messed up.

"Something's happening."

I turned at the warning in Tyrius's voice. "What is it?"

The cat's fur rose on his back until it bristled all around him. His nostrils flared, taking in a scent, and his ears flattened on his head. "I smell necromancers."

And then as one, the soulless people in the barn, young and old, all turned and fixed their attention on us.

"That can't be good," I breathed.

Tyrius took a step back from the person he was smelling. "Uh—Rowyn. Is it me, or did all these yellow-eyed people just *turn* on? Like someone flipped their switches?"

"Tyrius, get away from them." My voice was tight with tension as I coaxed the cat with my free hand while keeping close attention on any of these yellow-eyed people, should one of them step out of line and decide to grab my furry friend. Some of my tension released as soon as the cat was safe behind me, but not that much.

I mean, there was creepy, like a ghoul feasting on an old corpse kind of creepy, and then there was this—a barn full of soulless, yellow-eyed people all staring at us at the same time with the same dull but intent expressions.

It was the motherload of all creepiness.

I stifled a chill. "I feel like I'm staring into my own horror film," I breathed as Layla and Gareth flanked me on either side.

"They're being controlled, navigated, like the zombies," said Gareth, his hands dripping with elf dust. "A necromancer is directing them."

109

"Like I said, someone just flipped their *on* buttons," mewed the cat at my feet.

"Animated puppets." I glanced at their faces, feeling sorry they were being used in this way. "The necromancer that's controlling them can't be that far away." It was a total guess, but it seemed to fit.

"Why are they just staring at us like that?" asked Layla. I could feel the uncertainty in her voice as she shifted from foot to foot.

"To freak us out?" It was a stretch, but I had no idea what was happening or why they were just standing there watching us.

"It's working," said the cat.

"If the necromancers are *navigating* these people," I said, "does that mean they can also see through their eyes?"

"Yes." Gareth's face was hard. "They can see us."

"Okay, then. Let's test your theory." I raised my hand and flipped them the finger.

As one, the soulless people charged.

Whoops.

They moved stiffly, their arms and legs twitching, as if struggling against the onset of rigor mortis. Their joints jerked, moving like toys that hadn't been assembled properly. It was the most horrid thing I'd ever witnessed, and I'd seen my share of nightmares.

"Does that answer your question!" squealed the cat as he ran out of the barn, his nails tearing into the wood planks.

More and more of them came at us with the same blank expressions, their charge gaining mass and momentum.

"Out! Out! Out! Hurry!" I shouted. I didn't want to fight them. But I didn't want them to kill us either, which was, without a doubt, what the necromancers wanted to do. But this wasn't those people's fault. They were being manipulated. Used.

"Get out!" Gareth pushed me out of the way. His hands blurred, their movements too fast to see as he hit the oncoming herd of the soulless with puffs of turquoise elf dust.

I backpedaled and sprinted out the doors. "Don't hurt them!" I shouted as I reached Layla and Tyrius just outside the barn.

With bursts of speed, the elf shot at the soulless with blows of elf dust, over and over again, never stopping, like an automatic weapon. He stood with his legs apart, his elf magic bursting out of him like a fountain of pixie dust.

The first line of the soulless sagged and then simply collapsed into a limp heap onto the floor. Then another. Then another, until the last of the soulless people went down, stacked above the rest like a horrid pile of dead bodies.

Fear clutched at my heart. "Please tell me they're not dead." I stared at the group piled over one another, Gareth had his back to us, his shoulders thick with tension.

KIM RICHARDSON

These people still had a beating heart. To me, that qualified as alive, and I didn't think Gareth would murder them all because their souls were missing.

Letting out a long breath, he turned around slowly and walked out of the barn. When he turned to look at me, his face twisted into a grimace. "They're not dead. They're just sleeping. It should hold for a few hours."

"Cool. Sleeping dust." Tyrius peeked at the pile of soulless people lying on the barn floor, not daring to step inside.

Layla sheathed her blade to her waist. "This is so messed up. We have to tell Father Thomas."

"Yeah. We do." I stared at the heap of people in the barn. Some had their eyes closed, but some I could still make out the yellow in them. These were mothers, someone's daughters and husbands, and children. These people had lives. And the bastard necromancers had taken them. They had no right.

"Who knows, maybe the priest can help them?" said Tyrius, his voice full of sorrow and his blue eyes glistening as he looked up at me.

I doubted that. I tried to smile at the cat, but I just couldn't. I felt sick with a feverish anger I couldn't tame.

"What do we do with them?" asked Layla, her voice quiet and rough, her face pale. "We can't just leave them here. They'll need to eat. Have water."

I stepped forward. "Well, we can't risk them getting out and mixing with the general population. Not until we figure out how this was done to them

112

and how we can reverse the process. We keep them here and we go get help." I fought against the bile that rose in my throat as I shut the hay doors and locked them inside. I tried to convince myself I was doing this for them and not for us or the general population. If they got out, God knows what the necromancers would have them do.

I was furious and tired as we made our way back through the forest to the temple. The four of us were quiet, all working out what we'd just witnessed in our ways.

Thoughts came rushing through me as I tried to order them. All those souls were taken from those poor people. If the necromancers didn't ingest them like demons did, where were their souls?

CHAPTER
12

My super plan of setting a trap for the necromancers by using the soulless in the barn came to an abrupt halt once the word was out.

Father Thomas and the other priests, horrified as they were to hear about it, would not let us use them as bait. Which, come to think about it, made sense. Instead, the forty-two soulless humans were picked up by helicopter—no joke—and transported to a facility owned by the church. They'd be looked after there until we figured out how to reverse the process. *If* we could reverse the process. That was a big *if.*

Part of me didn't believe we could. I'd never even heard of something like it happening before. Every story I'd heard about when the soul leaves the body,

114

no matter the circumstances, the body died. The soul would either travel to Horizon—the place where all souls went after a mortal died—or it was simply gone, dead, eaten by the demon who'd ingested it.

Souls were like batteries. They held power. Lots of power. Which was the main reason demons hungered over them. But I couldn't let my doubts be known to Father Thomas who'd taken the soulless into his care. He seemed so adamant that all would be resolved in time. I wish I had his optimism.

"I know you can do this, Rowyn," Father Thomas had said, and the conviction in his voice had made my chest tighten. "We can't let these innocent people die. Think of them as having a disease. A virus. And you need to find the vaccine."

Okay, if you put it that way, it sounded easy peasy. It wasn't.

The necromancers weren't stupid. If they could remove a person's soul, keep them alive, and then pilot the body, these bastards were as smart as they came. Perhaps smarter.

But I was a bulldog. I wouldn't stop until I found them. That's a promise.

I didn't know if the necromancers could only inflict their soul removal curse or spell, (because that's what I thought it was) to humans or if half-breeds and angel-born could also become their puppets. I still had so many unanswered questions, and it seemed the deeper I dug, the more confused I became.

Sitting on my couch, I wrapped a strand of wet hair behind my ear. I stared at the wine glass on the coffee table, which was filled to the rim with a generous amount. I thought after a long bath I'd feel better. I didn't.

"Are you going to have some wine or are you just going to stare at it all night?" Gareth sat next to me on the couch. The warmth of his thigh against mine was pleasant and soothing. He reached out and rubbed my back in slow, even strokes. It felt awesome. He was awesome. But I couldn't shake this feeling in my stomach, this sick feeling that the necromancers were onto something, and the situation with those poor people was just the beginning of something much worse.

"You barely touched your food." Gareth's eyes were wide and uncertain, and I knew he was worried about me.

He'd made dinner. Chicken curry. It was amazing, and my taste buds had had a party inside my mouth, which left me feeling even more guilty that I'd had maybe two bites.

After watching the last church helicopter take off with the last of the soulless people, we'd all gone home, mentally exhausted, and frustrated. Danto came to pick up Layla from my place and Tyrius had excused himself in a hurry, wanting to be with his wife and kids and my gran.

"Talk to me. I hate seeing you like this." Gareth reached out and pulled my hands so that I turned around and faced him. Wow. A man who actually *wanted* to talk. I was in heaven.

I reached over and pinched the skin on his arm. Hard.

He barely reacted. I just got a cocked eyebrow from him. "What was that for?"

I shrugged and smiled. "Just checking to make sure you're real."

Gareth laughed, the deep sound vibrating through me. The intensity in his dark eyes sent tingling jolts all over my skin, making my blood pound.

I opened my mouth and then closed it again, trying to figure out how to word what I was feeling without sounding mad. "I have this feeling," I tried again.

"What kind of feeling?"

I gave a small laugh. "A very bad one." I angled my body toward him and draped my leg over his.

Gareth propped his head on his elbow. "You can tell me. I can take it."

A smirk lifted my lips. "Well, since you're *badgering* me and everything... I have this tightness in my gut, like what we discovered today is a glimpse of something a lot worse. When I think of all those people... I mean, what the necromancers did to them is sick and twisted, but they were locked up there for a reason."

Gareth was silent for a moment. "Part of a bigger plan."

"Exactly." I traced my eyes over his face. "I can't stop thinking about it. So, we need to figure out what this bigger plan is before the necromancers start replacing those soulless people with more of them." It was a guess, but I had a feeling it was a very good guess.

The elf put one of his big hands on my leg. "They must have another temple somewhere in the city or close to it."

I raised my brows. "I hadn't thought of that. You think Cynthia would know?"

"We can ask her. It's worth a try."

I laced my fingers with his. "While you're at it, you should ask her about the people in the barn. If she was raised in that *community*, she might know why they were put in there in the first place. Maybe she knows how the necromancers can steal a person's soul and keep them alive. She probably knows a lot more too."

Gareth rubbed his thumb over my hand. "I'll call Father Thomas and see if he can arrange a meeting with her."

I nodded. "That sounds good."

"You know what else sounds good?" The elf slipped his free hand around my waist and pulled me on top of him so I was straddling him. Then his hands slid down my sides to grasp my waist, tugging me closer.

I ran my hands up the smooth expanse of his back. Reaching upward, my fingers played with the hair at the nape of his neck.

"You naughty elf," I whispered staring at his mouth. I couldn't help it. My body demanded I do something. I obliged and slipped my hands under his shirt, feeling his hairless chest and the hard muscles beneath my fingers.

The elf made a low guttural sound. He pressed closer, his heat obvious through the thin material of my shirt, and smacked his lips on mine. His lips were soft and warm and demanding. His stubble rubbed my face, sending tingles over my skin. Heart pounding, a soft sound of real bliss escaped me. My tongue found the smoothness of his teeth, and his muscles under my hands tensed. I pulled my tongue away, teasing.

Feeling it, his breath came and went in a pant. His eyes were dark and full of desire.

I smiled wickedly at him as I fumbled with his belt—

A knock came from the front door.

I froze and looked up at Gareth.

"I don't remember making plans with anyone," I said, turning my head toward the front door. "Maybe it's Layla or Father Thomas," I told him, remembering how the priest had just showed up at my door yesterday.

"Don't these people have phones?" grumbled the elf, his voice rough with traces of need still in it.

I showed him my teeth, smacked my lips against his, nibbling the bottom one, and swung my legs off of him. I rushed to the front door, glancing out the window in the hall as I went. I recognized the black clothes of the priest.

Relaxing somewhat, I pulled open the door. "Hi Father—"

A man stood on the front porch, but it wasn't Father Thomas.

He was tall, like Gareth, and heavy-chested. Perhaps forty years old, his ordinary brown hair was going gray in uneven patches. His black shirt was wrinkled, and his jeans were stained with mud. And where Gareth carried his weight with a confident and commanding gait, this man's posture was limper and duller, with his arms hanging loosely at his sides.

Light from the front porch glinted off his eyes, which were touched with crow's-feet at the corners and the same shade as the people in the barn.

My heart slammed in my chest.

Holy hell.

His yellow eyes told me everything I needed to know. Except *why* he was here.

The stranger began to walk deliberately toward me, and I jerked back on instinct. My hands brushed my waist, only to realize I had taken off my weapons belts earlier, upstairs in my bedroom.

Crapola.

I backpedaled, keeping my body facing the soulless man, as my heart thrashed against my chest and my mind tried to make sense of what was happening.

"Gareth!" I howled as I moved back in the hallway and stumbled into the living room, the soulless man following me.

I heard the elf curse and the sound of his heavy feet hit the hardwood floor behind me. I could see his black trench coat hanging behind the soulless man on the coat rack at the entrance. We were both weaponless.

When I hit a hard body behind me, I stopped, and Gareth moved to stand next to me.

The soulless man halted, his yellow eyes darting from me to Gareth and back to me. His mouth twisted into a smile and he began to laugh. The sound was a mix of a guttural grunt with an echo, as though two voices laughed at the same time, which was seriously creepy.

Goosebumps rose on my flesh.

"You stole my subjugates," said the man. I could hear two distinctive voices rolling out of his mouth as though this wasn't one but two people standing before us. And then I realized the necromancer was speaking through him.

Oh, this was going to be good.

A burst of anger coated some of the disturbing sensations running through me. "You can't steal people, asshole."

"They were my property. And you took them." His eyes flicked to Gareth who'd taken a step away, leaning towards the hallway. I knew he was trying to go for his coat.

I gave the soulless man a hard look. "You took those poor people and shoved them in a barn without any food or water, you dick."

"The dead don't need to eat."

I felt a growl escape me. "They're not dead. These people are *alive*. They would have died if it weren't for us." And somehow, I was going to save them, but right now, I had no idea how I was going to do that. That image of the little boy in the barn would haunt me forever if I didn't do something.

The soulless man's face wrinkled in what I suspected was a thoughtful expression, but it came off stiff and mechanical, like a robot trying out its facial expressions for the first time.

"The subjugates have no souls," said the man. "You call them people, but they are not." He gave me a lazy, wicked smile. "Not anymore."

Grinding my teeth, I wanted nothing more than to kick this guy in the head. But I wouldn't be hurting the necromancer. I'd be hurting that innocent man.

"Why don't you show yourself instead of hiding behind this man? What? Are you afraid of a mere woman?" From the corner of my eye, I saw Gareth step further toward the hallway. Good. I had to keep this guy busy talking. I could do that.

The soulless man just stared at me with his yellow eyes, his face crinkling in an eerie smile.

"What's your name?" I ventured. "Which one are you?" I tried again. "Are you the same necromancer who set the zombies on us? Or are you the leader. This... Lord Krull?" When he didn't answer I asked, "How did you know where I live?" I hated that he'd figured out who I was and showed up here, but I hated even more that my gran, Tyrius, Kora, and their kids lived just across the street from me.

Something occurred to me. If the necromancers could see through the eyes of the soulless they piloted, it meant they'd heard our entire conversations back at the barn. They'd heard everything. And now they knew who we all were.

Crap.

The soulless man smiled again. "I know everything there is to know about you, Rowyn Sinclair."

I cringed. So, I was right. "Is this about me giving you the finger? Grow up. It's just a finger." I knew it had been a bad move, but too late now. Though, it didn't explain why he piloted the soulless man to come all the way to my house. Why even bother? Unless he wanted something.

The soulless let out a laugh that had the hair on the back of my neck rising. His eyes flicked to Gareth, who'd managed to sneak a good ten feet farther from me. "I know about the elf as well."

Gareth froze, his face hard. "You don't know anything about me."

The soulless chuckled again. "You can use your elf magic on my subjugates. But it won't change anything. You can't touch me. Your reach is not long enough."

It was my turn to laugh. "How 'bout you step out of that body and we'll show you how long."

His head moved from side to side, his yellow eyes widening when he saw something of interest in my living room and kitchen like he was gathering information about my house, about me.

I stepped into his line of sight. "What the hell do you want?" Anger made my muscles stiff. He might be using this poor bastard's body, but if he didn't stop his spying, I might do something stupid, like kick his face in.

The soulless man bared his teeth. "At last, an intelligent question." He lifted his hands and clapped. The movement was stiff and mechanical, reminding me of a manikin. Then his arms dropped to his sides again. "I was beginning to lose hope for you. I thought we'd never get there. You are, after all, just a Hunter. You track and kill. That's the entirety of your skills. Isn't that right?"

"You've got five seconds before I smack you unconscious. Better make it count." I wasn't going to stand here and let this necromancer insult me in my own home. He was creepy, but I could still kick his ass without any weapons. I still had my killer looks.

I cocked an eyebrow at him. "Oh… I know… You *want* me." I smiled, showing a slip of teeth. "I get it. If I were you, I'd want me too."

The man smiled, pulling his lips over his gums. "You stole something of mine, and now I want it back," said the necromancer, his yellow eyes rolling over me.

"Or what?" I challenged and pressed my hands on my hips. "You're going to kill me with your bad breath? You don't scare me, little puppet." In my peripheral vision, I could see Gareth was nearly at his coat, but I didn't want the necromancer to say nightnight just yet. I needed more information.

"You cannot win this, Rowyn," warned the necromancer. His tone was dry yet somehow filled with venomous undertones.

"Yes, I can." I had no idea what we were talking about. When in doubt, go with a know-it-all attitude.

The soulless man cocked his head as fury wrinkled his brow. "Give back what you stole, or you and everyone you know will die."

I rolled my eyes. "Like I haven't heard that one before."

"This is your last chance."

Savage fury made its way into my gut and stayed there. "Nice try. I'm not afraid of you. And there's no way in hell I'm going to return these people so you can abuse them. Like you're doing to this poor bastard. You're sick. And if anyone's going to die… that'll be you."

The soulless man's yellow eyes fixed on me. "Soon, you will see."

"All I see is a coward," I said, and Gareth's attention snapped to mine. I could see him moving his lips at me, but I kept my gaze on the soulless man. "You're not that strong. Are you? You're afraid. You hide behind this man because you're afraid."

"You," said the necromancer. "Are a mindless Hunter. You have no power."

"And you do?" Of course he did, but I wanted to piss him off. It seemed to be working.

The yellow-eyed man twitched and spread his arms again. "Controlling of the mind is the greatest power—a skill you cannot comprehend with your mindless Hunter brain."

"Okay then." Since we were on a roll, might as well keep him talking. "If I'm so clueless, how about

125

you tell me how you removed their souls. With a spell?" I searched his face for any indication I was on the right track. "A curse? A ritual? Did you use some sort of weapon?"

Gareth's hands dripped with turquoise elf dust as he made his way toward the soulless man as silently as a baal demon. *You go, elf.*

The soulless man spun his head around, seemingly having eyes in the back of his head. He glanced at the elf and then turned and focused on me again. "All of you will die. And in death, I will find you."

I frowned. "I'm sorry, what? I don't speak dumbass."

The soulless man reached up and grabbed his head—

In a blur Gareth flung the turquoise dust on the man.

But it was too late.

There was a horrifying crunch as the soulless man snapped his neck and crumbled to the floor.

CHAPTER
13

We sprinted across the parking lot of Saint Mary's Abbey with Tyrius on my heels and Gareth next to me.

The building was of a modest size and built in the Romanesque and Byzantine architectural styles. The perfectly balanced design was crowned with three domes raised on stone pillars. Warm yellow light leaked from above the many windows and doors, illuminating the abbey like a precious jewel. It was huge, the size of a four-story hospital. It was an architectural beauty, but I wasn't here to admire the view.

When the necromancer had said I'd be sorry, I never expected it to be so soon.

Minutes after he'd snapped the neck of his own subjugate, I got a phone call from a frantic Father Thomas. Apparently the other soulless people had broken free from whatever confinement the priests had put them in and were running all over the abbey attacking priests, monks, and some nuns.

I'd called Layla and left her a message. It would take her at least an hour to drive north to Thornville. Gareth and I were closer.

After picking up Tyrius, we piled into Gareth's infamous 1970 Ford F100 light blue pickup truck and sped toward the abbey.

There was no time to do anything about the dead guy in my living room. I'd deal with him later.

My thighs burned by the time we reached the entrance, which was a pair of wooden, nine-foot-high doors.

Tyrius galloped past me, dipped his head, sniffed the doors, and said, "Clear!" as he bounced back.

I hit the door with my shoulder because I hadn't been able to stop my forward momentum. I winced and then turned the handle and jerked inside.

We hurried into a large entryway the size of my dining room and living room combined. A giant, double staircase led to the upper levels, flanked by doors and hallways that stretched in both directions. The furnishings were few, but they were exquisitely crafted of polished wood and gleamed in the light. Four large chairs of deep, polished wood and rich brown leather sat in the foyer.

It reminded me of Father Thomas's church. It was surprisingly well-lit with large chandeliers and sconces lining the walls, which were a mix of stone, drywall, and wood beams. The place was huge. It would take a day or so for a complete tour. Again, no time to play the tourist.

Tyrius whistled. "Nice crib. The kids would love to play hide and seek in here. Might burn a few rugs and drapes, but all in good fun."

"Where to?" asked Gareth. His eyes shone dark and sexy under his fedora, and his long black coat draped over his wide shoulders, spilling with little bursts of multicolored elf dust.

"I have no idea. I've never been in this place before." I looked past Gareth to the endless hallways and rooms. "Father Thomas was supposed to meet us at the entrance." The fact that the priest wasn't here didn't settle well with me.

"You think something happened to him?" asked Tyrius, his ears low on his head, pulling the thoughts right out of my head.

I didn't want to have to think about that. The necromancer had been pissed at us for taking his subjugates. And now, he might have killed Father Thomas for revenge. Or just because he could.

A second later, what sounded like the screams of a gang of rabid animals filled the air.

I gave the elf a look and jerked out my soul blade. "Follow the screaming."

And we did.

The three of us raced across the stone floor, my heart about to burst out of my ribcage as I pushed my thighs as hard as I could, slipping now and then on the polished floor.

Tyrius sprinted ahead of us in a blur of beige and black, like a miniature cheetah. He might be small, but the Siamese cat was like Roadrunner on steroids.

The scent of blood reached me before I saw the trail of red with smeared footprints.

It ran down the hallway and disappeared abruptly around the corner. I followed the blood, large puddles of it zigzagging in a peppered line. That was *a lot* of blood.

My jaw clenched, tension pulling at every muscle as I neared the corner. *Please don't let it be Father Thomas.*

I reached the junction and turned.

On the floor next to the wall was a man. He lay flat on his back, his dull brown eyes open and staring at the ceiling. A trickling stream of red washed down from his middle to pool around him. A mix of pale flesh and blood peeked from ribbons of his black shirt. A small, silver handle from a knife stuck up from his chest, and red splatters stained his white collar.

But it wasn't Father Thomas.

"Thank god," I muttered, immediately regretting it. This was a life. And from the defense wounds on his arms and hands, he'd fought hard. He didn't deserve this.

"Poor guy," said Tyrius, stepping carefully around the body so as not to touch the blood. He stopped at the piece of silver sticking out of the priest's chest. "That's a butter knife." Tyrius turned and looked up at us. "Who the hell kills someone with a butter knife?"

"A very sick person." A sense of dread filled me. If the soulless could kill someone like that with a butter knife, I'd hate to see what they would do if they got their hands on the priests' swords.

"Looks like he fought hard." Gareth came around and knelt next to the dead priest.

"Whoever did this did a serious number in his gut," commented Tyrius. He met my gaze. "If this is the soulless's handiwork, it's worse than we thought."

I gripped my soul blade harder. "They didn't do it. The necromancers did this. Don't ever forget that." I took a breath. "Let's keep going."

We doubled back and rushed down the hallway toward most of the voices and the screaming. We passed more bodies, another priest judging by his white collar, had a fork perforating his left eye, and a younger man in his twenties had his throat cut. He wore a white T-shirt and jeans, so he wasn't a priest.

I had no idea how the soulless had gotten their hands on the cutlery, but if we didn't stop them soon, the abbey would be a blood bath.

My imagination provided me with a great visual of that yellow-eyed mob tearing at Father Thomas while he tried to save them. Yeah, I bet he was trying, and it was going to get him killed.

I put on some speed, my adrenaline soaring as I pushed my legs faster. Tyrius galloped ahead of us while Gareth and I pushed ourselves to catch up.

We didn't have to run for very long.

We reached the end of the hall and pushed open a set of swinging double doors, which revealed a large, sunken area I suspected had once been the abbey's cafeteria. But now it looked more like a refugee camp with rows of sleeping bags over cots (the ones that weren't turned over), and some makeshift clinic at the back separated with folding walls.

And the cafeteria was at war.

"Oh my god," I choked as my adrenaline spiked.

Screams rose, and sounds of genuine pain and terror filled the large room. Forty-two strong soulless people battled what I could only guess was about six priests and a dozen other people I didn't recognize.

They fought with the mindless efficiency of being controlled, like robots programmed only to kill. Some hacked their way through the line of priests, and some just used their hands to try and grab a leg or an arm. I did not want to think about what they'd do with them if they caught one.

The screams rose, high-pitched, and terrible. I wasn't sure what was more disturbing—a horde of zombies ripping apart and munching on innocent humans, or a throng of humans hacking and stabbing innocent humans under the control of necromancers. I thought it was the latter.

Even though I kept comparing the soulless with zombies, an undeniable difference separated the zombies and the soulless. Zombies killed anything that moved, mindless killing instruments, but the soulless were controlled and activated, moving with purpose and the intelligence of the puppeteers, the necromancers.

Which made them a far greater threat than mere zombies.

Cold enveloped me when I spotted Father Thomas pinned in a corner against a far wall, fighting off two women who were trying to stab him with what I believed were spoons. You could laugh, but spoons in the wrong hands could be just as deadly as knives.

I could see a sword hanging at his waist, swinging in its sheath. He wasn't using it to defend himself.

"Damn priest," I growled. "He won't fight them."

"He's going to die if we don't do something," urged Tyrius.

He was right. I had to reach him before they killed him.

"I get that he doesn't want to harm them," I said. "Gareth. Do you have more of your sleeping elf magic?"

"I do." Gareth shifted his weight next to me. "If we can group them all together, maybe using the tables as barriers and enclosing them inside, I could dust them all at once. I might get a few priests, but at least it'll stop the fighting."

It wasn't the best plan, but under the circumstances it could work. "Good enough for me. Come on!" I shouted and sprinted forward.

A soulless woman turned as I neared the group. She was in her sixties with a mess of blonde hair and had no expression, none whatsoever, on her face. But her yellow eyes widened at the sight of me.

"Rowyn," said the woman in that same necromancer voice I'd heard in my home from the now-dead dude on my living room floor.

Yeah. Totally creepy and unnatural, and I nearly tripped as the sound came out. It would give me nightmares for years to come.

Her body jerked into motion and she lurched herself at me, her hands going for my weapons belt.

I don't think so, creepy lady.

I spun. Using the butt of my blade, I hit her hard on her left temple and she went down.

I walked around the woman. "Sorry. But you had those *crazy* eyes."

"One down, forty-one to go," muttered Tyrius, his body shimmering in that bright white light as he began his transformation into his alter ego.

"Rowyn."

The sound of terror from Gareth pulled my eyes away from the woman on the ground and I followed his gaze.

Then I noticed how quiet it had become.

I let out a little scream inside my head at the mass of yellow eyes *all* staring at me.

The soulless stood motionless, their faces blank as they watched me, watched us. The soulless weren't individuals. They shared a consciousness—like the

Borg from *Star Trek* but without the mechanical parts woven in and around their flesh. Spooky, nonetheless.

A low growl pulled my attention to my left. A giant, black panther pulled back its lips, revealing rows of sharp teeth the size of kitchen knives.

"I know," I told the panther. "I don't like this either."

I let myself relax a little when I spotted Father Thomas, alive and free of those two women who'd turned their attention on me with the rest of the yellow-eyed herd.

What happened next was even more disturbing.

The entire mass of soulless people opened their mouths. "You will perish," they said in unison, the same necromancer voice rolling off their tongues and magnified as though with magic. "Embrace what is inevitable. Embrace your true master. Embrace Death."

"Great pep talk," I told the group, my voice echoing around the cafeteria. "Motivational speaker of the year. I think the local mayor's office is hiring. You should check it out."

Tyrius snorted next to me, but as a panther it sounded more like a short growl. So cute.

And then, as one, the soulless lunged.

CHAPTER

14

If I thought hearing them speak as a whole was creepy, it didn't even compare to them moving all at once with the exact, twitchy gait and pace, their legs and arms jerking at the same time. I wanted to scream like a banshee, but I couldn't. Hunters didn't scream like little girls. We usually *caused* the screaming.

I was in hell. An army of human-sized puppets was coming to get me.

What's a gal to do? Run, silly. And so, I did.

I broke left while Gareth broke right. And Tyrius, well, Tyrius charged into the oncoming herd like a bulldozer. The soulless went scattering like pins hit by a bowling ball, creating a clear path behind him. He wasn't using his claws or teeth, which was great, and the soulless he hit would only suffer a few broken bones. They could heal from that, as soon as I figured out how to return their souls.

For now, they either stayed on the ground stunned, or their legs were broken. It sucked, but I'd take that over their deaths anytime.

I threw myself forward as the moans and hissing grew louder, hauled ass over what I thought was a dead priest on the floor, covered in blood, and made it into the center of the cafeteria just as maybe twenty soulless came rushing at me. I grabbed the nearest foldable metal six-by-four table, spun it around, and pushed it against another table so they were corner to corner, like I was making a longer table with the two.

I looked up and found Gareth pushing two tables together across from me. We were doing our best to try and herd the soulless into one spot.

I couldn't risk shouting our master plan to Father Thomas or the other priests, but when I saw two priests—the redhaired one who had put a sword to my neck and another I recognized from Father Martin's office—pushing and steering some of the soulless together in the center of the cafeteria, I knew they understood what we were planning to do.

I saw a flash of white and whirled to see Father Thomas throw what looked to be a tablecloth over three of the soulless. They stopped moving. Smart. If the soulless couldn't see, neither could the necromancers. What a clever little priesty. Love him.

Father Thomas turned to me and I gave him a thumbs up. "You got more of those? Use them!" I shouted and turned as the priest ran to what looked like a storage room at the back of the cafeteria.

I caught a glimpse of something large and black. Tyrius was going around the cafeteria in great bounds, knocking over any soulless that came at him or just any he felt like. I thought the big cat was enjoying himself a little too much, especially when a roar erupted from him that sounded like a laugh.

Some of the soulless watched us, and I could make out the realization of what we were doing as it flashed behind their yellow eyes. They stopped, putting up a new tone of a disapproving howl. Limbs jerking, they went around the others, trying to break free and come after me from the opposite side.

"Oh, no you don't." I lurched to the side and grabbed another table, yanking it as hard and fast as I could. It hit the corner of the other table with a loud bang and blocked the soulless from reaching me. They stumbled against the table barrier, limbs jerking.

Obviously it wouldn't hold. They could easily climb over the tables, but they weren't. And I wasn't going to wait and see if they would either. We just needed them together for a few seconds, long enough for Gareth to dust them with his elf magic.

Humans didn't possess supernatural abilities like the strength of the werewolves or vampire speed. And these soulless humans were no different. Thank the gods. However, I did notice the few seconds' lag of reaction as the necromancer or necromancers—who knew if this was just one controlling the humans or if this was a team effort—piloted the humans. It was the only thing I could use against them.

The necromancers couldn't anticipate my movements. I needed that.

Panting, I kept going and didn't stop. I kept ducking and grabbing table after table until Gareth and I had formed a u-shape with the assembled tables, trapping the soulless inside.

"It's working!" I shouted over to him before I thought better of it.

Three soulless broke away from a priest who was trying to push them further into the center and turned toward me.

Oops.

Their yellow eyes focused, and I could almost see the necromancer behind them as they made for me. There was a sense to them of something quiet and still and dangerous—of something vile and malicious beyond the scope of any human—and it scared the crap out of me.

The soulless came at me, and it took a strenuous effort not to use my soul blade and slice it across their throats.

Innocent humans, Rowyn, I told myself. *We don't kill the innocent.* It was a one-way ticket to the Netherworld for me if I started to slice them down.

But it didn't mean I couldn't punch them in their faces.

A soulless beefy man with a brown beard held a silvery fork in one hand and a knife in the other.

I sheathed my blades so I had the use of my hands. "I'm getting mixed singles here. Either you're up for a fight, or you want to eat me."

He lunged at me.

I sidestepped, landed a left hook into his midsection, and gave him one hell of an uppercut with my right hand across his jaw. He stumbled back and then I kicked him in his manly parts. When in doubt, aim for the balls.

I hadn't been sure the soulless even felt pain until I saw the man cover his groin with his hands and fall to his knees.

Okay then. Good to know.

As soon as he fell, another soulless woman came at me. Her long brown hair reminded me of Layla.

She came at me with spoons, one in each hand, manipulating them as though they were sharp blades. Her movements were fluid and not jerky, and I was guessing the necromancer who was navigating her was focused on her, putting all his mind into control of this body. No doubt because he wanted to kill me.

"Bring it on, Spoons." I made a gesture with my right hand. Not that it mattered. She'd never stopped coming at me.

Her face was spread in a wide manic smile as she attacked, striking, spinning, and slashing, driven by some unseen force within her. I kept jumping away, and she kept missing.

I slowed my momentum, figuring I was a step ahead of the necromancer.

Big mistake.

As I slowed and waited for her to jab right, she feinted and jabbed left, catching me on my side with one of her spoons.

I cried out and stumbled, feeling wetness where it also burned.

I straightened. "You *spooned* me!" Yeah, I knew how that sounded.

The woman's face went blank as she opened her mouth. "You're a wild animal that needs to be put in her cage. Then your soul will be mine, Rowyn Sinclair," said the same voice I recognized from the soulless man who had appeared at my doorstep.

"Not going to happen." I leaped forward, ducked, spun, and kicked her in the knee. Something snapped and she went down. "Told you."

"Rowyn!"

I turned at the sound of urgency in Gareth's voice. He was pinned behind a table with twelve soulless pushing against it. Their arms flailed as they tried to get ahold of him.

I swooped down into the masses and punched and kicked with precise, measured jabs, sending the nearest soulless into a tumbling sprawl. But more just vaulted over those on the floor and kept coming.

"Do something! Hurry!" Gareth shouted. "I can't keep holding on!"

"I know!"

Damn it. A sea of soulless stood between me and Gareth. Worse, half of the herd were still on the other side of the table trap we were trying to build.

"Rowyn. Catch!"

I whirled around and caught the end of a thick rope with my hand. Father Thomas held the other end, thirty feet away at least.

I looked at the priest, and I knew exactly what he was thinking as he coiled his end of the rope around his arm to secure it.

Following his example, I did the same.

"Tyrius. Get back," I shouted, catching a glimpse of black fur in the middle of the mob.

And then we were moving.

We ran, our rope slack between us. I looked around wildly as I zigzagged my way around the soulless, catching them with the rope and winding it around them. We worked fast. We had to before the necromancers caught on.

When I figured the runaway soulless were all tangled in our rope, all lassoed up and unable to move, I dropped the rope.

"Let's see how long it takes you to get out of that," I said to no one in particular.

I spotted Tyrius and my breath caught. "Tyrius. Put that man down!"

A man hung in the panther's maw. He was hitting the panther's face with his hands repeatedly.

Tyrius the black panther raised an annoyed brow, moved to the center of the cafeteria, and spat the man out. The man hit the floor and went still. With his tail in the air, Tyrius waddled past me, his head high and proud.

"Any time now, Gareth," I said, seeing that the priests, bloodied and battered, had moved away from the soulless to give Gareth a wide berth. I stepped away as well, not wanting to get hit with Gareth's sleeping dust.

"I hate this," said Father Thomas as he came to stand next to me, breathing hard and looking disheveled. Horror pulled at his usual handsome features, making him look grim and gaunt. "This isn't right. These are people."

"I know." Guilt hit hard. "I hate it too. But this is the best way we can help them before they hurt anyone else or themselves."

Granted, if I couldn't figure out how to return their souls, it was going to get a hell of a lot worse.

I watched as the elf pulled his fists from inside his jacket, turquoise dust seeping from between his fingers.

And then something strange happened.

The soulless backed away from him, moving together until they were joined by the ones Father Thomas and I had lassoed together.

The herd parted, and from within it stepped a single person. No, not a person, but the little boy I'd seen in the barn.

Gareth made to move—

"Wait," I cried. "Let him speak." Who knew, the necromancers might slip up and give us something we needed.

Gareth frowned at me, but he stilled, his hands still dripping with elf dust.

The little boy's yellow eyes met mine as he opened his mouth and spoke. "Blood will be spilled. Death will be eternal, and balance will be restored."

"Bite me," I answered.

The boy stared at me for a second, and then the light in his yellow eyes dimmed, like it had been extinguished. It looked as though whatever spark of life was still in him had vanished, and he collapsed on the floor.

Oh, no.

My throat tightened with dread as I watched the scene unfold. The seconds ticked by as though in slow motion. There was nothing I could do to stop it.

Gareth flung out his hand, hitting the herd with his dust.

But it was too late.

All around us, the light left the soulless' eyes, as though someone had switched off their life switches. The herd fell, crumbling over themselves onto the floor in a lifeless heap of bodies.

They were all dead.

CHAPTER

15

"**Y**ou think they'll show up?" Tyrius pulled another piece of pizza into his mouth and began chewing.

"They better." I rested my arms on the kitchen table, my half-eaten slice of vegetarian pizza staring up at me from my plate. I loved this pizza from Giorgio's Pizza, a local joint, but I just couldn't bring myself to have another bite.

"When did you call them?" Gareth sat with his arms crossed over his chest, the tips of his pointed ears peeking through his thick, tousled dark hair. Behind him were stacks of boxes that we still hadn't unpacked.

My shoulders slumped, and I pulled my eyes away from the boxes before I got too depressed.

I leaned back in my chair. "Last night when we got back."

Tyrius choked on his pizza and sat up on the table next to me. "Blistering demon balls! You called the angels? Please tell me you didn't try summoning one again. Rowyn? You didn't, right?"

"I could have." I eyed the cat with a tight smile on my face. "But I didn't. I have to go through the proper channels now. I'm working for the Council, and they have protocols to follow. If I want to keep my post, I *have* to follow them."

"Good." The cat chewed and then he swallowed. "That's good. Well, it's past noon. When did they say they'd show up?"

"They didn't." That's the one thing I hated about angels. You never knew when or if they'd show up. They would show up when they wanted, when it was convenient for them, not for you.

Angels. I had a love-hate relationship with them.

But the Council had assured me my case had been bumped up to priority one, with all the human deaths and the necromancers still MIA. The Council had also decided to put four other teams of angel-born Operatives on the case to help find the necromancers responsible or any leads that could help.

I was happy and surprised by the Council's decision. I was going to need all the help I could get.

"What about Layla?" inquired the cat, staring at my plate.

"I told her to stay home. I'll fill her in later." No point in dragging her back here without something solid. She and Danto had showed up at the abbey last night, a half-hour after the necromancers had killed all the soulless.

The cat leaned over my plate and sniffed it. "You gonna eat that?" He put his paw on it as though he'd claimed it already.

"Not anymore, now that you've added your DNA to it." I pushed my plate at him. "You can have it. I'm not hungry."

The baal attacked what was left of my pizza as though he hadn't eaten in months. I couldn't help but laugh.

"Not so fast, Tyrius," I said shaking my head. "You're going to make yourself sick."

"Nonsense," said the cat as he swallowed. "Have you ever heard of a baal who'd eaten himself sick?"

"Maybe."

"Liar." The cat snorted and tore into my pizza again, sending splatters of tomato sauce all over his face and nose and this time making Gareth laugh.

I looked up at the elf. I hadn't heard him laugh since yesterday, and I missed it. All I wanted was to crawl into bed with him and feel his warm, hard body against mine. But now wasn't the time to get worked up with thoughts of a naked sexy elf.

It didn't help that all my sexy thoughts got smashed with the visual of that little kid's lifeless eyes replaying in my head. I'd barely slept all night. How could I when we still had a group of demented, murderous necromancers on the loose somewhere in the city?

Bile rose in my throat at the thought of all those dead people lying in a heap in the abbey's cafeteria. It had seemed so easy for the necromancers to control, so easy to take their lives as though they meant nothing.

"What about John Doe over there?" asked Tyrius between chews. "He's starting to smell. And not in a rosy sweet kinda way either."

My eyes moved past the kitchen to the body in the living room. It was wrapped in a tight cocoon of transparent plastic sheets—the same ones we'd used to wrap our furniture with—in an attempt to keep the body from decomposing over our newly finished hardwood floors.

"The Council said to leave him. Apparently, the angels want to inspect the body." No wonder I couldn't sleep with a dead guy in my living room.

"I guess it's the same for the bodies at the abbey?" asked the cat as he began to lick his paw and wash his face. My plate was empty and gleaming it was so clean.

"I don't know. I think Father Thomas is planning on identifying each body so he can contact their immediate families."

"What will they say was the cause of death?" asked Gareth.

"I think I remember him saying a virus or something." No one would believe the truth. Not unless they were members of the paranormal community.

Gareth uncrossed his arms, his face troubled. "He's going to have to explain how they all ended up in the abbey. These people weren't related. They could be from anywhere in New York or even out of state."

I nodded. "The story he came up with is that the local hospital moved them to the abbey, not having enough space for them, and not wanting to contaminate other people or the nurses and doctors."

"That would work." Tyrius let himself fall on the table and roll onto his back with his legs splayed. "I'm stuffed like a turkey on Thanksgiving. Do I look fat to you?"

"Yes."

"Rowyn?" asked Tyrius, and I could see a little pot belly forming.

"What?"

"I can't move anymore."

"Why am I not surprised?"

The elf got up. "I'll make some coffee," he said, smiling. I watched his very fine behind as he made his way to the kitchen and filled the coffee pot with water.

"Good idea." Coffee sounded amazing right about now. I watched Gareth for a moment before my eyes moved back to the dead body. "Those were a lot of soulless people."

"Yup. A crapload," said the cat. "Is it normal that I can't feel my mouth anymore? Oh my god—I can't feel my whiskers."

149

I shifted in my chair. "We still don't know how the necromancers manage to remove the soul from a body without killing it."

"That, we do not." Tyrius hesitated. "Does my voice sound weird to you?"

"I mean…" I leaned forward and rested my elbows on the table. "All those people, all those soulless people. How did they manage so many at once?"

"Maybe they used a weapon or something," commented the cat. "See that? I do sound different. I'm like a Barry White version of me. Kora's going to love this."

I stared at him for a moment. "Forty-two missing people in one day? The human police would have been all over that, but I haven't heard anything about missing people reports in the city."

"And who knows how long they were kept in that barn." Gareth placed one of the two cups of coffee he was holding on the table for me and sat down.

"True." I felt Tyrius's eyes on my cup as I brought it to my lips. "Don't even think about it, little kitty."

The cat rolled his eyes. "I didn't even say anything."

"You didn't have to." I took a sip of coffee, and my eyes widened at the glorious bitter taste. I quickly took another sip. "What I'd *really* like to know is why? Why do this in the first place?"

"It's that damn prophecy, that's what," mewed the cat.

I let out a sigh. "Guess we won't know much until we find a necromancer and beat it out of him."

"Preferably with my boot up his ass," said the elf, and I beamed at him.

"I'm rubbing off on you," I teased. His dark, sultry eyes rolled over my face, and I couldn't believe he was mine. All mine. Yay for me.

Gareth wrapped his long fingers around his coffee cup. "Do we know if Cynthia has said anything else about the necromancers that could help us?"

I leaned over and checked my phone. "Nothing yet. Father Thomas is supposed to let me know, but I think right now he's got his hands full with all the dead bodies. I don't expect to hear from him today."

I felt bad for the priest. Two of his Knights of Heaven had been killed, though I didn't know which ones. They were tight. They were family.

This whole situation had gone from bad to a hell of a lot worse in a short amount of time.

Restless, I drummed my fingers on the table. I needed to do something. I was a doer. I didn't sit around and wait for the directives of others. That wasn't who I was. I might work for the angel-born Council, but I was still a Hunter. And Hunters got crap done.

The longer I waited for the angels to show up, the more uptight and angry I became. If they didn't show up soon, I might have to take matters into my own hands. Screw the Council. Lives were at stake.

I *was* going to summon an angel.

Call me crazy, but I couldn't sit here and do nothing.

I took the last gulp of my coffee and stood up. "I can't wait any longer—"

There was a sudden pop of displaced air.

I spun around, and in my kitchen stood a man next to a white German shepherd.

Angels.

Tyrius rolled to his side. "Oh, goodie. The halo police are here. We're saved."

Chapter

16

The man was tall with a pleasant face. He looked to be in his early forties and in great physical shape. His light gray suit was tailored perfectly to his broad shoulders and narrow waist, where I could spy his double soul blades. A shaved head gleamed in the light from the kitchen window and over his mocha-colored skin.

I'd seen my share of angels, but it was always a bit of a shock to see that underlining glow beneath their skin, as though millions of tiny white lights lay just below the surface. Their meat-suits glowed. Not kidding.

The memory of my own experience as an angel came rushing back. I'd worn an m-suit myself. It had felt like I was wearing a thin layer of someone else's skin on top of my own. It had taken a bit of getting used to. But the feeling of power that radiated from it had made all the difference. My angel body had resonated with power, and I was fast. Vampire fast, if not faster.

I'd been a Dark angel for a day. And it had been awesome.

My gaze moved to the white dog that could easily pass for a wolf. He was magnificent with fur the color of new snow and a large muscular body. His golden eyes watched me with an eerie stare that glittered in a heightened intelligence.

The dog was a Scout for the Angel Legion. And my friend.

All my pent-up anger from before vanished at the sight of a friendly and familiar face.

I smiled and stood up. Pushing my chair back, I walked over to the gorgeous white dog. "Hi, Lance. I'm glad to see you again." The last time I'd seen him was at the battle of Lucian's Hellmouth. I went to rub his head, like I normally would any dog, but yanked my hand back at the last minute, choosing to clasp them in front of me instead. I didn't think Lance would have appreciated that.

"I'm not sure whether to applaud or call animal control," spat Tyrius as he leaped off the table and padded over to stand right in Lance's face, making a show of his sharp nails as he tapped the wood floor.

Great. Just freaking great.

Lance kept his gaze on me. "It's nice to see you again too, Rowyn. Gareth," said the dog, ignoring the cat. "This is Shane."

The angel Shane gave a slight nod of his head. "Hi."

"We're here to see the body," said the dog. "I take it it's the human sushi roll in your living room."

"Aren't you clever," said the cat. "What other dead body is there? Do you see another dead body lying about?"

"Tyrius," I warned, wanting to nudge him with my foot. "Don't. Not now. I mean it." I knew angels and demons were archenemies, and it used to be like that for me until I became an angel. Which made it nearly impossible for me to explain to my furry friend how my view of the angels had changed. I wasn't sure if he just didn't get it, or if he just refused to even try.

The cat made a face but kept his mouth shut.

I moved to the living area to unwrap the body, but Gareth beat me to it. The elf carefully untangled the body from the plastic sheet. He frowned and covered his nose as he peeled away the last plastic layer.

I jerked back at the stench. "Wow. That's potent." I rushed to the windows in the living room and pushed both up to get some much-needed fresh air. I'd smelled my share of dead bodies—zombies, ghouls, you name it—but something was just horribly pungent about the smell of this rotting body, like the smell of New York City's sewer system on the hottest summer day times a hundred.

"I think the plastic made it worse," said the cat, keeping a very good distance between him and the dead man.

When I could breathe again, I inched closer to the body. His eyes were closed, something Gareth had done before we'd wrapped him up. The dead man's head was at an awkward angle, evidence that his neck had been broken.

I had to agree with Tyrius, wrapping him in plastic had somehow sped up the process of decomposition. With that horrid smell came the horrid condition of the body. The skin had the stiff, waxy look dead bodies got. Worse, I could see a thin film over it, like sweat, though I knew it wasn't. It was the body's own fluids escaping through the pores of the skin.

This close, and even with the windows open, my eyes watered at the stench. Though John Doe smelled like a sewer, I felt sorry for him. Somewhere in this city, he was missed by his family. And they had no idea what had happened to him.

Surprisingly, Shane didn't seem that much affected by the smell as he knelt next to the body and inspected it. His hands went straight to the dead man's face and he pried open his left eye.

"The soul has been taken," said Shane, his voice monotone, though not unpleasant.

"No shit," said Tyrius with laughter in his voice. "Tell us something we don't know."

I glared at the cat and raised my eyebrows at Gareth who was smiling at Tyrius's remark. He caught me staring at him and gave me a "what?" look.

Shane placed his hands about four inches above the dead man's corpse, his face set in concentration. "I am sensing the necromancer mark on this human," continued Shane as though Tyrius hadn't interrupted him.

Tyrius let out an exasperated huff. "Rowyn already told you cosmic nitwits it was the necromancers. What else do you want? Do you want us to do charades too? Would that help speed up the process?"

"There's a procedure to how we operate, catnip," growled Lance. "You don't like it… you can leave."

"And miss the dude's Jedi tricks?" mused the cat as he sat down on his haunches. "You'll have to drag me away, you flea-bitten mutt."

Gareth turned around, his shoulders moving in what I suspected was laughter. Man, these two. I wanted to kick both their butts.

We were very lucky the angels actually came. Though it had taken more than twelve hours, it was still a win. And I was going to work with that.

"What else can you tell me about his soul?" I leaned forward a bit and retched at the stink.

"I can sense the soul was removed from the body and held somewhere. It was alive for a few days. And then the soul died."

I raised my brows, seriously impressed. "Wow. You can tell all that by doing your Jedi trick?" What? I couldn't resist. Tyrius *had* started it.

A smile pulled at the corners of the angel's lips, and I could tell he was proud. "Yes. A residual aura of what was taken. Fingerprints, if you will."

157

"Nice." I wanted to smile, but the smell kept interfering with the muscles in my face.

"I can remove most of the smell with my elf dust, if you want," said Gareth, looking at me. "Maybe that'll help?"

"That won't be necessary." The angel kept his attention on the dead guy. "Your magic would remove valuable information about how this person was controlled, about what is left of his aura, about the remnants of his soul and the necromancer who navigated him. Smells are natural. So is the decomposing of flesh. It doesn't bother me."

Tyrius mumbled something under his breath and I shot him a look.

I was in the presence of two angels, and I wasn't going to show them the weakness of my mortal body. If he could work next to the stinky John Doe, so could I.

Trying to convince myself that the corpse smelled like roses and lilacs, I knelt next to the angel.

"You said the soul was held somewhere," I prompted, breathing through my mouth. "What does that mean exactly?"

Shane met my gaze. "Every soul has its own mark or imprint. It differs for each person. Their individuality, if you will. Imagine... every single person on this Earth has a number. I can sense the life of this soul, so I can track its number, follow its path."

"Like a GPS?" asked Tyrius.

The angel looked at the cat. "Exactly."

"Okay, I'll admit, that's pretty cool," said Tyrius, and I swear I saw Lance's lips pull back in a smile.

Shane looked back at me. "With that knowledge, I know this man's soul was removed and held somewhere. It wasn't ingested or killed, which is usually what happens when demons kill a mortal."

I nodded, knowing this all too well. "But the mortals weren't killed. Not at first."

Shane pressed his lips together. "And neither was the soul. His soul lived for three days. That, I am certain. And then it just… died. Quickly."

I leaned back a bit from the body, hoping to catch a bit of fresh air. "How can they do that? The necromancers? How could they trap a soul? It doesn't make sense."

Tyrius cleared his throat. "Don't forget they removed the souls *and* kept the bodies alive."

"Right. That."

The angel shrugged. "My guess is with Death magic. But I'll have to do a bit more examining to be sure. Necromancers use the dead as weapons. I've never heard of them using souls. And in this way."

"Now you have," said Tyrius.

I looked at the angel. "Where do you think they were holding the souls? Could they have been holding them in their temples?" How do you even hold a soul? In a jar? A room? I was having a really hard time trying to imagine it.

"Again, I'm not sure," said the angel. "Souls are basically energy. To be able to capture a soul and keep it alive and hidden somewhere takes great power. It's possible the necromancers figured out a way to do this at their temple… and it's also possible the souls were kept… *elsewhere*."

"Elsewhere?" I asked, not missing the hardness in his voice. "You mean the Netherworld?"

The angel's dark eyes met mine. "It's also a possibility. But again, this is all just speculation."

Son of a bitch. This was bad.

My tension rose, stiffening my shoulders. "You think they made a deal with a demon?"

The angel looked down at the body. "I would have said no before seeing this with my own eyes. Demons trade in mortal souls. And they do have the power to keep souls for a few days, even weeks. But it's usually for something greater like power over their world and, of course, more souls. But a demon making a deal with a necromancer? What could the necromancers offer the demons in exchange? If not the souls in question, then what? Necromancers are mortal. They mean nothing to demons. And from what I can see, the soul wasn't tampered by demons. There are no demonic traces. None."

I rubbed my eyes. Now I was even more confused. "It might just be a theory, but it's something."

"The best *something* we've got so far," said Tyrius, and I was surprised he was agreeing with the angel.

If the necromancers had indeed made a deal with demons, I might be able to break that deal if I knew the demon in question. It would help to know what the necromancers offered the demons as well. One thing was for sure. This necromancer ordeal kept getting worse.

Tyrius twitched his tail behind him. "Well, at least we know no more people got their souls hijacked."

"That we know of." I looked at the angel. "The Legion keeps track of souls, right?"

"Yes."

"It's part of the job description as a guardian angel."

"It is."

"So," I said. "Then you were aware that some souls were missing?"

The angel shook his head and stood up. "It's not how it works."

I got up, not wanting to look up at him. "Really? Okay. Explain it to me." If the Legion knew about the missing souls, why didn't they do anything about it?

"We know when souls die," answered the angel, and I saw Gareth cross his arms over his chest, watching the angel with a curious expression. "We keep track of every living soul. When a single soul dies, even among the billions, we know about it. But a missing soul… is not a dead soul. We had no way of knowing the necromancers were doing this. Not until the angel-borns approached us."

It was not what I wanted to hear. "So, the Legion won't be able to warn us if the necromancers start stealing souls again."

Shane shook his head. "I'm afraid not."

Tyrius cursed under his breath. "This is not good, Rowyn. How are we going to find these sick bastards if we don't know where or when they'll strike again?"

A beep sounded from my phone, and I pulled it out of my pocket. My heart thrashed as I read the text. "I just got a 911 from the Council." I looked up and met Gareth's intense gaze. "The necromancers have been spotted in Times Square, New York."

"Stop your grinnin' and drop your linen." Tyrius leaped into the air, his tail high and slashing behind him. "Let's roll!"

Smiling, I rushed to the hallway, wrapped my weapons belt around my waist, and slipped my jacket over it. Only when I had my boots on did I remember the angel and the dead body.

Oops.

I hurried back to the living room. "Are you two coming with us?" I asked, glancing at Lance and Shane.

"I'm coming," said the white dog. "You're going to need my help."

"Like we need a flea bath," muttered Tyrius.

Shane gave me a tight smile. "Go. I need to take the body back with me to Horizon. We need to perform some tests and see if we can figure out how the necromancers were able to keep the body alive without the soul."

Made sense. "Thank you for your help."

The angel smiled. "My pleasure."

Before I could ask the angel how he was planning on taking the corpse with him, he said, "Go. I'll take care of him. I presume you have a bathtub, right?"

"Yes," I answered, knowing the angels needed water to transition back to Horizon. It still didn't explain how he was going to transport the body, but it wasn't my call. I was needed elsewhere. "All right, then."

When I looked back, Gareth, Tyrius, and Lance were waiting for me by the front door.

I smiled, imagining the surprise on the necromancer's face when my fist connected with his jaw. *Got you, you son of a bitch.*

Feeling slightly better about this outcome, I rushed out the front door.

Chapter
17

We ran through the rush of humans along West 42nd Street in Manhattan. Enormous stone and glass buildings rose around us on either side. Massive billboards and television screens the size of cars blinked down at us. The busy street overwhelmed my ears with loud honks and running motors. The smell of grease and beer from the pubs reached me, and so did the roasted peanuts, asphalt, and the stink of exhaust.

Thousands of locals and tourists scrambled along the streets, laughing and enjoying the city life. The street was packed with the usual business types: women and men in expensive suits, carrying café lattes in one hand while chatting on their cell phones with the other.

"Do you know where on 42nd street?" came Tyrius's voice in my ear. The cat's body was wrapped around my neck like a scarf.

"Near 9th Avenue," I panted back, aware of a human woman eyeing me strangely. Then her eyes widened as she spotted a large white dog jogging next to me when I rushed past her.

Okay, so we looked a little weird. It wasn't every day you saw a man in a fedora hat and a long black trench coat, a woman with a cat wrapped around her neck and a white wolf running alongside without a leash or collar. We were a true motley crew, and that's how I liked it.

The green sign with 9th Avenue written in white letters came into view. "There. We're here," I said as I halted at the corner of the street, my lungs about to burst out of my chest.

Tyrius shifted around my shoulders. "I'm not seeing any necromancers. Mutt? You getting any necro vibes down there?"

Lance looked over at the wave of humanity. "Would it surprise your whiskers that I do?" I wasn't alarmed that the dog had spoken right in the middle of a cluster of humans. To them, it sounded just like an ordinary dog barking and not the voice of a person.

"Don't you bring my whiskers into this," mewed the cat.

Gareth brushed up against me. "Where are they?" His long coat swung around him like a cape, a super-elf.

The white dog cocked his head to the side. "Right here."

A human man walked by and patted Lance's head. "Cute dog." He flashed me his teeth and walked away.

It was really hard not to laugh at the expression on Lance's face, part horror, and part anger. What did he expect? He'd chosen to wear the guise of a dog, and a big *white* one at that. He was bound to get some attention.

"Here?" Tyrius moved to my left shoulder. "We're *here*. And I don't see them. Looks like you're not as smart as you think you are, Benji."

The dog's ears flattened on his head. "I'm telling you. The necromancers are here. I can sense their energies."

"Their energies," I repeated, wishing I had those powerful angel senses again. I kinda missed that. And my superspeed. I knew angels had heightened abilities to sense the supernatural, but in a crowd of thousands of mortals with their own energies, that was seriously impressive. "How many are there?"

"Three," answered the dog. "I'm sensing three distinctly *different* energies."

Three. My heart slammed in my chest as I spun on the spot with my hand on my weapons belt. I wasn't about to take out my blade in broad daylight, not yet, and not unless I had no other choice. I caught sight of one of the angel-born teams across the street from us, all in black gear with identical frowns on their faces. They hadn't spotted the necromancers either.

If Lance said they were here, they *were* here. I believed him and I trusted his angel instincts. The necromancers were here. I just had to find them.

"Maybe we should split up," said Gareth. "We might be able to spot them better if we separate. It's impossible to see anything with all these people." He frowned at a group of young men who'd purposely hit him in the shoulder as they moved past us.

"The elf does have a point," said Tyrius. "This place is crawling with humans. We'll never pick them out of a crowd like this."

"We will." I threw my gaze over the heads that crowded our side of the sidewalk. "I'm pretty sure I can spot them." I don't think I could ever forget the gaunt faces the necromancers shared. "They don't have glamour magic." Or did they? I hoped not.

"No." Tyrius's hot breath brushed my cheek. "They have Death magic. It's worse."

"I'm not seeing any zombies at the moment." The dread I'd been feeling since I jumped out of Gareth's truck intensified. Why were the necromancers here in the first place? What about 42nd street attracted them?

"Well," said Tyrius, and I felt him lie down on my shoulder and shift until he was comfortable. "I'm going to take a nap. Wake me up when the action hits."

"Just like a cat," mumbled Lance.

"Exactly." Tyrius nudged his cold nose against my neck. Though I couldn't see his eyes, I was certain the little kitty had them closed.

I let out a long sigh and looked around, seeing wall-to-wall human bodies but no necromancers. Were the necromancers hiding? Had they spotted us and run away?

"How gentle do you want me to be if I happen to catch one of them?" asked Gareth, a hint of mischief in his voice.

I flashed the elf a smile. "Just as gentle as I would be, honey."

The elf beamed, transforming his handsome face into a sexy visage. "That's my girl."

"Will you two shut it," moaned the cat. "I'm trying to get some shut-eye. Not nightmares, thank you very much. I think I just threw up in my mouth."

I laughed, which was totally inappropriate at the moment, but it did ease some of the tension I was feeling.

I didn't know how long I stood there watching the wave of humanity roll up around us. We kept getting looks from passersby. Lance was drawing a lot of attention. The animal lovers went right up to him and scratched his head while the pooch gave me a deathly glare. But most of the humans gave us and Lance a wide berth.

When I felt myself relax a little, I saw her.

In the middle of a wave of people, not a hundred feet across from me stood a necromancer.

She was tall, freakishly tall for a woman. Maybe six-four, give or take a few inches. Even from where I stood, I could see her face clearly. Her features stretched, her cheekbones sticking out above pale, sunken eyes that rested below a hairless brow. Her face was gaunt and pale, like she'd been starving herself on purpose for years. But this wasn't anorexia. This was, I guessed, what happened to your body when you played around with Death magic. You ended up looking like a corpse. Like death.

Her bony shoulders were draped with a black robe, her face partially hidden with her cowl. She reminded me of the Sith characters from *Star Wars*. If she thought wearing that would make her blend in, she was even more stupid than the notion that shaving her eyebrows was a good thing. Trust me. Shaved eyebrows didn't look good. Period.

And she just stood there, facing me while people milled around her. She held herself straight with brisk purpose, confidence, and calculating eyes. She wanted me to find her. Okay, so that might be part of her plan.

But I was still going to kick her bony ass.

Her pale eyes focused on me and her face stretched into an all-too-tight smile, like her skin was about to crack open and bleed.

"There!" I shouted, pointing to the necromancer who hadn't moved. When I saw both Gareth and Lance had seen her too, I took off at a run.

No point in waiting.

Tag, I'm it.

Hands out, I knocked humans out of the way as I rushed toward the necromancer. She was mine. All mine.

"A little warning would have been nice!" cried Tyrius as he hung around my shoulders, his nails piercing into my flesh as he hung on for dear life.

"I did. I said 'there.'"

"Not. Good. Enough," the cat howled.

The necromancer spun around and slipped through the crowd. It didn't matter. I had eyes on her. She wasn't going anywhere.

"Move! Out of the way! Move!" I shouted as I pushed humans from my path not so gently. A big bearded man cursed me out. I didn't blame him. I'd have cursed me out too.

"Sorry," I cried as I kept going.

I spotted a slip of her black robe before she disappeared into a crowd of teenage girls. She was fast. How'd she manage to move that fast with all these people in the way? I rushed to where I'd last spotted her. Nothing.

Cursing, I plowed forward, vaulting around humans up the street until I saw her again. The necromancer spun around. Her eyes were completely white, and her lips moved as she raised her hands as though in a chant. A dark mist emanated from her hands, spreading out, over and around her like a glowing black sphere.

"Watch it, I feel a spell coming," said Tyrius.

"I don't care. I can reach her before she finishes." Fury bubbled up in me as I was rushing towards her—

Something grabbed me from behind and I was pulled into a hard chest.

"Don't," hissed Gareth in my ear, his hands around my waist, pinning me to him.

"Why? I have her." I struggled in his grip, confused as to why he'd grabbed me. A flash of white appeared in my line of sight, and Lance was there, next to us. His ears were low, and a deep growl emanated from his throat.

Gareth's lips brushed my cheek. "You don't. Look."

The back haze-like sphere had spread to a circumference of about a hundred feet, enveloping at least a hundred or so humans. The scent of rot was overwhelming and snuffed out every other scent in the street.

It only lasted for a few seconds, and then the sphere fell.

If Gareth hadn't grabbed me when he did, I would have been inside that sphere.

With her hands still held high, the necromancer smiled at me. Well, I think she was smiling at me, but without irises, it was hard to tell who she was looking at.

And then something strange happened.

All those people who'd been cloaked inside the circle froze. After a moment, the skin on all of them sparkled, as though it was painted with millions of tiny diamonds. The diamonds then detached themselves and hovered above each person, slowly coming together into a ball of light, like a tiny sun. Souls.

Oh no.

I knew what this was, and I could do nothing but watch as the souls were ripped away from the innocent people. Then as one, the souls all sprang towards the necromancer. At first I thought she was going to grab them somehow, but then she simply snapped her fingers and the souls vanished.

"Rowyn," said Tyrius. "What the hell just happened?"

"She took their souls. That's what happened." I pulled out of Gareth's grip, my eyes on the necromancer bitch. I yanked out my blade, pointed it toward her, and mouthed *you're dead*.

When I looked back at the humans, they were all staring at me with yellow eyes.

Tyrius's nails cut through the skin on my shoulder. "Uh—I think this is bad."

Still smiling, the necromancer lowered her hands and spoke two words. "Kill them."

And then the wave of soulless humans spun around, their yellow eyes locked on to us, and charged.

CHAPTER
18

Have you seen the movie where the mob of soulless people comes crashing down on you on 42nd Street? Yeah, me neither.

The three of us sprinted in the opposite direction right after Gareth flung out two shots of his sleeping elf dust, which, unfortunately, only landed on maybe twenty or so of the soulless. They fell, but then a mass of soulless behind them just hurtled over them and came at us again.

It gave us a few seconds' head start, and we took it gladly.

I was also glad I had on my light boots, which were perfect for running. The image of me trying to run in those six-inch heeled boots Layla always seemed to wear would have killed me or broken an ankle. Probably both.

"I just *love* an afternoon jog," I panted as I picked my way between two men in dark business suits who hadn't yet noticed the mob approaching behind us. "Um—where are we running to?"

Gareth sprinted next to me, his long legs moving with ease. "My truck."

"Are we going to run them over with your truck?"

"No." A frown spread over the elf's face. "My truck is going to get us out of here."

Right. I stole a look behind me and felt some relief. The soulless mob was still a bit behind us. Gareth's truck was only two blocks away. We were going to make it.

Screaming rose from the other side of the street.

"Rowyn! Look to your left," cried Tyrius.

From across the street came another mass of rushing, yellow-eyed humans. *What in the—?*

"There!" shouted Lance, bounding ahead of us on the sidewalk.

Another herd of soulless was fast approaching from up ahead, their limbs stiff and mechanical but moving rapidly.

"How did this happen?" I cried. Gareth stood next to me with his eyes wide.

It was as though all the people in Times Square had all lost their souls and were now under the control of the necromancers.

And we were surrounded.

Call it angel-born mixed with demon essence intuition, but I saw them. Standing on either side of the street dressed in identical heavy black robes were two more necromancers.

Great.

One necromancer junky was bad enough. Three, well, three was just a hell of a lot more complicated.

"Come on. This way," shouted Gareth, as the elf took a left on 8th Avenue and headed south, away from the madness.

Lance and I sprinted after him. I held on to Tyrius with my hand as I pushed my legs as fast as they would go. I wouldn't risk him falling and then getting trampled by the mob.

My heart thrashed painfully against my ribcage. I watched Lance gallop effortlessly ahead of us, his muscles contracting and beauty in the way his legs flowed. His body was built to run and had me wishing I could shift into a dog just this once. Four legs were far better than two.

"Rowyn! Rowyn! You can't hide from us," chanted the soulless close behind us. The voices of the necromancers magnified as though they were speaking through a megaphone.

And then they all laughed. Because, let's face it, they were psychotic. And creepy as hell.

The sound had all the hair on my body rising. It was the creepiest sound, and even Tyrius had clamped down on my shoulder hard.

"Soon it will all be over," chorused the voices. "Life will be eradicated. Death shall rise."

I ran for maybe thirty seconds, gritting my teeth as the mob of soulless charged from behind. I was a good runner, but I couldn't keep up a full sprint forever.

The sound of the heavy tread of the footsteps behind me shifted, becoming louder and unsteady. Closer. Damn. I didn't know how close they were, but they sounded close. Too close.

I chanced a glimpse over my shoulder and then wished I hadn't.

Three or maybe four hundred strong soulless—all of mixed ethnicity, age, and gender—rushed behind us like a nightmarish, killer puppet show. Their limbs were jerky and stiff, and their faces were all blank. But their eyes were bright with a common intelligence and cunning.

"Don't look back!" shouted Tyrius. "Just run! Run!"

He didn't have to tell me twice.

With a new surge of adrenaline, I found my second wind, and I was running like the devil was at my heels. In a way, he was.

Gareth's truck came into view up ahead. Lance reached it first and waited. Then the elf was there, and he vaulted over the hood of his truck like a Hollywood stuntman. He came up on the other side, opened the door, and he and Lance slid in. Impressive.

Four seconds later, I pulled open the front passenger door and jumped in, Tyrius leaping off my shoulders as I shut the door.

Boom!

The truck shook and rocked as hundreds of soulless threw themselves against it repeatedly, the sound of metal crushing as fists hit it exploding around us.

Gareth cursed as he slammed his hand on the door lock knob. "Lock the doors."

It was an old truck, so we had to do everything manually.

I whirled and reached for my door's lock knob—

My door inched open.

My heart raced as a soulless man's face appeared at the window. His hand clamped around the door's metal edge as he pried it open a little more. In a flash, I had my hand on the door handle pulling, but the man was stronger. Then, to my dismay, another soulless appeared next to him, her hands on the door as she pulled along with him.

Crap. Crap. Crap.

"Rowyn!" yelled Gareth.

"I know," I yelled back, pulling as hard as I could on the door handle with my right hand.

Having no other choice, I yanked my blade free with my left hand and came down hard on their fingers. The door jerked free and I yanked it closed, smacking down the lock knob with a *thud*.

I looked down at the seat. Five bloody fingers stared back at me.

Whoops.

Boom!

I cringed as the soulless threw themselves at my window, their faces bloodied as their skin tore and cracked under the sheer force, leaving thick trails of blood trickling down the glass.

A loud thump came from the truck's roof, as many feet pounded from above. The light from the afternoon sun was snuffed out as hundreds of soulless clambered up on the truck and surrounded us from all sides. The truck jerked and I turned to see the soulless climbing into the truck's bed and banging at the rear panel with their fists.

"Demon balls!" shrieked Tyrius. "They're trying to break in!"

Lance growled and barked at the soulless pounding behind us.

Fear sank into my gut. I looked at Gareth, finding his eyes on me, and his expression grim.

The elf stuck his key into the ignition, and the truck roared into life.

"Yeah, that's right!" cheered Tyrius as he straightened up on my lap. "We're gonna plow through these bastards! Onward, elf!"

I grimaced, looking at Gareth, but his eyes were in front of him, on the dozen or so soulless that had clambered up on the hood and were now smashing the windshield with their hands and heads. Not pretty. And really scary.

The glass behind us shattered. I winced and had my blade up as I turned around. The glass had a web of cracks in it, but it was still holding.

"It won't hold for long," I said. "If we don't leave now… we're not going to make it." *No, because these puppets are going to tear us apart with their own hands.* The thought of their cold hands on my body made bile rise in the back of my throat. I wasn't going to let that happen.

"Gareth. We need to move."

The elf's hands were tight on the wheel. "These are innocent   people."
"Who are probably already dead," I reminded him, the words feeling horrible as they came out of my mouth. "If we don't leave, we die. If we die, how are we supposed to stop the necromancers? The Council needs us. The humans need us. We need to leave. Now." Before the necromancer puppets shred us into ribbons.

"I don't know about you, man," said Tyrius. "But I've got four kids and a wife. My kids need me. My wife needs me. Hell, I need me!"

The elf's face was twisted in horror.

I slipped my arm around Lance and placed my hand on Gareth's shoulder. "We can't save them all, but we will save some." The truck rocked again, pulling high on an angle, and for a horrible moment I thought we were toast. But then the truck fell back straight and bounced.

"Looks like they want to tip us over," said Lance. He looked at me. "I can slip through the window and get help."

"Yeah, right," interrupted Tyrius. "By the time you come back, all that'll be left of us is red soup and shredded skin noodles."

Gareth's eyes narrowed. "There's only one way out."

"Yeah. Through them," said the cat, and my chest tightened.

The elf dug his hands in his coat pocket, and when he pulled them out, they dripped in black elf dust.

"What's that?" I'd never seen that color before—though black wasn't technically a color—but who cares.

"Something that'll go boom," said the elf.

"I love things that go boom," said Tyrius, his eyes wide, and Lance laughed. Weird. Were the two bonding?

With his hands closed around elf dust, Gareth rolled down his window.

I straightened. "Gareth. Don't." The elf was mad. "They'll get in."

Ignoring me, Gareth leaned over the opened window, punched a few soulless in the face to clear a path, and then he flung his hands over the hood of the truck.

He ducked inside. "Hang on!"

"What?"

As soon as the dust hit, there was an explosion.

The truck bounced and I swear we were airborne for a few seconds.

My ears rang, but when I looked around light spilled through the windshield. The soulless that had been at the front and over the hood of the truck were lying on the sidewalk, away from the car. They were stirring, ready to get up.

Not bothering to close the window, Gareth put the truck in drive and slammed on the gas.

I jerked back as the truck's tires squealed and we sped up 8th Avenue.

"Netherworld be damned!" cursed Tyrius as he leaped up behind me and stood on the backseat's headrest. "Dude. That was awesome."

A smile twisted on the elf's features. "I know."

I laughed and ran my hand over Lance's head. He gave me a narrow look, but I didn't care. We were safe.

As the truck sped up 8th Avenue, I turned around and looked back.

The elf hadn't killed even a single one of the soulless.

Now, *that* was impressive.

CHAPTER
19

Father Thomas's office felt stuffy and five times hotter than the last time I was here. The room smelled of male perspiration and fear. I stood with my arms crossed over my chest, leaning against the bookcase at the far wall—first because the air seemed less stuffy here and second because I had a good view of things that were going down.

My muscles were stiff with tension, and I'd developed a neck pain on my left side that throbbed down and across to my shoulder. I knew it was stress, but I couldn't do anything about it for now. After the soulless mob attack yesterday in Times Square, I'd barely slept, maybe two hours tops, which could also explain the neck pain.

So, when the priest had texted me about an emergency meeting at one in the afternoon, I grabbed my weapons belt, jumped in my subbie, and drove to the church.

"New York City's in lockdown," Father Peter was saying, sitting in Father Thomas's chair behind Father Thomas's desk. *Dude. That's just rude.*

Father Thomas sat in a small office chair to the right. If he was upset about the other priest invading his space, he didn't show it.

The other Knights of Heaven all gathered around the office, some sitting in chairs brought in from other rooms and others on the couch. Six priests had gathered, counting the redhead I owed an ass-whooping.

"It's all over the news." Father Peter leaned over the desk, interlacing his fingers. "They're calling it a 'super-virus,' and people are scared. They're quarantining themselves in their homes, afraid of coming out and catching the virus."

"Which works in our favor," said one of the priests with short blond hair whose name escaped me. "The more who stay at home, the less chance the necromancers can infect them."

He was right. I hated to see my city in such disarray and hopelessness, but the truth was, the humans were safer if they stayed home. For now.

But the necromancers couldn't hide forever. And they were going to get what was coming to them. That was a promise.

"Where are all the soulless right now?" asked the redheaded priest.

"In the streets," answered Father Thomas, his voice hoarse. "Still roaming around Times Square. They've been there since yesterday, fighting the New York Police officers who are trying to contain them to get them to the hospitals."

Father Peter shook his head. "They can't. There are too many of them. There are more than two thousand soulless in the city right now."

I sucked in a breath through my teeth. Damn. I had no idea it was that many. Only a few hundred had attacked us, but it seemed the necromancers had stayed busy stealing innocent souls.

Frustrated, I opened my mouth and turned to my side, expecting to see Gareth but seeing only a bookshelf next to me. *Ooops.* Feeling foolish, I clamped my mouth shut and pretended to be interested in a book before turning back around.

I'd asked Gareth to stay with my gran, even though Tyrius and Kora were with her. With everything going on, it didn't feel right leaving her without extra protection. Gareth loved my gran, and he'd give his life to protect her. I was still shaken by what had happened yesterday, and if Gareth hadn't stayed behind with my gran, I would have declined Father Thomas's meeting. Sorry, but my gran came first, and the priest could always give me a recap over the phone.

Following the incident in the truck, Tyrius had been really quiet, no doubt contemplating how close we'd come to dying and thinking of his kids. When I'd dropped Gareth at my gran's, the Siamese cat had asked if I minded that he stayed behind with Kora and the kids instead of coming with me to the church. My heart had clenched at the fear that reflected in his beautiful blue eyes.

"Yeah. You should stay with your kids," I had told him. "I've got this. It's just a meeting. I'll tell you all about it when I get back."

"We'll save you some pizza," the cat had replied, visible tension leaving his posture.

I'd doubted that. His kids ate more than him. If even a crust was left behind, I'd consider it a miracle.

"Did you hear back from the mutt?" Tyrius had asked.

"Not yet," I had told him. We'd dropped off Lance at a nearby pond yesterday, his way home to Horizon. He promised he'd be back as soon as the Legion had new intel regarding the soulless and the necromancers. It seemed to me like the angel mutt was growing on the demon catnip. The thought had made me smile all the way to the church, but the feeling hadn't lasted.

"I spoke to the mayor," continued Father Peter and my eyes snapped to him from across the room. He hesitated as his expression turned bitter. "They're going to call in the National Guard to *remedy* the situation."

"Remedy how?" asked one of the priests with a short beard and dark circles under his eyes that shone through his glasses.

Father Peter was silent for a moment. "Eradicate the infection before it spreads."

He didn't have to spell it out. We all knew what that meant. They were going to kill two thousand people. Kill them to protect millions.

I was expecting a collective outrage from the priests, but they all just sat there silently, with identical grim expressions.

Damn. This was bad. The National Guard had no idea what they were up against. They didn't understand this. They couldn't. This wasn't a typical pandemic. This wasn't a virus. This was Death magic, but they didn't know that. To protect the rest of the population, they were going to kill all those soulless.

But maybe there was a way to save them.

"How soon until the National Guard shows up?" I asked to no priest in particular. The theft of all those souls weighed heavily on me.

Father Peter's eyes focused on me. He hesitated, like he was contemplating whether to tell me.

"When?" I asked again. I didn't care that my tone was demanding, nor did I care if he didn't like me. I wasn't here to make friends. I was here to do a job, and that's exactly what I was going to do.

"Tomorrow morning. Nine a.m. sharp," said the priest finally, though his lips twisted in distaste like revealing this information had left a bitter taste his mouth.

I leaned back against the bookcase, and spines poked through the fabric of my jacket. That didn't give me much time to track down the necromancers, but it was all I had. I clenched my jaw. I would make it work.

Father Peter was still staring at me like I was a useless bug he wanted nothing more than to swat. So, I kept staring at him until he finally looked away.

You don't scare me, priest.

"The church is sending reinforcements." Father Peter leaned back in the chair, his gaze flicking between everyone in the room except me. "They'll be here tonight."

"How many?" I asked as I waited until he looked at me. "How many will the church send?"

His jaw clenched. "Fifty."

I raised a brow. "Fifty? Are you serious? Fifty isn't enough. Not nearly enough." I didn't care to hide the skepticism from my voice. Fifty was a joke.

"That's right," challenged the priest. "Fifty Knights of Heaven. Fifty *skilled* warriors of the church," he added a note of casual disdain to his voice.

He was an idiot if he thought that would somehow stop the thousands of soulless. They would be slaughtered, but I wasn't about to start a war with the church.

"And what about you?" argued Father Peter, his eyes narrowing as he looked at me, and I felt all the other priests' eyes focus on me as well. "What is the angel-born Council doing to help us?"

"Well, for one thing," I told him. "They have every available angel-born Operative out there looking for these necromancers. That's about two hundred, if not more." It wasn't thousands, but it was better than fifty.

Silence. Okay. This was not going well, and I was glad Gareth wasn't here to witness it.

The tension in the room was thick, and I didn't blame them. We were all feeling it.

"Rowyn," said Father Thomas, and I moved my gaze to him. "You said something to me earlier about how you saw the necromancers stealing the souls. Can you tell us more about that?"

I swallowed and took a breath. "Before it happened," I began as the visual of the necromancer woman's lips moving in a chant came rushing back. "The necromancer said a spell. I was too far away, and with all the noise from the street, I couldn't hear the words. But it was definitely a spell. I'm guessing a Death magic spell."

A chorus of outraged gasps and exasperated cries from the assembled priests filled the room. Amateurs.

"Rowyn?" Father Thomas gave me an encouraging nod to continue.

I waited for the room to settle. "She raised her hands—"

"She?" said one of the priests, the only one with his hair pulled back into a low ponytail. "The necromancer was a she?"

"Yes. *She*." I looked at their shocked expressions. "Looks like the necromancers don't discriminate with the sexes." I let that sink in a moment. "Then she raised her arms and produced some kind of black mist that spread out over a crowd of people." I took a breath and added, "Then I saw their souls."

"You *saw* their souls? How?" asked Father Peter.

"I saw their souls leave their bodies. I saw them… hovering in the air."

Father Peter's gaze cut into mine. "And where did the souls go?"

I knew this was coming. "I don't know. She snapped her fingers… and they were just gone."

"Just gone?" questioned Father Peter incredulously. "Souls can't be *just* gone. They either reach Horizon, or they are killed and don't go anywhere."

"Well, these ones were *just* gone," I said, starting to get pissed off at his attitude. "Look. I'm not making this up. I saw it with my own eyes. So did my friends. The souls disappeared. Where? I have no freaking idea. But the necromancers do."

If awards were given for the "scowl of the year," Father Peter would have been a true winner.

"You are a very insolent young woman," said the priest.

I curtsied. "Thanks, hon."

Father Thomas cleared his throat. "Where do you think they are, Rowyn?"

"Well, Shane—the angel who came to look at the body in my living room—seems to think maybe the souls were taken to the Netherworld."

Wait for it…

The congregated priests let out another round of exasperated cries of outrage. Father Thomas stood up and glared at the other priests. They stopped their hissy fits but kept glowering.

"The angel," said Father Thomas as he clasped his hands together before him, "believes the necromancers are working with the demons?"

I shrugged. "It's a theory. He told me he'd get back to me later with more intel. But for now, it's the only thing that would make sense. I mean, the souls aren't here, in this world. If they're not here, they've got to be somewhere else. That somewhere else is pointing to the Netherworld." Because we didn't know where else they could be.

Father Thomas's dark eyes searched my face. "What about how the necromancers can keep the bodies alive without a soul? Or how they can pilot them?"

I shook my head. "He doesn't know. He told me he'd have answers for me once he had more time working on the body." Yup. Really lame, but it was the truth and it was all I had at the moment. "You can glare at me all you want," I told the other priests, my gaze flicking between them. "It won't change the fact that right now we've got a whole lot of nothing, and thousands of people are going to die if we don't stop the necromancers."

"These people are already dead." Father Peter watched me. "Once the soul leaves the body, it cannot return."

I turned to Father Thomas, my eyes narrowing. "What's he talking about?" I didn't like the expression on the priest's face. "Is that true?"

Father Thomas sighed through his nose. "I'm afraid so, Rowyn. Once the soul leaves the body, it has already started its new path. A soul will only leave when the body is truly dead. Souls enter the body when a new life is born. And they leave when the body dies."

Bullshit. "But these people are not dead." I curled my fingers into fists and felt pain sear my flesh as my fingernails cut into my palms. "They're walking and breathing. They have heartbeats. That's not dead. That's *alive.*" *You white-collar douches.*

Father Peter gave me a disdainful glance and then snapped, "People don't come back from the dead."

"I did," I blabbed before I could stop myself. The archangel Raphael had never specified my resurrection as a secret. My face was hot with a surge of bubbling fury. "I died. And here I am. In the flesh. So, how do you explain that?"

Father Peter smiled. "You're a liar."

It took all my strength to remain still and not vault across the room to land a sidekick into the priest's throat.

My blood pounded in my ears, and I matched his smile instead. "I'm not lying." But the priests all looked away from me, dismissing me like I was crazy. Okay, I did crazy things sometimes, but that didn't make me crazy.

Father Peter's mouth hardened into a firm line. "Necromancers animate the dead. It's what they do. As a Hunter, I would have assumed you knew this. It appears they've mastered this skill as they have reanimated thousands of the dead."

"Thousands of alive," I shot back. I couldn't help it. "These people are alive."

The priest's face took on another darker shade. "Why are you here, Hunter, if you are not willing to help?"

"I am trying to help."

"It looks to me like you're just wasting our time. We're here to discuss how to save the lives of those who matter."

I raised my voice. "Those who matter?"

Father Peter looked at Father Thomas. "The people who live and are in danger of the necromancers' Death magic. The other thousands who are at risk if we don't put a stop to this."

"So, let me get this straight. You're going to do nothing?" I glared at them all. "You're just going to let all those people die?"

"It's extremely taxing to have oneself keep repeating the same thing over and over again. I'll tell you one last time. Those people are dead. Forget about them. Think of those who are alive."

I'd had enough. "You're wrong. And I'm going to prove it." I stormed out of the office.

"Rowyn! Where are you going?" shouted Father Thomas.

"I have a sudden need to take a shower," I shouted back as I cleared the doorframe and headed down the hall. *To wash this filth off of me.*

The priests' voices rose in anger behind me. Father Thomas and a few others I couldn't recognize were in a shouting match. I was so mad I could barely see straight, and I practically kicked the side door open and marched out. The cooler air was welcome on my hot cheeks as I made my way to my Subaru in the parking lot. I had no idea if my theory was right, if somehow the souls were returned to their bodies, life would breathe into them again. Yet, I had a feeling it would. I couldn't explain it. I just couldn't accept what the priests were telling me. *I* had died and was brought back again. If it had worked for me, wouldn't it work for all those people? Granted, I'd been killed for a purpose, to become a Dark angel no less, but the principle was the same. Wasn't it?

If anyone was an expert in souls, the angels were. Shane would know and the next time I saw him, I was going to ask him.

By the time the hooded figure stepped into my line of sight, it was already too late.

CHAPTER
20

"Okay. I'll admit it. You got me," I said to the necromancer because, let's face it, he really did. But it didn't mean I still couldn't kick his ass.

And yes, it was a *he* this time. Though he looked like a crackhead, I recognized him as the same necromancer who'd sicked his zombies on us in the temple. This was going to be fun!

Though his hood kept most of his face in shadow, his white skin seemed to glow in the sunlight. It had that pasty, waxy corpse quality to it. Something that could have been black eyeshadow covered most of his eye area and framed his pale eyes, giving him a raccoon look. Though I'd seen him before, the no eyebrows and eyelashes still creeped me out. The stench of rot was the worst. He smelled like he slept with the dead. Hell, maybe he did.

Instincts kicking in, I cast my gaze around the parking lot and the neighboring buildings. I couldn't see any zombies or soulless anywhere. Though it didn't mean they weren't there hiding, waiting for the perfect moment to ambush me. I seriously doubted he'd show up alone. From what I'd witnessed with the necromancers, they never fought alone. They always had an army at their disposal. A dead one. Or worse, a soulless army.

I yanked out my soul blade. "Where are all your dead pals? Thought you guys never left home without them." I smiled. "Did you guys have a fight?"

The necromancer's gray lips spread widely. "I thought we could do this, just the two of us." He arched a hairless brow. "You know… one on one."

The way he looked at me, like he wanted me—not to have sex with me, but to eat my soul—was a million times more eerie and disturbing. Not to mention gross.

"I gotta thank you." I laughed. "You've just made my job a hell of a lot easier."

His face, wrinkled and haggard like it had been in the water for months, cracked a smile. "Really? And what job is that, Rowyn?"

"To kick your ass, silly." I flashed him my teeth. "Are you going to tell me your name, or do you want me to make one up again. I've got loads of really good ones. Please say yes."

The necromancer chuckled. "You can call me Lord Rath."

I chuckled back. "I'm not about to call you *lord*. No, Rath it is. Kinda sounds like rat. Doesn't it? Yeah. That name suits you. Good choice." I gave him a thumbs up.

Lord Rath folded his hands in front of him. "I'm going to make this easy for you."

"Do tell, Rath. Rath. Rath. Rath." I was liking saying that name for some reason. "The suspense is killing me." *But I'm going to kill you first. Stinker.*

The necromancer flashed me his yellow, rotten teeth. "Give me back the ferro ex mortuis now, and I will let your soul live. Refuse, and I will torment your soul until the end of time with the rest of them."

I cocked my hip. "The what ferro? Sorry, I don't speak douchebag."

"The blade at your hip," answered Lord Rath, his voice short. "Give it back."

Ah ha. So, this blade was important to him. Why? One thing was for certain. If it was important enough to seek me out, no way in hell I was going to give it to him.

"Rath, Rath, Rat—oops, I mean Rath. You need to respect the rules, buddy. We all do."

The necromancer's face was blank. "The rules?"

I waved my blade as I spoke. "Finders keepers, losers weepers. Come on, you know it."

Lord Rath's gray lips twisted into a snarl. "The ferro ex mortuis doesn't belong to the nonbelievers. You've already soiled it, having it next to you like that. You should have never touched it with your filthy hands."

I stared at my fingernails. "Okay. So I might need a manicure, but I wouldn't exactly call them filthy." A thought occurred to me. "Is that why you came to my house?" I'd thought it was because we'd freed the soulless from the barn, but now I wasn't so sure. "You came for your blade? For this?" I made a show of my weapons belt with the necromancer blade snug in its new sheath.

Lord Rath said nothing, but I took that as a giant yes.

I tapped the ferro ex mortuis with my finger. "Why is it so important? It's just a piece of stone. It is stone, right? Granted, it's very pretty. Make another one. I'm keeping this one right here."

The necromancer dipped his head. "You'll never understand, but the blade is useless to you. Only in Death can the ferro ex mortuis shine."

"Right," I answered. "And you were going to use it to sacrifice that poor woman, Cynthia."

Lord Rath's smile was a wintry thing. "Cynthia chose willingly to sacrifice herself to Death. No one forced her. She was happy to do it."

I sucked in a breath through my teeth. "Happy to do it? The woman was brainwashed since she was probably just a kid in your creepy cult. She had no idea what she was agreeing to. You were using her. Her life meant nothing to you."

"On the contrary," said the necromancer. "Her life meant a great deal. Unlike yours, hers has a *true* purpose."

Now, why did he have to go and say that? "My life does have meaning, you skinny bastard. It's meant to kick your ass."

Lord Rath laughed. "The only thing you have that's worth anything in this world... is your soul. Souls are powerful tools."

I wanted to vomit at how sick he sounded. "Since we're on the subject of souls," I began, "which demon did you bargain with?" If I knew the demon, maybe I could strike a better deal somehow. It probably wouldn't work, but I was desperate. I'd do anything to get the souls back.

The necromancer lost some of his smile. "Demon?"

"Yeah. The one who's keeping all those souls you stole in the Netherworld for you."

At that, the sinister man laughed, and the sound sent a wave of pricks over my skin. "Necromancers don't make deals with demons." He laughed again, and this time I wanted to punch him in the face. "And we'd never give them any of *our* souls. Why would we give them the source of our power?" He stared at me for several seconds. "You really don't know anything about us. Do you?"

Okay, now I was really confused. If the necromancers didn't make a deal with the demons, and the souls weren't kept in the Netherworld, where were the souls?

I flashed him my teeth. "How about you tell me, and then we can argue about that too." I doubted he was going to spill the beans, but it was worth a shot.

Lord Rath remained calm. "You don't have the knowledge you need to understand, Hunter. It would be a waste of my time."

"Yada yada yada. I'm getting bored." Partly true. "Are we going to fight or what?"

Lord Rath gestured with his right hand. "Give me the blade," he threatened. "I won't ask you again."

I waved my soul blade at him. "Come and get it, Rat." I wasn't going to make this easy for him. After what they'd pulled on all those humans, he deserved a good ol' ass-whooping.

Lord Rath's lips moved in a silent spell. A wind rose and so did the smell of carrion and sulfur. The necromancer blinked and his eyes had gone completely white.

Crap. Not this again.

A sudden noise pulled my attention toward the back of the church, to the graveyard beyond. People moved around the gravestones, their tread stiff and slow. Not people. Zombies—about fifty of them.

Damn.

I arched a brow and glanced at the necromancer. "A herd of zombies in broad daylight. You're ballsy. I'll give you that."

"Thank you," said the creep.

"You never intended this to be a fair fight." I knew the odds of surviving a herd of fifty zombies were slim, even for me. I had a better chance at fighting just this necromancer death junkie. "Can't do it. Can you? You're too pathetic, too weak to know how to make a fist and use it?"

His eyes widened, frustration evident on his face. "I don't need to use my fists. Does a king need to fight when he has an army at his disposal?"

King? That was a giant ego right there. I shrugged. "I've done the zombie thing before. It's getting a little too cliché for me. How about you give me something new. How about you show me your giant necromancer balls and fight." Yeah, that didn't come out right, but you get the picture.

Lord Rath lowered his hood. His bald head gleamed, and parts of his scalp had black marks on it like he'd taken a piece of coal and smeared it on his head and along the sides of his neck. "Have it your way then," said the necromancer. "I didn't want to have to do this just yet, but you've changed my mind." There was silence for a moment. "It amazes me that an idiot such as you were a Hunter once."

"I'm still a Hunter, asshat," I said, and I couldn't keep the anger or frustration out of my voice.

"Not for long." He mumbled a word under his breath, and the mass of twitching, shuffling zombies halted just beyond the border of the church's parking lot.

I breathed a mental sigh of relief. It wasn't a huge win, but I took it.

I didn't like the smug smile on the bastard's face. "Why are you smiling? The fighting hasn't even started yet."

Lord Rath regarded me with an expression somewhere between irritation and satisfaction. "You took something from me, and now I've taken something from you."

I felt something of a chill at his words. He was arrogant, looking at me as though he'd already won the fight. He wasn't a fighter, not in the one-on-one sense of the word. He was a thinker. Thinkers were the worst kind of enemies. A smart enemy didn't have to be stronger or faster than you. He just had to outsmart you.

And that's exactly what he was thinking.

I swallowed hard and lowered into a fighting stance. "You've got nothing on me."

Lord Rath tilted his head and began circling me as I moved accordingly. "I took it," he said, making a fist of his hand. "It's mine now. It will always be mine."

Gotcha. He meant my soul. "I still have my soul, dumbass."

He eyed me, a faint glimmer of humor somewhere in the look. "I wasn't talking about yours. I'm talking about the soul of a loved one. Someone precious to you."

Another chill spiraled up from my lower back to my neck and stayed there. "What did you say?"

"You gave me no choice, Rowyn. You should have given me back the ferro ex mortuis when I asked you."

Oh, my god. Gran.

201

My knees buckled and I nearly fell. "Did you…" No, I couldn't even say the words. It couldn't be true. "You're lying." I should have stayed with her. I should never have come.

Lord Rath cocked his head. "You know I'm not. And it was so easy. Almost a joke, at how easy it was to take the soul. I barely lifted a finger."

Rage thumped into my blood. "I don't believe you! You're a liar. Liar!" I snarled, pointing my blade with barely controlled fury. "If you did anything to her… I'm going to kill you and all your freakish brothers and sisters." I tried to focus through the fog of my rage, but the image of my dead grandmother squished all the reason from my brain.

"It's over," said Rath, and then he sucked on his fingers like he was licking the icing from a cake. "The soul is mine. It will always be mine. Forever."

The steady rage inside me flared into a full-blown madness and will to kill.

I tapped into my Hunter skills, homed in on my abilities, and flew forward, my soul blade aimed at his throat.

His arm came up and his fist opened, tossing something into my eyes.

I stumbled as searing pain exploded in my eyes like he'd doused me with acid. Cursing, tears spilled on my cheeks. It burned like hell. I blinked, but it was like my tears were made of sand.

I could see, but just barely.

I laughed, turning to the silhouette I hoped was the necromancer, but it could also be a lamppost. "You're a dirty fighter."

"We never established any rules," said the necromancer. Okay. Definitely not a lamppost. "I thought you knew all the tricks, Hunter."

"Me too." I regretted my arrogance at my fighting skills. Now with my impaired vision, it wouldn't be as easy as I thought.

Something silver flickered in his hand. It could be a knife or it could be a chain.

In a flash, the necromancer, what I could make out, came at me, black robes unfurling around him.

Blinking fast, I dodged and struck at his side. He parried. Our blades connected and shock pierced my arm. He might be skinny, but he was strong and quick.

But my rage was still pounding, fueling my limbs with my sweet friend adrenaline.

He thrust and we clashed again. My eyes burned, begging for me to stop and squirt water into them.

Something flew at me. A knife? A fist? I had no idea.

When I felt the sting on my thigh, I knew. The bastard had cut me.

Lord Rath laughed somewhere to my right. "How does it feel to be powerless?"

"How does it feel to be a giant jackass?"

"You call this fighting?" asked the necromancer. "You look more like you're trying to fish and failing. And you think you can beat me?"

I dropped my guard and twisted to the side. He took a tiny step forward, off balance. I knocked his left arm up and thrust, hitting him with my left fist. Rath jerked back. The skinny bastard was faster than I thought.

He laughed, baring his teeth, and I could make out streaks of blood. At least I'd hit him and not the lamppost.

Half-blind, I raged and whirled. My soul blade flashed as I cut and sliced, putting everything I had into my speed since I could barely see.

A shape moved. I went for his arms. If he couldn't hold his blade, he couldn't fight.

His boot caught me. The blow knocked me back, and black stars blocked what vision I had left.

Ow.

I hit the ground, my face wet with tears, and my eyes felt like they were melting. Not cool.

A shadow danced before my eyes. He wasn't going to fool me again.

I jumped to my feet, slashing my blade before me. My eyes still burned like a sonofabitch, but now I could see better, like I was staring from underwater.

Lord Rath stood with his arms out, words spilling from his mouth. His lips moved, whispers of a language I'd never heard before reaching me. It was guttural, almost demonic—a Death magic chant.

Oh shit.

I wasn't the smartest Hunter in the world, but I knew when to split. Like—right now.

I turned, my feet slid and I fell to my knees. As I tried to scramble up, the necromancer's chanting grew more intense behind me, louder, the words more sinister. I knew I was in serious trouble when I choked on the sulfur in the air.

I needed to get to my subbie.

Panic filled my mind. I could see my subbie just up ahead, and I pushed my legs harder, my heart pounding.

And then the world slowed. I slowed.

It was like I was stuck in a world of cotton. Everything around me was hazy, even my mind. A cold feeling settled around me, slow and thick. Gradually, the magic grew and spread through me, flowing out from my chest into my skull and toes. It spread until it consumed me.

Lord Rath kept whispering. I could hear him clearly, pouring power into the words.

I blinked. Numb, my body wouldn't respond to my mind. When I looked at my hand, a silent scream erupted in my throat though I wasn't sure it came out at all.

Tiny brilliant lights covered my skin as though I'd painted myself with liquid diamonds.

I felt it then. The pull on my soul.

Lord Rath was stealing my soul. And I would become one of his soulless puppets.

Fear was close in my heart. I tried to move, tried to run away, but my body would not respond.

No! I was going to die. I would never see my gran or Tyrius or Gareth ever again.

I could hear laughter. I guess it was kind of funny. Me, the extraordinary angel-born Hunter having her soul sucked out of her. This wasn't how I'd pictured myself dying.

I blinked, the brilliance of my soul particles bright like suns.

Do something, Rowyn!

But I couldn't. A speck of anger was all I had left. A single tear slipped down my cheek.

The necromancer appeared in my line of sight. I could see clearly now. I could see his laughing face as he said the last of his Death spell.

Lord Rath's smile was bright and wicked. He opened his mouth widely, and the Death chant spilled through it—

And then a sword came thrusting out from between his teeth.

Blood spewed from the necromancer's mouth, his eyes wide with fear. Then he fell forward on his face.

Father Thomas pulled out his gleaming silver sword from the back of the necromancer's head. The expression on the priest's face was pure rage, his mouth twisted in a snarl.

I shivered as a cold feeling flowed out of me in a deliberate rush, leaving me feeling sick with a bitter taste in my mouth, like rotten meat. The Death magic rushed out in a steady flow, and then it was gone, except for the faintest whisper of an echo.

I fell to my knees and put my hands out as a wave of nausea hit. As soon as I could, I checked my hands. My olive skin stared back at me. It wasn't glowing. It was over. I still had my soul.

"Rowyn!" Father Thomas knelt next to me, and I felt his hand on my shoulder. The sharp clang of metal hitting the pavement rang out as he dropped his sword. "Are you all right?"

I coughed until I found my voice. "I think so. Thank you," I said, my voice harsh and rough. I was glad the handsome priest had just saved my life. I met his dark eyes. "How did you…"

"I came out looking for you." Father Thomas let out a sigh. "I wanted to apologize for the others. We might not always agree, but their hearts are in the right place."

I smiled, glad to feel the muscles in my face working. "Not sure they have hearts."

"I saw you with him. Saw you two fighting. I rushed back to get my sword."

"I'm glad you did." My eyes found the necromancer. "He tried to take my soul," I said, my lips trembling.

"I know. He won't hurt anyone ever again." Father Thomas wrapped his arm under me. "Can you stand?"

"I think so."

The priest helped me to my feet. I swayed a little, but after a moment I could stand firmly as the strength returned to my limbs.

"What happened to your eyes?" Concern creased the priest's features. "They look bad, Rowyn."

"Rath threw something at my eyes." I resisted the urge to rub them. "I don't know what it was, but it hurt like hell."

"Come inside," said the priest. "I have a doctor on call who works for the church."

"No." I felt stronger with every breath. "Will you take care of this bastard's body?"

Father Thomas frowned. "Yes, but—"

"I have to go. Something happened to my gran."

"Rowyn, wait!"

I barely heard him as I shambled forward toward my subbie, the image of my dead grandmother playing in my vision. Guilt, fear, anger—I shoved them all aside, focusing on walking straight without falling on my face.

Gritting my teeth, I forced my legs to move faster and faster. And then I was running, and I didn't stop till I reached my subbie.

CHAPTER

21

"**G**randma? Gran!" I cried as I burst through my grandmother's front door, sweating with spit flying out of my mouth. I felt like a rabid dog. My face shone wet with tears as the fear of losing my grandmother became all-consuming. I felt nothing else. I was numb with a fear so strong I was afraid it'd tear me from my life and throw me into a dark place, alone and blind.

"Gran!" I shouted again as I stumbled into the kitchen—and halted.

Gran, Kora, Tyrius, and their kids, Krystal, Tyson, Kaia, and Titus were all sitting, either on chairs or on the kitchen table. Born all with white fur, I was glad their colors were changing as they matured. Without their different markings and color, I wouldn't have been able to tell them apart. Plates were littered with splatters of tomato sauce, green peppers, mushroom bits, and crumbles of the crust as the only evidence that pizza had been served.

"Damn, Rowyn," said Tyrius, blinking several times. "You look like you walked into a carwash."

"Rowyn?" My grandmother stood up from her chair. "What's the matter? What happened to you?"

I stared at her beautiful big blue eyes, my lips trembling as I tried to reel in my emotions. I said nothing. I couldn't speak as I just staggered into her and hugged her as tightly as I could without snapping her spine. I breathed in her scent of lavender soap and wine.

"You're okay," I said to her hair. "You're okay."

"Of course, I'm okay," said my gran. "But if you don't let go of me soon... I'm going to suffocate to death."

I let go of her and stepped back. "Sorry."

My grandmother watched me. "You better start talking, young lady. I want to know why you thought something was the matter with me." She pointed a finger at my face. "And don't even think of lying to me. I've got six baals that'll tell me if you do."

Tyrius snorted, and his kids all started laughing. "She's got you there, Rowyn."

"A necromancer happened, that's what." The image of Rath's face sent a wave of anger through me. He'd lied. Lied to rattle me, to get my guard down. It had worked.

Tyrius jumped up on the kitchen table, his fur bristling around him. "A necromancer? Where? I thought you went to see the priests?"

I nodded, feeling suddenly tired and hungry at the smell of cooking. "He jumped me in the church parking lot."

"Dad, let's go take him out," said Titus. He was the largest of the baal kids and the one that looked the most like his mother with a fluff of pure white fur and large golden, fierce eyes. My heart just melted at the ferocity in his voice. "I'm ready. I know I am."

"I want to go too!" said Kaia, who was the spitting image of her dad. Apart from the fact that she was more petite, she was his little clone.

Krystal pressed her paws on the edge of the table. "If Kaia's going, I'm going too!" She was also white but had stunning streaks of gray wrapped around her legs and tail, like the pattern of a lynx.

"I'm the eldest," said Tyson. "I should go." Though, he wasn't as large as Titus, his fur was a mix of white and beige with dark gray around his face, ears, legs, and tail. He looked more like a blue point Siamese rather than a seal point like his sister Kaia.

The four young baals all cheered. I smiled at the cute, deadly furballs.

"Thank you, guys," I told the teen baals, seeing Kora's mood darken as she flashed Tyrius a glare. "But Father Thomas took care of that."

"Father Thomas? No way." Tyrius's ears perked up. "Now I'm psyched. Give me more."

My grandmother pulled out a chair. "Sit before you fall. Let me get you a slice of pizza and a nice glass of wine."

Pizza sounded fantastic, and I swear I started to drool. I dropped into the chair.

My grandmother's firm hand pressed on my shoulder as she leaned over me. "First, I need to take care of those eyes."

Tyrius padded to the edge of the table and stared at me. "Demon balls, woman. What happened to your eyes?"

I shook my head. "Rath threw something in them."

"Rath?" laughed Tyrius. "What a stupid name. But then again, he is a necromancer." His kids all burst out laughing. The sound felt so natural and lovely that I felt myself relax a little.

I leaned back into the chair. "Yeah, well, he wanted me to call him *Lord* Rath. That wasn't going to happen." Again, the kids burst out laughing. I had my own audience. It felt amazing.

My grandmother stepped closer to me and examined my face. "Your eyes look bad, honey."

"It's fine. They'll heal on their own," I dismissed her, knowing that one of the perks of having angel blood was my super healing abilities.

"You don't know how your body reacts to this Death magic." My grandmother gave me that motherly stare. "You want to take that chance with your eyes? You don't get another pair."

"Fine."

She moved to the sink and turned on the tap. "Here." My gran tossed me a cold cloth. "Press that on your eyes. It'll get the swelling down."

The swelling? How bad do I look?

Tyrius sat right in front of me. "How is el padre mixed up in all this? The suspense is making me shed." He made a show of shaking his body.

I pressed the cloth on my eyes. That did feel better. "Father Thomas saved my life."

"How so?" inquired Tyrius. "What did the necromancer want?"

I peeled the cloth from my eyes for a moment just as my grandmother set a plate in front of me. Pressing the cloth back on just my left eye, I grabbed the slice of juicy veggie pizza in my free hand and took a bite. My taste buds exploded. Man, I was ravenous.

I swallowed, not caring about the grease spilling down the sides of my mouth. "He wanted his knife back." I tapped the dark blade at my waist. "Apparently, it's important. I have no idea why, but it is. Enough for him to seek me out... twice." I switched the cloth to the other eye. "He's the same one who sicked his zombies at us at the temple."

Tyrius made a growl in his throat. "That skinny bastard. I should have ripped open his jugular when I had the chance." The kids burst out laughing again, which turned into hushed, nervous giggles once they caught the glare coming from their mom. I smiled. Kora was a great mom. She was strict when she needed to be, but she was also gentle and kind to her children.

Tyrius cleared his throat, and my warm and fuzzy feeling died. "Any thoughts about what this blade can do?"

"No idea." I bit into my slice of pizza again and swallowed. "I'm getting some supernatural vibes from it, but nothing that could tell me why it's so important to the necromancers. He called it the *ferro ex mortuis*."

"Knife of the dead," translated Tyrius, his whiskers lifting as he made a face.

"Fits, doesn't it." I switched the cloth on my other eye. "It kinda looks like a death blade, but it's not. For one thing, it doesn't give off the same energy, and it's not made of metal. More like it was carved from a stone."

"Rowyn, can I see it?" prompted Kaia, her blue eyes peering from her seat across from me.

"Yeah. I want to see it too!" said Titus as he leaped from his chair onto the table and padded over to Tyrius.

"If you're going to see it, I should see it too. I'm the one with the brains." Krystal flicked her tail from side to side.

Tyson snorted. "Brains? You've got the mental power of a bird."

Krystal shot him a look. "You're just jealous because I'm smarter than you."

Tyson hissed. "Say that again."

Krystal laughed. "I said—"

"O-o-o-kay, guys," I said, seeing Kora's fur rising and her nails peeking out from her front paws, looking like she was about to swat a couple of her kids. "Uh—maybe later. I'm going to hang on to it until Shane gets back. Maybe he knows about it."

Tyrius stared at the crust that was left on my plate. "Good idea. Did the divine princess say when he'd be back?"

I opened my mouth to answer but then shut it. Something was missing. I cast my gaze around the kitchen.

My heart stopped. The wet cloth slipped from my hand.

I stiffened. "Where's Gareth?" I couldn't believe I hadn't thought about him. Guess having nearly lost one's soul would do that to a person. He was supposed to be here.

"He's fine." My gran came over and squeezed my shoulder. "You just missed him. He went over to your place to fetch some more wine. He wanted me to taste that Portuguese wine he can't stop raving about."

Thank the souls. I let out a long breath as my heart jumpstarted again. "Okay. Okay. He's okay."

Tyrius nudged my shoulder with his nose. "Are *you* okay?"

"I'm fine." I scratched under his chin. "Just a little shaken up. I'm better." I didn't think telling them about how I nearly lost my soul to the death junkie necromancer would do anyone any good. It would only make things worse.

My grandmother turned from the kitchen cupboards, her hands on her hips, reminding me of myself. "Have you seen my large plastic container with the red top?"

"Yeah. It's at my place. You lent it to me three days ago with some of your lasagna leftovers. It's clean. Let me go get it and I'll grab Gareth on the way back."

My gran smiled at me. "Good. I'll have some ointment for your eyes when you get back."

I pushed my chair back and stood. "Be right back," I told the baals, Tyrius regarding me with narrowed, suspicious eyes, and I walked out of the kitchen before he suspected I was holding something back.

I shut my gran's front door—apparently I'd left it open this whole time—and walked across the street to my house. The pizza had filled me with some much-needed energy, but I was still woozy and all the muscles in my body ached like I'd just stepped out of a fighting pit after combatting twenty beefy demons.

One look at me, and I knew the elf would work up some of his healing elf remedies. And I would gladly accept them.

A shadow moved across the front window, and I recognized my sexy elf's silhouette.

I stepped up to the front door and pushed in, not bothering to close it. I just wanted to see him and hold him. It was crazy how much I needed his comfort. It was even crazier to imagine what I'd do without it.

"Gareth," I called as I walked through the living room to the kitchen.

The elf stood at the kitchen sink with his back towards me.

"Gareth? Didn't you hear me?" I stared at his fine behind. I was going to smack it.

"Gran is expecting that wine you told her about—"

Gareth turned around, his motions slow and stiff like his joints pained him with that simple turn.

A heart-wrenching wail pierced the air. I fell to my knees, unable to get enough air into my lungs as my world crumbled around me, shifting with a nauseating spin.

I looked up to my elf, my beautiful, strong, wizard elf.

And his yellow eyes stared back at me.

CHAPTER
22

"Rowyn? You need to snap out of it. Don't make me whip your ass, woman. You know I'm good for it."

I knew it was Tyrius's voice. I recognized it, but he sounded so far away, like he stood on the edge of the world, on a cliff, and was shouting back to me. Weird. Why was he so far away? Why was I so far away? Was I dreaming? Was this a dream? It felt like a dream.

The scent of demon energies sifted through the upper levels of my thoughts, skimming through my hazy dream state. I was warm and comfortable, though my mattress was hard, almost like wood. Strange. But I didn't want to wake up. I didn't know why, but this felt better. *Stay asleep. Stay here.*

"She's lost it," I heard Tyrius say. "She's cracked. She's all packed up and ready for the loony bin."

"Rowyn? It's Layla. Can you hear me?" This time Layla was speaking to me, her voice faint, nearly a whisper. Why was everyone so far away?

Hi, little sister. I can hear you. What's up?

"You need to come back to us," continued Layla, her beautiful voice drifting around me like the sound of rippling leaves in a wind.

"Look at her," came Tyrius's voice again. "She's in shock. She needs a doctor. She needs Pam. We need to call Pam. Like, right friggin' *now.*"

Pam? I know that name. Something cool touched my cheek and then my forehead.

"She's really warm. She might have a fever," said Layla, her voice higher than usual. "What did you say happened with the necromancer?"

"She fought him and then el padre saved her by killing him," answered the cat. "She didn't go into specifics, which, come to think about it… sounds a lot like she was hiding something. Which could only mean… it was really bad."

You clever cat. So clever.

"Could he have made her sick like this?" I heard Layla ask. "Did he put a spell on her, you think?"

"I don't know," said the baal demon. "She seemed better at Gran's. Her eyes were still bad, but she ate some pizza. No. This happened after she saw Gareth."

Gareth… where is Gareth?

"She looks really bad, Tyrius," came Layla's voice again, though softer this time. "I'm scared."

"Me too. But sitting here won't help her. We have to do something. Before it gets worse."

Someone clapped their hands together. "Wake up, Rowyn." Layla's voice hit my ears again. "We need you. I need you. Gareth needs you."

Gareth? Why did he need me? Where is he? I can't hear him.

The sound of feet slapping on wood neared me. "We'll take her to Pam's. I'll carry her into the car," said a voice.

Is that Danto? Danto is here? Hi, Danto! Wait a minute... where is here? This is a dream. Isn't it?

"Or... we can opt for the faster option," said Tyrius.

"Which is what?" questioned Layla's voice, tight and small.

"When in doubt, go for pain."

Something as sharp as needles pierced my skin, and pain exploded from my arm. I screamed and yanked my arm from the attacker. My mind moved from sleep to awareness. I blinked, my gaze a bit unfocused, into the face of a Siamese cat staring down at me. "Tyrius?" I pulled my arm into my line of sight. Four tiny holes dripped with blood. "You bit me. Why did you bite me?"

The cat gave me a smug smile. "You're welcome. Now get up."

"What?" Only then did I realize I was lying on the floor, staring up at the ceiling. I pulled myself to a sitting position. I was in my kitchen.

Gaze still unfocused, I pressed my palms on the floor for balance just as I remembered doing before the panic took me.

"How long was I out?"

"About an hour." Layla sat next to me and grabbed my hand. Her warm fingers felt nice against my cold skin. "I came as soon as Tyrius called."

"Tyrius called you?" I spun on my knees. Danto stood in the living room, looking like a male model in one of those cologne commercials. His open black shirt revealed a tanned, muscled chest. His handsome face was twisted in grief, and his dark eyes gleamed with sorrow.

Behind him was a man tied to a chair. The tips of his pointed ears poked from a mass of tousled, dark, wavy hair. A slip of black cloth was wrapped around his head to cover his eyes.

Gareth.

I felt the walls of the kitchen closing in on me, and then everything started to spin again as the events of what had happened earlier came rushing in… his large, yellow eyes staring at me.

My chest contracted.

Gareth.

He sat in one of the kitchen table chairs. His hands and feet were bound with rope, and a few extra loops of rope circled his body. He was moving his head from side to side like he was trying to listen.

Lips trembling, I stood on shaky legs. My grandmother's pizza rolled up in my throat, but I forced it down before I starting spewing chunks. I remembered screaming. My eyes closed, and I felt the emotions all over again.

My heart seemed to die right there and then all over again. *Please, no*, I thought, tears blinding me as I stared at him.

I felt a brush on my leg and I looked down to see Tyrius rub up against me. My furry buddy was trying to comfort me.

"I'm so sorry, Rowyn," said Layla, her voice filled with grief. I wouldn't look at her. If I looked at her, I would lose it again.

My eyes burned, but I would not let the tears fall. This wasn't the time to cry.

Danto walked over to me. "I thought it was best to cover his eyes. In case one of the necromancers showed up."

"It won't shut the necromancers out completely, but it'll help," commented the cat as he bounded over to the elf. "At least, for now. Until we figure out what... what to do."

I nodded, not able to bring myself to speak. This was my fault. I'd brought this on. Gareth was without a soul because of me.

"Rowyn?" Layla rubbed my arm. "Please say something."

My throat burned. Guilt. Regret. Anger. Sorrow. They were all competing, and I didn't have a winner.

I stood there in silence, staring at the man I loved, at the man who loved me back with all his being.

I'd ripped out his soul. The necromancer had actually done it, but it might as well have been me.

Danto rubbed his jaw. "Should we contact his family?"

I found my voice. "What do you mean?"

The vampire crossed his arms over his chest, staring at the floor. "Well. Shouldn't we tell them what happened?" His perfect face pinched in distress. "They're his family. They should know that he's… lost."

Anger won the emotional battle. "Why are you talking like he's dead," I raged. "He's *not* dead." I was practically shouting. I didn't feel any guilt anymore. I was only angry. How could they not see that the elf was still alive, still breathing, still…

Swallowing, I took a hesitant step forward toward Gareth. "I have to fix this," I whispered.

"This isn't your fault, Rowyn." Tyrius appeared at my side. "You can't blame yourself."

I gave a bitter laugh. "Oh, yes, I can. *I* did this. If I had given Rath back his stupid knife, Gareth would still be…" What? Complete? Whole? Mine again? "He would still be Gareth. Not this."

"You don't know that." Tyrius shook his head, his ears low on his head. "You don't know that the necromancers wouldn't have done it anyway. They're toying with us. With you."

My eyes rolled over Gareth's face. His lips moved, not with words, but with nothing, like the mumblings of a mad person.

"Why?" My voice shook, and I hated it. "Why are they doing this? What do they want?"

"I think I can help you with that," said a familiar voice.

My heart leaped to my throat and I whirled around.

Shane stood in the kitchen, and next to him was Lance.

CHAPTER
23

I stared at the angel Shane. His skin seemed darker in the dim light of the kitchen, making it almost the color of dark chocolate. He wore casual clothes, all black, with a military-style jacket. "Help me with what exactly?" My voice came out hoarser than I'd wanted. My Godzilla persona was getting the best of me.

Shane took a moment, seemingly giving me a few seconds to collect myself. His eyes moved behind me. I saw the shock in the angel's eyes when he caught sight of Gareth and heard the tiny whimper from Lance's throat that nearly sent me to my knees again.

Shane turned to me again and said, "When did this happen?"

I opened my mouth to tell him, but my jaw just hung there, the words evaporating in my throat. I couldn't help the emotions that came cascading down on me again. It was like I was reliving the shock of seeing Gareth without a soul, all over again... and again... and again...

"About an hour and a half ago," said Layla, and I let out a little breath of relief.

Danto took a firmer stance, his hands clasped before him. "We had to restrain him so he wouldn't hurt anyone... or himself."

Tyrius edged forward and sat next to Gareth's leg, his ears low and his eyes narrowed dangerously, looking like a guard dog, or rather, guard cat. "It was the necromancer called Rat. He wanted Rowyn to suffer."

"It worked." I rubbed my face, trying to get my muscles to work again. I moved my hand to my waist and pulled out the necromancer's knife. "Because of this." I showed the angels the blade. "He called it the—"

"Ferro ex mortuis," answered Shane. "It's a sacrificial blade the necromancers use during their death ritual. They call it The Passage. The transition of life into death."

I frowned. It had to be more than that. Or maybe it wasn't, and Rath was just a giant bastard who didn't want to share his toys with others.

Tyrius made a sound in his throat. "Well, at least now we know what that means." He bobbed his head to the angels. "What other heavenly news you got for us? Are you receiving the divine messages right now?"

I looked at Tyrius. I couldn't be mad at him for patronizing the angels. It was the only normal in my life right now. I needed all the normal I could get.

"It doesn't matter anymore." I slipped the blade back on my waist, wondering why I even bothered to keep it. "He did this to Gareth because I wouldn't give it back. There's nothing more to it."

"Rowyn," growled Tyrius. "Don't do this. You know it's not the only reason."

"It is, actually." My temper flared, and I caught a glimpse of Layla staring at the floor. Her miserable expression was accompanied by tears in her eyes.

Danto watched Layla, his toes flinching like he was contemplating taking her into his arms to comfort her. I knew he wanted to do it, but he was holding back because of me.

My stomach knotted. I'd give anything to feel Gareth's strong arms wrapped around me. My own eyes burned. Damn it. I would not cry. I'd already had one breakdown today. I would not suffer another. Gareth needed me. I *was* going to fix him.

Blinking fast, I moved my gaze between the angels. "What did you find out?"

Shane came forward. "We know why the necromancers are taking the souls."

"And where they're stashing them," said Lance. His golden eyes flicked to Tyrius, daring him to say something snarky.

227

Tyrius raised his brows after a moment. "Is this *free* intel, or are you waiting for us to pay you or something? Go on. Spit out the saintly dribble."

"Remember when I told you that souls are filled with power?" Shane was speaking fast.

"Yes," I answered. "Everyone knows that."

"Right. It's one of the reasons they're so attractive to demons."

"Dude," said Tyrius. "I'm getting mixed signals here."

Shane exhaled slowly, a mortal gesture. "To perform their Death magic, the necromancers need a great amount of power—a huge amount. They need the sum of enough power to control and maintain the bodies of the living. Only souls can lend that kind of energy."

I crossed my arms over my chest. "So far so good. I'm waiting for the part where I'm supposed to be intrigued." Okay, that was harsh, but I was running on my Godzilla bitch fuel, and I couldn't turn it off. Not even for angels.

"When the body dies," continued Shane, "the souls return to Horizon."

"When they're not eaten by demons," interrupted the cat.

"But the necromancers found a way around that," continued Shane.

My interest piqued. "Go on."

"With their Death magic," said the angel, "they can store the souls in a place where the souls can't escape. A place where even the demons can't reach. A place where the necromancers can use the power of all the souls they've stolen."

"Hang on to your butts," said Tyrius. "Here it comes."

I swallowed. "What place?"

"A new realm," said Lance, and Tyrius cursed.

The baal spit on the floor. "You need to stop smoking that heavenly crack, dog-breath. There's no such thing as a *new* realm. There's here, there's your joint, and there's the Netherworld. That's it."

The white dog shook his head. "Not anymore."

"That's a truckload of cosmic crap." Tyrius's blue eyes met mine. "Do you believe these celestial freaks? Tell them, Rowyn. Tell them this is not cool."

Pulse rising, I flicked my gaze between the angels. "If you're lying to me…" I didn't want to complete that sentence. I had a feeling I would regret it.

Danto and Layla, both feeling my mood, came to stand next to me.

Shane didn't even react to my outburst. "I'm not lying to you, Rowyn. There is a new realm. We've only just discovered it."

My lips parted. "A new realm? You're serious?"

"Very," said Lance. "We were able to retrieve some echoes of memory through the human body that had been connected to the necromancer. It's how we knew the necromancers were storing the souls in that place. A place they call Death."

Of course it was called Death. Because Sunshine was already taken.

Tyrius nudged my leg. "I think the halos are running out of air up there."

I shook my head. Tyrius didn't say they were lying, more like they were nuts, and believed in their nuttery. Did that make it true? "What do you mean, a new realm? How's that even possible? Necromancers are humans, unless you know something I don't. And humans can't create realms," I said, my horror mixing with confusion.

Lance looked up at Shane. "Do you want to tell her, or do you want me to tell her?"

I raised a brow. "Tell me what?"

"Go ahead," said Shane.

"Gods and Goddesses can create realms and realities," began the dog. "Just like this realm, Earth, the realm of the living, was created."

Tyrius hissed. "We all know the story, mutt. Get with the program."

"There's another entity. You can call it a god or you can call it by its true name." Lance blinked a few times. "This entity is called Derrigor."

Tyrius whistled. "This keeps getting better and better."

"Hush, Tyrius." I glanced at the angels. "Let me guess. This entity, Derrigor, the necromancers made some kind of deal with him?" I went with male since the name sounded male.

"That's what the Legion believes," said Shane. "Derrigor has the power to create realms. The necromancers must have discovered this and raised him somehow, or simply woken him."

It all made a lot of sense.

"They hid this new realm well," said Shane.

"But not well enough," commented Lance. "They couldn't hide all those souls forever. Their energy started to slip through the cracks of this place, sort of like how Rifts open. It's how we found it."

A thought came to me. "How can the necromancers steal the souls from these people and keep them alive while they manipulate them?"

"Think of this place as a giant powerplant," explained Shane. "And the stored power, the souls, have a direct link to their bodies. Like an electrical box with wires connecting to each person, feeding them with energy."

Lance's golden eyes gleamed as he met mine. "We think it's the reason why the bodies are still alive. That power feeds into the mortal bodies. Sustaining them."

"But for how long?" I looked over to Gareth, who hadn't moved since the angels arrived. "How long can the souls live in that place?"

Shane shrugged. "It's hard to tell. Years maybe. Until the soul is drained completely."

A burst of angst lit through me. "Those people don't have years. They've got less than a day."

Lance and Shane shared a look. "You mean the people in Times Square?" asked Lance.

"They're sending in the human troops," said Tyrius. "They think it's a virus. They're going to kill all those people for fear of it spreading."

Danto swore under his breath and ran a hand into his luscious black hair. I knew it as his signature gesture when he was nervous or edgy. Layla was next to him in a second, her fingers interlacing with his.

I felt despair rush in. For all those people's souls, for Gareth's. My heart seemed to cease. I felt nothing but pain. It was all I was. All I had left…

But I still had one more card to play.

I clenched my jaw, struggling to keep my fear and despair from showing. "You said that place, Death, where the souls are being stored—used—and not killed is the reason why the bodies are still alive. Right?"

Shane nodded, his face thoughtful. "Yes, yes that's right."

I paced the room as ideas welled inside me, and thoughts and ideas made connections into bigger plans.

"So… the souls are alive as well. Right?"

"Yes," answered Shane.

I pursed my lips as I continued to pace. "*If,* hypothetically, the souls were freed from that place…" I took a breath before asking the question I'd been dying to ask. "If they were freed, could they find their bodies and be whole again? Be the person they were before?"

I waited, desperate hope almost painful as it clenched around my heart. I glanced at Tyrius, now shifting awkwardly.

For a moment there was silence. Either the angels didn't know the answers, or they feared my reaction to those very same answers.

Lance finally answered. "Technically, and I really *mean* technically, 'cause I've never heard of this happening before…" The dog blinked. "I would have to say… yes… Yes, the souls would find their bodies and breathe life back into them."

The hope that I could bring Gareth back to me was desperate and painful. But the angel's words were all I needed to hear.

"But that's a very big *if*," said the dog, having seen something on my face. "Like I said, it's never been done before."

Tyrius cocked his head. "Or you just never heard of it happening before. Doesn't mean it won't work, fleabag."

Lance pulled up his lip to show his teeth. "I never said it wouldn't, kitty cat."

I bit my lip. "Well. That's good enough for me."

"Rowyn," said the cat, "you've got that expression you get when you're cooking up ideas in that large brain of yours."

I threw my gaze about the room. They were all staring at me. "It's just… maybe if—"

"Why, isn't this little group gathering delightful," came a voice I did not recognize.

A chill rolled through me, like icy fingers slowly wrapping around my neck and choking me.

I turned around, already knowing what to expect.

Gareth's face was pulled into a smile. "Though I cannot see you, I do recognize your voice. Hello again, Rowyn Sinclair." The elf's lips had moved, but his voice wasn't what came out.

It was the necromancer's voice.

CHAPTER
24

I didn't know whether to scream, to cry, or to run over there and jump-kick the man I loved in the face just to make the voice stop.

It was wrong. All wrong. This wasn't supposed to happen. Not to me. Not to Gareth.

I took a breath, trying to stay upright, though the room was starting to waver again. Gareth's face was all smiles, though I knew the elf wasn't smiling, but the necromancer. Gareth was just a tool, a marionette for the puppet master.

My eyes closed, and a lump filled my throat. Grief slammed into me, and I staggered to stand. I would not fall. Not in the presence of the man who took Gareth's soul.

With shaky legs, I walked over to the elf, using the movement to hide my trembling body. I took another step closer, wanting to fall on my knees and pull him to me, to breathe in his scent, just to feel his warmth.

Instead I looked down at him, knowing he wasn't in there, knowing a parasite was inside him.

"Which one are you?" I demanded, my voice trembling with barely controlled fury. Gareth's head turned towards my voice. When he didn't answer I said, "Are you the one called Lord Krull?"

The smile on Gareth's face widened. It was eerie and cold, nothing like the one I'd grown so attached to. There was no warmth. It was mechanical. It was wrong.

"Very good," said the necromancer named Lord Krull. His voice was hoarse and rough, like a man way past his hundredth birthday. "I saw you with the priest. I saw what he did to my brother, Lord Rath."

"Rat," interjected Tyrius. The Siamese cat was at my feet. "Rat is dead, dumbass."

Gareth's head moved from side to side as though the necromancer inside was trying to find the source of the voice but failing to do so.

"Spying or peeping?" I asked.

"Peeping," said Tyrius. "I can smell it on his peeping voice."

Loved that cat. "I see," I said, making sure to speak directly at the necromancer. "You were peeping through the eyes of those zombies at the church. You like to watch." *You disgusting dirtbag.*

"We are always watching," said Lord Krull. "We are always listening. We hear and see *everything*."

Tyrius sniffed and spat on the floor. "Is it me, or does this sound a lot like a demented version of Big Brother?"

"You're not wrong." I had a plan. And for my plan to work, I needed some questions answered.

I turned to the sound of feet approaching to see Layla and Danto coming to stand next to me, both with mirrored severe expressions. The angels stayed where they were. *Fine by me.*

I leaned forward, trying to rid the pain in my chest so I could think clearly. "What's the meaning of all this? What do you want from the souls?"

Gareth laughed, or rather, Lord Krull did. The sound was like the gurgling of a dying animal. Unnatural. "This world is wasted with the filth of humans. Their bodies are weak, but their souls… well… their souls are power."

"But you're using their bodies too. Aren't you?"

"Until they wither away, yes," answered the necromancer. "But their souls will live on, fueling us with unimaginable strength and power."

Guilt seemed to stop my heart, and I looked away before I did something stupid, like use my boot to shut his mouth. Tyrius sat next to me on the floor, miserable with his whiskers twitching in irritation.

I pulled my eyes back to the elf. Half his face was covered with the blindfold, and I was glad of it. That way I could pretend it wasn't him. I could almost make myself believe it wasn't Gareth. Almost.

"Does it have to do with that prophecy?" I asked. "Yeah, I know about it. Cynthia blabbed. She blabbed *a lot*." Total lie. The truth was, she'd barely given us anything apart from reciting cult scriptures and more nonsense. I searched what I could see on his face, but I didn't know whether he was frowning or not.

The necromancer took a harder line. "Cynthia was a gift to the Master. Taking her was a mistake. Her life was not her own. It belonged to him. You had no right to take that gift."

"Cynthia is a person, you dick. She's not a thing."

"Her life served only one purpose. She'd accepted that purpose. She wanted it. And you took it from her."

"I gave her life back to her." He seemed to be on a roll with the blab, and I didn't want to stop it. "The prophecy. The Death Walker. What's that about?"

The necromancer straightened in his chair. He lifted his head and said, "The Death Walker will break down the wall between life and death. And when that happens, all life will perish. And then the dead shall rise."

I pressed my hands on my hips. "Let me guess. You're this so-called Death Walker, right?"

Lord Krull-Gareth's face twitched into a wide smile. "I am."

"Lovely."

"Blood will be spilled," continued the necromancer. "Death will be eternal, and balance will be restored."

My pulse had yet to settle, and his chanting just pissed me off more. "If I kill you, your prophecy won't come true. All your hopes and dreams," I snapped my fingers, "will vanish."

Gareth's dark hair fell over the blindfold. "The prophecy will come to pass," said the necromancer. "There is nothing you or your little Scooby-Doo gang of misfits can do to stop it."

"Dude. Scooby's awesome," mewed Tyrius.

"We'll never stop," said the necromancer. "And you can do nothing to stop us. Just like there was nothing you could have done to save the elf's soul." Lord Krull-Gareth smiled and ran his tongue over his bottom lip. "And I'll take your grandmother's soul next."

Gran.

Tyrius hissed and growled, his fur brimming on his back, and his claws out for the kill.

An awful pressure ground on my mind. Gran, the only connection to my parents. If something were to happen to her…

My instinct to protect and kill was overwhelming. Fear and fury wound about my mind in white-hot ribbons. In a rush of pure fury, I lashed out.

"You bastard!" I cried. In a flash, my hand wrapped around his neck before I realized what I was doing.

"Rowyn! Stop!" Layla bumped against me, her hands over mine as she tried to peel them off the elf's neck.

I kept squeezing.

KIM RICHARDSON

"It's Gareth," cried Layla. "You're hurting Gareth. Rowyn. Stop!"

You're hurting Gareth.

Breathing hard, I let go of his neck and saw tubular red marks on his skin, my handprints. I stared, both horrified at what I had done and angry that I let my emotions drive me.

The necromancer tsked. "Careful there, Rowyn" he wheezed. "You don't want to hurt your beloved elf. Do you? Another love-squeeze like that and you would have made my job a lot easier." He laughed, and the sound sent an icy quiver to my soul.

I reached up and yanked the blindfold off. I wanted this bastard to see my face before... what? I killed him? I couldn't do anything. This was Gareth. The necromancer knew I'd never hurt him—apart from throttling him a little bit.

Yellow eyes peered up at me. Gareth's face was ragged, his skin a little too gray, a little too pasty, as though he had a fever. The parasite in him was slowly draining him of his life.

I unclenched my teeth and put my face in his. "I'm coming to get you, Lord Krull."

The necromancer's eyes lit up, the color of old urine. He opened his mouth to say something—

And then my fist connected with his right temple. Gareth's head snapped back and then fell forward.

"Damn, woman," laughed Tyrius. "That's going to leave a seriously wicked bruise. What the hell did you do that for?"

"I did what I had to do." *I'm so sorry, Gareth.* I pulled the blindfold back up and covered his eyes. Then I turned and faced the angels, who—no surprise there—stood in the exact same spots.

"If I kill every goddam necromancer," I said, closing the distance between us, "will the souls free themselves?" I already had a feeling what the answer would be, but I had to ask.

Shane and Lance traded a look. Their silence was my answer.

It left me only one choice. My last card.

I planted myself before them, my hands on my hips, and said, "Tell me how to find this new realm."

CHAPTER
25

"**A**re you insane!" shouted Tyrius, and for a second I thought he'd Hulked out into his alter ego, the black panther. He ran up next to me. "Rowyn. I think you're the one who got hit on the head because you're talking *crazy*, woman."

I nodded. "Yeah. Guess I am."

"He's right," said Layla, her voice tinted with dread. Her eyes bugged widely and the concern on her face had my chest contract. "You can't be serious."

"Very." I turned back to the angels. "And? How do I find it?"

Shane ran a hand over his bald head. "Even if we tell you, you can't enter."

"If there's a doorway... I can." Who did he think he was talking to? I'd died and become a Dark angel. There was nothing I couldn't do. Or at least, nothing I wouldn't try.

Shane shook his head, and frown lines marked his face. "It's not a realm for the living, Rowyn. It's a realm of death."

"Hence the name," said Tyrius, his ears swiveling on his head. "If it was called Happy Hour, there'd be no problem."

"Rowyn." Lance padded forward, his tail low. "Your mortal body can't get through. It would be physically impossible for you to enter. I'm sorry, but it won't work."

My mouth went dry at the enormity of what I was about to say. "But my consciousness will."

Layla drew in a sharp breath. "What do you mean?"

I blinked and said, "Astral projection."

"Netherworld be damned." Tyrius smacked his forehead with his paw and fell to his side, stiff like a catsicle.

They were all looking at me like I was nuts. Okay, maybe I was a little bit. "I used to do it all the time when I was young. I can't tell you why I can do this—maybe it has to do with my demon heritage—or my angel—or maybe neither. I just know I can. Tyrius can tell you. I grew out of it eventually, but I remember how it works." *I think.*

Layla cocked her hip and glared at the angels. "Would that work?"

Shane looked down at Lance. "Yes," said Shane as he pulled his eyes back on me. "Rowyn's consciousness or spirit can travel to that realm." He narrowed his eyes. "However. It's a *huge* risk. We don't know much about this new realm. You don't know what you'll face once you're there."

"I'm willing to take that risk," I said. Tyrius was still on the floor, but his head was shaking over and over and his lips were mouthing the word "no."

"If something happens to her consciousness," said Layla. "If she dies there… does that mean she dies here as well?"

Now she just burst my happy bubble.

"Yes." Lance slumped his shoulders. "One cannot live without the other."

Layla turned on me, her pretty features tight and angry. "So, basically you want to go to this Death realm alone. Risk your own life? You don't even know if it's going to work."

"It's the only way."

Layla's face was turning another shade of red. "We should try to kill all the necromancers first," she said. Her bottom lip quivered, and it pained me to see her so upset. I knew she was worried about me.

"It won't work," I told her. "Even if we do kill them all, the souls will still be trapped. Gareth will still be trapped." My throat constricted, and it took a gargantuan effort not to start bawling my eyes out.

I cast my gaze behind me. Gareth, or what was left of him, was still out cold. If I didn't at least try, I could never live with myself.

I met Layla's dark eyes. "I'm going there, and I'm going to free the souls. We can eliminate the necromancers when I get back."

"No." Tyrius sat up, his blue eyes gleaming with demonic energy. "You're not. Forget it. If I have to tie you up like Gareth, I will."

"Did you hear him, Tyrius?" I was shouting, my nerves getting the best of me again. "Did you not hear him say he was going to kill Gran? Who's next? Father Thomas? You? Kora and the kids? You know I have to stop this. I have to do this."

"No, you don't." The cat's eyes were bugging out. "Why does it always have to be you? Can't it be someone else's ass on the line here? You don't need to save the world all the time."

"This time I do," I told him. "Because this time…" my eyes flicked over to Gareth and back. "It's personal."

"I care about him too," muttered Tyrius. "But I don't think he would want you to do this. It's too risky."

"Are you going to stop me?" I growled. "Gareth wouldn't hesitate to do the same for me. He'd travel to Death and back to save me. And that's exactly what I'm going to do."

Death… here I come.

Tyrius mumbled something under his breath that I couldn't catch. But the kitty had stopped his tantrum. Good.

I looked at the vampire. "Danto," I said, my heart thrashing in my chest. My blood pressure was rising and transforming into a giant headache. "You need to keep Gareth safe until I return. Can you do that for me?"

The vampire nodded, a faint smile on his lips. "No problem."

"Tyrius." I stared at the cat. "You need to keep Gran safe. You heard what he said. So you need to keep an eye on her. Got it? I'm counting on you. Don't let me down."

The cat frowned. "What do I look like? A chicken? Of course I can keep her safe!"

I smiled. "Good kitty."

"Yeah, yeah, yeah." Tyrius pouted, his ears flat on his head.

I exhaled long and low. "Layla." I looked at my sister. "I need you to call Father Thomas and tell him what's going on. Tell him to be on the lookout for the necromancers, zombies, or more soulless." I took a breath. "Then. I need you to keep my body safe while I'm in that place. Okay?"

"I'll do it," said Layla. "But are you sure, Rowyn? What if something happens to you over there. What if you... don't come back?"

I knew what she was getting at. I had thought about it. For exactly three seconds. My mind was made up.

I shifted my weight. "Then I don't come back. I have to do this. There's nothing you can say or do to talk me out of it. My mind's made up."

"I know." Layla looked away from me, emotions playing on her pretty features. "Just… come back to us. Okay?"

"Trust me, I'm not planning on staying there." Hell no. I was going to free the souls and then I was going to kick some necromancer ass. I was looking forward to it. There was no way in hell I'd miss that chance.

"Shane. Lance. I need you while I do this. You'll have to direct me to this new place. Okay?"

"Yes," said Shane, and Lance nodded his head.

I rubbed my hands together. "Okay then. Oh, before I forget," I said. "Is this Derrigor persona in that realm too?"

Both Shane and Lance answered at the same time. "Yes."

I smiled. "Awesome."

CHAPTER
26

I had to admit, astral projecting my consciousness into the realm Death—a new plane of existence that no one apart from the god who'd created it had even seen—was pretty stupid. Scratch that. It was completely foolish, irrational, and reckless.

And yet, here I was, on my merry way to possibly my demise.

I lay on top of my bed, fully dressed, fully weaponized (not sure that it would help since I'd never tried to bring any weapons when I'd performed astral projection as a kid) while Lance rested at the foot of the bed near my feet, and Shane sat on the edge of his chair next to me, looking pale with his knee bouncing off the floor.

"Can you stop with the leg thing," I told him. "You're making me lose my concentration."

Shane gave me a smug smile as he stilled his leg. "Sorry."

I turned my head against the pillow and looked straight. With her arms crossed over her chest, Layla leaned against my dresser, her whip at her waist, looking like she was itching to use it.

I let out a long breath, trying to rid all the tension in my body, and trying to clear my mind to focus on what I had to do. It'd been hard to see Tyrius leave, especially since the cat wouldn't look at me. He was furious with me, I knew that, but he was more worried.

My eyes closed in the swirl of conflicting feelings. I pushed all the thoughts, the worries, the pains away, and went to that place inside me, that familiar place where I used to escape as a child. Where the pains of losing my parents and being different couldn't touch me. That place was my escape.

I focused on my breathing, emptying my mind as I visualized myself rising without moving my physical body. Like a thin brush of cold fingers, I felt the gathering power. It tickled through me, and my breathing slowed as I recognized the familiar feeling.

It was easier than I thought. It seemed the skill of astral projection was just waiting for me to use it again, like an old bicycle forgotten in the garage under all the clutter.

I focused my consciousness to stay there, hovering in the room, like a ghost.

"I'm ready," I said after a moment, my voice low and drifty, like a whisper. Tyrius hated this part. If I kept thinking of Tyrius or anyone else, I would lose the connection. "Take my hand." I reached out with my right hand. "And tell me about the realm of Death. You have to show me as best as you can. Show me where it is. You need to open your mind and let me see it. Does that make sense?"

Granted, I'd never tried this before with anyone, so I had no idea if my brilliant plan was going to work. I'd always projected on my own, usually with Tyrius on the bed next to me, swearing as loudly as he could in the hopes it would break my concentration. All it did was reinforce my skill and talent to transport my spiritual me somewhere else.

"Yes. It makes sense." Shane gripped my hand. The skin on his palm was cold and rough, making me realize how close to the real thing these mortal suits were. "I don't know where the souls are in that place. You're going to have to find them on your own."

"Fine," I mumbled, trying to not lose the connection.

"It's a big place Rowyn. If you find yourself in trouble... come back. We'll find a way." When I said nothing, the angel muttered, "Good luck. Here goes."

With our hands connected, I slipped my awareness to Shane's. My skin tingled everywhere his aura touched mine, the different charges raking over my consciousness like silk on sand. I felt a slip of energy as Shane's thoughts connected to mine, like we were sharing a memory inside our heads. What he saw in his mind, in turn I saw in my mind.

Next, I visualized myself rising again without moving my physical body until I had lifted off the bed, up past the roof of my new house, until I was just beyond the stars.

It was an awesome feeling to float, to fly, and I wondered why I had ever stopped. Puberty? Who knew?

I couldn't feel Shane's hand wrapped around mine anymore. I couldn't feel the softness of my pillow or the snugness of my mattress. I felt nothing.

That was the worst part. Until I focused on a place, "the nothing" as I called it, always gave me the creeps. I never stayed there long, making sure I always had a place to go.

I hung there for a moment, waiting for something, waiting to be transported to the realm that was in Shane's head.

And so far, there was diddly-squat.

Just darkness, all around me. Like I was stuck in a giant black box with no light, no walls, just an abyss of nothing. *Where the hell is it?*

Can you see the doorway, Rowyn?

I flinched as I heard Shane's voice inside my head. Yeah, that creeped me out just a little. I was not used to having another voice talking inside my head apart from my own.

It will look like a portal. It should stand out. Can you see it?

I did what I was told and looked for a light in this gargantuan blackness. If this was a glimpse into Shane's mind, there was a whole lot of nothing.

And just like that, I saw it.

A spec of light, the size of a pea, flickered like a single bright star in a black sky. It pulsed slightly, visible streaks rotating clockwise around it with greater and greater speed.

"Okay, Rowyn. You know the deal. Move toward the light," I told myself.

Using the light as my guide, I willed myself forward. And I went.

This was the best part of astral projection—the superman, or rather, superlady (because superwoman was already taken) superpower—where I could fly. I would have loved to have a cape right now. Purple, not red. Oh, and the knee-high boots to match too. But you could forget about the tights. No one wants to see that. Even on my spirit-self.

The light shimmered and grew as I neared it until it was as large as a garage door.

It wasn't a doorway per se, more like a whirlwind vacuum of light that had sucked in everything around it. And I was the idiot going to go in.

"Just like the light at the end of the tunnel," I whispered. "Nice."

What was that, Rowyn? I'm having trouble understanding you. I heard Shane say again.

Oops. I forgot to turn off my internal walkie with the angel. Whatever I said out loud, those near my body would hear.

"Nothing," I said out loud, articulating the word, just in case it didn't come through smoothly.

You saw a light? Came Shane's question.

"Yes. I'm going toward the light now." And hoping it wouldn't eat me.

Be safe, Rowyn.

Fear felt the same with my spirit body as it did with my physical body because fear was feeling, a mental state. And right now, I was scared shitless. I'm not going to lie. I had to be mad to travel into an unknown new realm occupied by some god. I knew if that Derrigor killed me in his realm, killed my spirit, my physical body would die as well. Me. My soul. My spirit. All of me.

If I didn't make it back, I knew Layla would gather up a team and kill the necromancers. I knew she wouldn't stop until she'd killed them all—or she would die trying.

That's what scared me the most. Part of me knew the necromancers were stronger. With the help of the souls' energy, they were an unstoppable force. What would happen if they reached a million soulless? Ten million?

The only way to stop them was to sever the link with their power. This place was a giant powerplant? I was going to pull the plug.

Remove the souls, free the souls, and they'd be powerless. Okay, maybe not completely powerless, but weaker and easier to kill.

Determined, I stared at the brilliant light. There was no turning back now. I was going to see this through.

"To the light!" I cried as I brought my legs together and threw my arms over my head in that superhero pose.

I shot forward like a rocket.

Whoops.

Like an astronaut in space, I was traveling in a straight line with the same momentum, no signs of slowing down—and right into the mouth of that beast.

"Ho-o-o-l-l-l-y-y cr-a-a-a-p!" I wailed with a half laughing, half terrified screech like a banshee.

I braced myself.

And then I hit the doorway. Or rather, I was *sucked* in.

CHAPTER
27

Have you ever been in that ride at the local fair where you're positioned inside one of those giant tops that keeps on spinning and spinning and spinning until you feel like you're going to spew up your lunch and your stomach?

This was much, much worse.

Even with my spirit body, I felt ill, like my head was about to snap off my neck. White light exploded all around me as I was wrenched through a giant vacuum cleaner. The jump through the portal hit me like a bucket of ice water, a slap right from the start with the shock turning into the sensation of being pulled in every direction.

I felt my body shatter, well, not my *physical* body, more like the particles that made up my spirit body. It wasn't at all the same feeling I'd gotten when I had been in Horizon and made the jump into that pool of water. Seeing my body disintegrate then had been a blast, and I wasn't scared. Now. I was terrified.

Shit. This was all wrong. I was going to get torn apart.

I strained to keep my cool. Freaking out now wouldn't help me. I kept my thoughts tightened into a ball, struggling to keep my spirit together.

And just when I thought I was about to literally explode, I hit something solid.

Solid?

I rolled onto something hard, definitely hard, as a tingling washed through me. Blinking, I waited for my eyes to adjust to the sudden light. When shapes were in focus, I looked around.

Rolling hills of blue sand spread out before me in all directions. A few trees scattered the landscape, and at first glance I thought they were dead. Then I quickly realized what I thought were dead, leafless branches, were the roots. Branches covered in red and orange leaves spread out at the bottom like a textured gown.

The trees were upside down. All of them.

Weird.

It was bright, seemingly to be around midafternoon. I looked up into the sky. There was no glowing disk that would account for the light, no sun. Of course not. This wasn't earth. The sky was a dead giveaway. It was green with streaks of yellow and orange, as though it had been painted by giant brush strokes. No white clouds either, but large, floating purple rocks hovered in the sky as though gravity didn't affect them.

Flocks of birds flew above me, their silver feathers a stark contrast against the green sky. They flew in a side-to-side motion, not the up and down flow I was used to. In fact, I couldn't even make out any wings, just large tails that seemed to propel them forward. When one flew close to me, I realized these were not birds. They were fish.

Schools of hundreds of fish were flying in a green sky with floating purple rocks, blue sand, and upside-down trees. This was all kinds of weird.

I felt like I'd just stepped into one of Salvador Dalí's paintings. It was an upside-down world. No, that wasn't the right word. This place was just… wrong. Like whoever created it wasn't right in the head. As though the creator was mad.

"This ought to be fun."

It was cold, and I thought it strange that I would even feel anything at all with my spirit body. Because *that* never happened. But it was there. All around me. An icy cold, like I'd stepped into a giant refrigerator.

I stared at my hands, and then I wiggled them. They looked…solid.

"Even weirder."

I grabbed a fistful of sand, which I should not have been able to do. The rough particles scratched my skin as I watched them spill through my fingers. I could sit here for hours wondering why this was happening, or I could get my ass up and start looking for the souls.

"I can have a good ol' freak-out later." Staggering to my feet, I stood, surprised at how real this body felt, almost like my real body.

And then it hit me.

This body was very similar to when I was an angel wearing a mortal suit. Like wearing the skin of someone else who kinda looked like you over your own. It was me, but it wasn't really me—a replacement, a stand-in, an avatar.

And this avatar was slightly different than the angels' meat suit. Here, I didn't feel the extra supernatural angel abilities or the strength that came with the angels' mortal suit. This skin was... ordinary.

"Bummer." It didn't matter. As long as it would take me to the souls, I could have been green for all I cared. Wings would have been awesome, though.

I spun on the spot, trying to determine where the hell the souls would be. I had imagined the souls trapped in a giant cage, together, where I could have picked the lock and set them all free. I was not that lucky.

"When am I ever lucky? Never. That's when." A thought occurred to me. "Shane? Can you still hear me?" My voice was much stronger now, well, at least to me it felt more normal and less whispery.

"Shane? Hello?" I waited for Shane's voice inside my head, but all I heard was a whole lot of nothing.

Our connection was severed. I was on my own. I'd known it was a possibility, but it still sucked.

Panicked, I tapped into my mind, into that place, that level of consciousness I'd always gone to when I astral projected—

And felt nothing. Not just empty air and drifting dust, but nothing. A cold and emptiness filled the space where my consciousness should have been. My own connection was severed. The connection between my spirit and my physical body was cut.

This was bad. Without that life-force string that connected my consciousness to my physical body, I didn't know how to get back home.

"Okay. Don't panic. I can fix this. Do *not* panic."

Too late. I was panicking.

I closed my eyes and counted to ten, trying to calm down. If there was a way in, there was always a way out. Meltdown aside, I opened my eyes.

"Okay. Where do I start?"

There was no East and West, or North and South. Without a sun, I had no idea where to look, and my sense of direction sucked. So, I picked a hill with a large rock formation that could be a mountain and made for it. Why the heck not?

I fell into a slow jog as the terrain permitted, traversing the mounds of blue sand and the occasional upside-down tree. I thought about calling out to the souls. But then, what would I call them? *Souls? Hello, souls?* That didn't sound right.

"Hello? People? Spirits of the people?" I called instead and winced at how stupid that sounded. But I stood for a moment, listening. I heard nothing but the constant push of the wind. Squinting, I tucked a strand of hair behind my ear as I searched the endless rolling blue dunes. The air stank, and the scent of sulfur mixed with a sweet smell caught deep in my throat.

Was that what *he* smelled like? This Derrigor?

Then I realized it was even more stupid to call out like that. Derrigor would surely hear me. Did he know I was here? That made sense if he kept tabs on the comings and goings of Death. Worry tightened my brow. Yeah. He knew I was here.

"Not smart, Rowyn."

I started to jog again. The souls were here. I just had to find them before Derrigor found me. Yup, piece of cake.

Not knowing how long my spirit could last in this new realm, I ran faster. Harder. Kicking up puffs of sand, I ran down a hill and then made the hard journey back up another. Yeah. This avatar sucked. No supernatural endurance in this crappy body.

I kept going, focusing on the mountain of rock in the distance and using it as my bearing. I was so focused on the mountain that when I hit the wall, I hit it at almost a sprint.

Ouwwww.

My forehead smacked first. Then, with the shock, I'd lifted my head, and hit my chin. After that, I did the disgraceful, face-on-glass slide to the ground because that was exactly what that had felt like. Me, walking into a wall of glass.

I stood with my hand on my forehead, which, surprise, surprise did not have a bump. But it had still hurt. That was weird, but not as weird as me hitting a wall in the middle of nowhere.

"A little warning would have been nice."

I reached out, and my hand pressed against what felt like a smooth surface. Glass? A mirror? Since I couldn't see my reflection, I nixed the mirror possibility. It was either *really* clean glass or a projection of some kind.

If there was one wall of glass, I had a feeling there were more. This was a prison—a giant glass prison. So, where were the souls?

A soft pop pulled my head up and I spun around.

A tumble of pebbles and rocks came from everywhere as five hooded figures draped in heavy black robes surrounded me. Their faces were hidden in the shadow of their hoods. Tendrils of black mist carried around them, as though they were wrapped in the aura of death. They were vaguely humanoid but more like an ape than a human with abnormally long arms and a slight bend to their posture.

I knew what these were. I'd seen them before. They were the same black specters I'd seen back at the necromancers' temple, right before they tried to sacrifice poor stupid Cynthia. Only this time, they were solid.

And they were coming straight for me.

Ah, hell.

CHAPTER
28

What do you do when you're facing an impending attack and you're backed up against the wall? You use your gift of gab, that's what.

I planted my feet and lowered myself in a crouch.

"Hey there, I'm Sasha," I told them. Rule number one when facing an enemy—never give out your real name. Rule number two—never show fear, but load up the sass. "I'm loving the dementors outfits. Or are you supposed to be ringwraiths? I could never tell the difference."

The five specters kept coming, closer and closer, their heads swaying from side to side as though they were trying to figure out who or what I was.

I lifted my hands in surrender as I stepped to the side and away from the wall. I needed space to fight, if that was going to happen. Yes, by the looks of it.

"So, what do I call you guys?" I asked, pulling myself forward another step.

"What do I call you guys," the five wraiths echoed their voices a mix of rough likeness to my own.

Yikes. That was creepy. Worse was the carrion-breath misting out of their mouths, or whatever was hidden beneath their hoods.

They weren't advancing as fast anymore, and I took that as a good sign. They were curious about me. That, or they were calculating who was going to attack first.

I flashed them one of my best smiles. "You wouldn't happen to know where the souls are? Would you? Maybe just point me in the right direction?"

The wraiths cocked their heads to the side.

"Right. Didn't think so."

"You are Rowyn Sinclair," said one of the wraiths, its voice low with a cruel tone.

I stiffened. "How did you know that?" *You specter freaks.* I didn't like that they knew my name.

"You passed through the realm of Death," answered the wraith. "Your soul is now connected to Death. To us. We know everything about you."

I pursed my lips. "That's nice. And you are… let me guess… the guardians of this place?"

The same wraith took a step forward. "We are the soul collectors."

"More like the soul jailors." I gritted my teeth at the way their heads kept lolling to the sides. "You're not getting mine, wraiths."

"We already have," said another of the soul collectors in a voice I was sure was smiling.

My Hunter instincts came through, and I brushed my hand against my hip, expecting to pull out my soul blade. Instead, I stared at the black necromancer blade in my grasp.

The ferro ex mortuis.

My face scrunched in surprise. Weird. My soul blade didn't follow me to the realm of Death, only the necromancer blade did. It was sharp and had a pointy end. That'd work.

Feeling a little brasher, I waved the ferro ex mortuis. "No. You don't. Na na na na naaa!"

The five wraiths hissed, their heads following the movement of the ferro ex mortuis, like a dog would when teased with a treat. But I had the feeling they didn't exactly like this blade. In fact, it seemed as though they hated it. Good. I'd use that too.

I gestured to each in turn with the necromancer blade. "Eeny, meeny, miney, moe, catch a tiger by the toe. If he hollers, let him go. Eeny, meeny, miney, moe." I pursed my lips. "Nah. I can't choose." I cocked my hip and flashed them my pearly whites. "Okay then. Who's first?"

Three of the five wraiths rushed forward.

"Hey, not fair!" I shouted as I angled myself, calculating my attack and defense strategy.

In a flash of black, slimy, corrupted fingers stretched forward, and I sliced through them with a great upward arc. Black mist poured out of the stump end of its fingers, making me pause. That was weird. Was that from the ferro ex mortuis or was it the wraith's blood mist? Though curious, I didn't have time to dwell on it. Not if I didn't want these wraith douchebags to take my soul.

The wraith hissed, halting for a second, which helped. Until the other two vaulted forward.

Crap.

Spinning, I demonstrated the stop-thrust jab I had been practicing with Gareth the past weekends. My blade arm straightened like one limb to its full extent. The dark knifepoint ripped through the nearest wraith's neck, and into twelve inches of air beyond.

The wraith screeched, its rotten fingers gripping the blade as it tried to pull itself free. Where its fingers touched the blade, white-hot sparks plumed between its knuckles.

And then the wraith exploded into a cloud of black mist.

And I mean *mist*—the wet, sulfur-stink mist that clings to everything and continues to smell even if you wipe it off. Nasty stuff. When demons exploded, it was usually ashes, but you did get the occasional slop of entrails now and then. This stuff was wet. *Ewww.*

"Gross," I cried. Spitting or trying to spit what I knew I'd gotten into my mouth, but all I did was hack air. You try to spit when you don't have any saliva.

A blur of limbs flashed in my line of sight.

I ducked. Too late.

I cried out as searing pain erupted from my arm. One of the wraith's hands was wrapped around my left arm, its touch like burning acid. Whatever body I had in this realm was like butter to these guys. I'd melt at nothing.

I felt like its touch was going to burn a hole right through my arm. I liked my arm. It had been a very good arm to me all these years. I still needed it.

With a swing of my right arm, I plunged the necromancer blade into the eye, or brain, or whatever was beneath that hood. I knew I'd hit something when the wraith let go of me and the pain stopped.

I pulled my arm up. Yup. A nasty black handprint wrapped around the skin of my arm. Apparently, this body could burn too.

"Now, look what you did. Bad wraith. Very bad wraith," I said and looked up.

The wraith I'd stabbed combusted into—wait for it—a cloud of black mist.

This time I was prepared.

I ducked and turned. When I came up again, the remaining three wraiths were not three wraiths anymore—but a wall of wraiths, a dozen strong.

"Figures." I raised my brows and shrugged. "Why is it that the bad guys never want to play fair? I know. Because fair would be me kicking your specter asses. And you know it."

The wraiths hissed and swayed from side to side in a sinister dance of death, a continuous stream of guttural moans emanating from them.

Well, I wasn't just going to stand there. I might be a tad crazy, but I wasn't an idiot.

I turned on my heel and ran.

I ran as fast as I could, which wasn't exactly an easy feat in the sand, but I'd figured I had maybe a few seconds' lead.

Something hit me in the back of the head.

Guess not.

I pitched forward, mouth open in surprise, and yes, shoveled up buckets of sand with my jaw as I went. Coughing, I rolled and kicked up with my legs, knowing a wraith would be there. My boots made contact with something solid and I had enough time to see the wraith fall back just as another replaced it.

Damn. This was not going as well as I had hoped.

Scooping as much of the blue sand as I could from my mouth with my fingers, I stood and swiped the necromancer blade like I would a long sword, hoping to slice a few wraiths before they had a chance to burn me again.

Dread was a sudden finality. There was no way I could fight all of these soul collectors, especially when it seemed they could just appear out of thin air in this place. I had a nasty feeling there were a hell of a lot more of them too if their job was to guard the souls, and there were thousands of stolen souls in here… well, you get the picture.

I was good. But I wasn't *that* good.

267

The wraiths seemed to relax a little. Either that, or they knew a victory when they saw one.

My shoulders slumped. I had failed. And I never even had a chance to find the souls, let alone free them.

I tried again to pull back into my mind, to connect into that place, that state of consciousness that allowed me to take this crazy-ass trip, wanting my ticket out of here. I floundered my mind again and again, but it was empty. There was nothing.

Shit.

"There's no place like home. There's no place like home," I muttered and clicked my heels. Nope. Nothing.

Damn. I was stuck in a realm without the means to get home. Worse. I was stuck in a realm without the means to get home *and* with a horde of ugly wraiths who wanted to take my soul.

If I had a heart, it would be thrashing madly in my chest. Yes, I was afraid, but a part of me went berserk with anger.

"Come on, you bastards."

I braced myself as the mass of wraiths came at me, rotten, skeletal fingers grabbing—

A blur of brilliant white light flashed before me.

Then another. Then another.

I stumbled back, staring in shock as thousands of small globes of white light attacked the wraiths like a swarm of giant wasps the size of tennis balls.

The white globes zipped and darted at the wraiths, moving like steel blades through the soul collectors and shearing through their bodies like cardboard. From all directions, in a whirling cloud of deadly fireflies, they struck hundreds of times in only a few seconds, black mist splashing into the air as the wraiths lost limbs and parts of their bodies.

I saw the sudden fear in the wraiths, their movements panicked and frenzied as they tried to beat the flying globes with their arms. But the globes were too fast, too strong, too many.

There was a collective shriek, and then all the wraiths exploded in a cloud of black mist. They were gone.

The brilliant globes hung in the air like giant-sized fireflies standing out against the dark green sky. I knew what they were. They were souls.

And they just saved my life.

A cloud of haze appeared in front of me. Within a heartbeat, the mist deepened. It shifted and then solidified, taking on the shape of a man.

"Gareth?" I choked.

CHAPTER
29

Gareth. My Gareth was standing before me.

I threw myself into his arms—passing right through him—stumbled and fell face-first on the ground.

I spat out some sand. "Not exactly the reunion I had imagined." I rolled over and stared up at the handsome elf, only noticing then that his body still had a kind of haze effect over it. And if I stared long enough, I could see the shadows of shapes through him, like a ghost. "I can't touch you. Can I?" I asked, though I already knew the answer as I got to my feet. I wanted so much to touch him, to kiss him, to wrap my arms around his large chest, and just lie there. But I knew I couldn't. Major downer.

Gareth's face was pained. "No, no you can't," he said, and I was glad his voice sounded the same.

I brushed some of the sand off my jeans. "This place is a trip. Isn't it? With the upside-down trees, the flying fish, the blue sand."

"You could say that."

I glanced at the elf. "Are those wraiths dead?"

The elf shook his head. "No. They'll be back." His gaze moved over the rolling blue dunes, his expression shifting to a darker mood. "They always come back. And then there's the other one…"

I moved my gaze over him. "You mean Derrigor."

Gareth watched me. "You know his name?"

I looked at the hovering souls. "Courtesy of the angels," I answered and glanced back at him. "Are you the only one who can… appear like this?"

Gareth met my stare. "No. But it takes lots of concentration and effort to maintain this body. It's much easier just to stay as a soul. What I am now…" He frowned at what he saw on my face. "This is just a representation of my body. I'm not here in the physical sense."

"Neither am I. But… why am *I* solid?" I stared at the necromancer blade I still held in my hand and slipped it back in its sheath against my waist.

"You're not the same as us," said the elf, and he gestured to the still-lingering souls. "You didn't enter this realm the same way we did. Your soul wasn't taken. You're still alive, Rowyn. We're not."

"Don't say that." I frowned nervously. "All of you," I said, looking up at the souls. "You're not dead. Your bodies are *very* much alive." I sighed, though no air came out. Weird. "But not for long."

"What are you talking about?" Gareth's face took on a hard edge, his posture stiff. "Rowyn. Why *are* you here?"

I knew he was mad, and I could tell by the deepening of his frown that he believed I did something very foolish. I pulled my face into a smile and said, "I'm here to save you, of course." I spread out my arms and said, "Ta-da!"

At that, some of the souls dropped a few feet in the air. Either they were shocked, or they too thought I was the giant idiot. If they had faces, their features would look just like Gareth's. I glared at them.

Gareth was silent. Fury seethed in him, anger and fear fueling his struggle to find the words. "That wasn't smart," snapped the elf. "Do you realize what you've done? How many times have I told you to *think* before you act? You're too impulsive. You've always been." He shook his head and began to pace. "Damn it, Rowyn. How could you do this?"

"And that's the thanks I get for trying to help?" Now I was mad.

"How?" Was the only word that left out the angry elf's mouth. Pity, it was such a pretty mouth.

"Astral projection," I said, a little proud of myself. Then I blurted, "Stop doing that!" At that, the souls that dropped another foot. Some even fell to the ground in fake deaths. "Seriously?"

"Astral projection," repeated Gareth. He didn't exactly look impressed. "If your consciousness dies here—"

"Yes, yes, yes. I know." I waved a dismissive hand. "I don't intend to die here. That's not part of the plan."

Gareth raised a skeptical brow, and I hated how real he made it seem, even with his ghostly appearance. "Oh, really?"

I pressed my hands on my hips and matched his exact expression. "Yeah. *Really*. Look, we need to get out of here."

"We can't." The elf ran a hand through his hair, the gesture casual and so genuine. "There's no way out of here. Not for us. We've already searched every inch of this prison. It's all we can do. But it's pointless. We can never leave."

"We can. We will." I took a step closer to him. "And we have to go soon."

Gareth's lips pressed together, his jaw clenched. "Why?"

"The humans think the bodies without souls are a result of some deadly virus. They're sending in the National Guard to eradicate the so-called infected."

"So?"

My face went slack. "So?"

"There's nothing you can do, Rowyn." Gareth gave a short laugh. "It's over. We are all just whispers of who we used to be." His eyes turned intense. "I tried. I tried to fight him. But he surprised me. And by the time I knew what was happening… it was too late."

It pained me to see him like this. I remembered what it felt like to have my soul almost taken from me. It wasn't pretty. If Father Thomas hadn't been there, I'd be just like Gareth and the lot of them.

Gareth went to grab my hand, and then realizing what he was doing, dropped his hand. "This is the end of the road for us, Rowyn."

"No," I started. "I know for a fact that's not true. The angels told me as much."

"The angels?"

"If I can get you out," I looked to the souls again, the thousands of them. "All of you, then you—your souls—will reconnect with your bodies," I told them, not knowing the proper terminology to use. Bond? Rewire? It didn't matter. By the look on the elf's face, I knew he understood.

Gareth was still frowning. "The angels told you this?"

"Yes." Not exactly. It was more of a "maybe" than a certainty, but they didn't have to know.

The elf turned to me, his eyes wide. "What about you? Can you project your spirit out of here?"

"Yeah," I shifted my weight. "About that. Um… there seems to be a tiny 'technical' issue with the ride back home."

"Rowyn?" Gareth's worried expression had my knees weakening. I loved that damn pointy-eared bastard.

"Not to worry. I'm not planning on staying either."
If only I could figure out how to get out of this place,
we were golden.

"What if you can't? What if you're going to die
here like the rest of us? Or worse, he'll just keep you
here. That's why he gave you a solid body. To inflict
pain."

"You mean Derrigor? I don't care about him right
now. I care about getting us out." I looked to the
hovering souls. "All of us."

The elf crossed his arms over his chest. "How?
There's no door or windows. This isn't your typical
prison."

"I get that. So, we… have to think outside the box.
Yes, I know how that sounded, but I'm telling you…
if there's a way in… there's a way out." There had to
be. "We just need to find it."

Gareth smiled. "If I could kiss you, I would."

"I know." I smiled back. "I'm just so damn
kissable." One of the hovering souls made a whirl and
I swear if it had eyes, it was rolling them right about
now. Somehow, I knew it was a woman's soul.

I pointed a finger at the soul. "You. Shove it.
You're going to thank me later."

With my hands on my hips, I spun around, my
mind working out a plan of escape. "Okay, you said
you've been over this entire place. Right?"

"Right."

"What stood out to you?" I asked my eyes fixed on
the fake rock formation in the distance. "What didn't
seem normal?"

Gareth made a face. "Have you looked around?"

"I get the weird aspect. Think *extra*-weird."

"Apart from it being a glass box prison?" The elf shrugged. "Not much."

It was my turn to roll my eyes. "No. I mean. If this," I spread my arms, "is your new normal. What *doesn't* fit." I looked to the souls. "Anyone?"

The soul I believed had rolled her eyes at me drifted forward. And the next thing I knew, she was standing in front of me, as a woman. Told ya.

"The sky is green," began the woman, whose red curly hair was pulled back in a long ponytail. She looked to be in her early thirties. She was a few inches shorter than me, fit and wore skinny jeans with a white blouse. "And have you seen the trees? I'm not even sure you can call them trees. If that's not extra-weird, I don't know what is. I'm Marla, by the way."

"It's nice to meet you, Marla." I looked between her and Gareth. For a human, she was taking this whole soul thing really well. Maybe she had no choice.

"Okay. What else?"

Marla gave an exaggerated shrug. "There's those creepy hooded monsters. And then there's the big one."

"Derrigor," I answered for her. "What else?"

"There's nothing else here," said Marla, her features twisting in anger. "It's just us, and all that blue sand. There's no door or portal or anything. We've already checked. We're stuck here forever." Her voice cracked. "I want to go home to my kids.

But I can't. Because no matter how many times I've tried, I can't break through those glass walls."

My jaw dropped. "That's it." I pumped the air with my fist, feeling like a fool that I'd actually done it for real, and the gesture didn't stay in my head.

"That's what?" laughed Gareth. The sound would have made my heart patter if I had one in this place. He had such a great laugh, and I'd missed it.

Reeling in my emotions, I said, "The walls. Whatever it is that confines us." I knew I was onto something. I didn't know how I knew this, but I was certain it was our way out. I beamed at them. "That's our way out."

"We've already tried that," said the elf and he looked at Marla. "We can't break them."

"You can't. But maybe I can." I turned towards the fake mountain. "We need to break the illusion." I looked back at them. "It's the only thing keeping you trapped here." It made sense. "This place is just a glass box. A container with a tight lid to keep you in here. We don't need a door. We're going to *make* one."

At that precise moment, a bell rang out. Not like a beautiful church bell but a more morbid, solemn sound that made me think of a funeral. It gave me the creeps.

Gareth stiffened, and his gaze fixed on something behind me. I hated the panicked look that crossed his face. "He's here."

I didn't have to look to know who he meant by "he." But I turned and looked anyway.

A misshapen shadow congealed not two hundred feet from us. It was ten or twelve feet tall, the body bleeding a pool of darkness. He had no shape now, but I could make out semi-human features in the flash of his darkness—eyes of white fire and a yawning mouth that was lined with burning coals.

The power coming from him pulsed in waves, lifting my hair from my head.

I knew my demons. This wasn't one of them. This was a god.

This was Derrigor.

Oh.

Shit.

CHAPTER
30

Derrigor was the most terrifying creature I'd ever seen. If I'd had my mortal organs right now, I would have peed myself.

A rolling wave of nausea went through me along with his power. The darkness around him was a shimmering blur, the glow of his eyes too piercing, his power suffocating. I found myself taking several steps back until that awful tide of feeling had receded, but I had to fight to stay standing.

Marla made a squeak that would have made a mouse proud as her body shifted and then collapsed into a ball of light. Marla the soul zipped high into the air and away from Derrigor. I didn't blame her. I would have done the same if I could transform into a pixie-like ball.

The other souls didn't make a sound, but they were zooming around like thousands of frenzied fireflies, flying behind me and Gareth.

Derrigor opened his mouth and spoke. "Come forward, little grasshopper. Hippity-hop-hop," he said, his voice a deep rumble. It was eerie, throbbing in strange tones while emitting a human sound from an inhuman throat. His white-hot eyes were focused on me. Yeah. Totally creepy.

"A curious little grasshopper, you are," said the god. "I sense a strong lifeforce in you. Curious indeed. But different. Yes. Different. You are not like the others. Perhaps I shall eat you now. Yes. That sounds about right. Come. Hippity-hop. Let me see into your soul, little grasshopper." Derrigor laughed then, a sound like a match igniting. There was an unmistakable note of pleasure in his voice.

I loosened whatever fake muscles I had in this body. "How fast can he run?" I whispered to Gareth.

The elf shook his head. "No idea."

"Little grasshopper? Come now. It is rude to ignore the host," continued Derrigor. "I let you into my home. If I did not want you to enter, I would have denied you entry. I let you in. I was curious. I wanted to see how you would fare in my world. I made this body for you. Do you like it?" When I didn't answer, he continued. "You will do as I say, and you will come to me. Come now, little grasshopper. Come play with me."

Yeah, right. Like I was going to obey this a-hole god.

I met Gareth's worried expression and said, "I have an idea."

"A good one, I hope."

"I guess we'll find out." I looked up to the souls. "Everybody! Run!" I shot forward, knowing Gareth was right behind me, and aimed for the mountain, where I knew one of the walls was. The souls whipped past me in a blur of white lights.

Derrigor's deep laugh followed behind me. "There is nowhere to run, little grasshopper. You are trapped. And your soul will be mine. Forever."

I don't think so. I ran faster. There was no adrenaline to help me, no supernatural strength. There was only my will. My will to live. My will to save Gareth and the others.

"Hippity-hop. Hippity-hop. Come out and play, little grasshopper," I heard Derrigor say. The god was clearly mad. It explained his choice of crib.

"Rowyn. Where are we going like this?" Gareth ran next to me, his feet never truly touching the ground and leaving no puffs of sand clouds or footprints.

I tried not to look. The more I looked the more likely I was to fall on my face again. "To the wall." I looked up to see the souls, hovering like Christmas lights, at what I thought was the edge of the wall.

"And then?" asked Gareth.

"Then we'll see if my plan works." *Or we all die.*

We reached the wall and the souls all gathered around, darting in fear and jittering in what I came to understand as impatience. They all wanted to see if I truly could get us out. Me too.

"Hippity-hop-hop-hop, little grasshopper," came the god's voice from somewhere behind me. "Hop, hop, hop. But you will be mine."

I looked over my shoulder. Derrigor was strolling his way towards us, his pace slow like he was out for a stroll in the park, admiring his screwed-up creation. The dude was really in love with himself. He didn't have to have a god complex. He *was* a god. His leisurely pace meant he didn't think we could get out. Good. It would give me the added precious seconds I needed. I was going to use that too.

Gareth stood next to me. "I won't be able to help you."

"You will." I loosened the necromancer blade from my weapons belt. "Keep an eye on the big guy and tell me if he gets close."

The elf stared at the blade. "A blade won't do anything to him. He's not mortal."

I pulled the blade up. "It's not for him. It's for us." My mind raced, matching the speed of the souls that were darting around my head, like annoying giant mosquitoes.

The necromancer blade had traveled to this realm with me. That had to mean something. Why that particular blade and not my soul blade? Because either Derrigor had forged it, or he had poured some of his power into it. The ferro ex mortuis was linked to this place. I was sure of it.

If I was right, it was also why the necromancer Rath had been pissed that I never gave it back. This blade was special. And now, I was going to test my theory.

I edged toward the wall, a quick glance behind me telling me that Derrigor was still too far away to see what I was about to do.

I stiffened with the necromancer blade held tightly in my grasp. "Guys, get ready," I told the souls.

And with all of my will and my desire to go home, I struck at the wall.

An explosion of brilliant white light detonated into a blinding blaze followed by a blast of kinetic force that blew outward in a cloud of sand. It hissed and I was propelled back to land on my butt, hard, legs splayed in the air and all.

I pushed myself up. Gareth hadn't even moved. He was staring at a spot on the wall.

I rushed over. Where I'd hit the wall with the blade, there was a tiny black hole, a slit the size of my thumb. Our way out.

"Yes! It worked!" I coughed, both exhilarated and shocked that I'd been right. The souls circled my head excited, and I had to resist the urge to swat them away.

I had expected the shattering of glass, but it was more like cutting through cardboard.

Derrigor let out a howl. "Grasshopper! What are you doing?"

I looked over my shoulder.

Obviously, he'd dropped the slow pace and was now in a full-fledged fury run. He was still quite far, but he'd be on us in less than thirty seconds.

Oh, crapper.

Gareth's smile froze in place. "You did it, Rowyn. You really did it."

"Don't get too excited just yet. I need to cut more." I'd only punctured a small hole. I needed to make a damn doorway to get us out. Me included.

I threw myself against the wall, hitting and slicing at the hole as fast as I could. Hell, I was even sawing it, slicing back and forth. It seemed to work better. The realm unleashed the light again, this time so brilliant I could barely see what I was doing. But the more I cut, the more darkness appeared through the hole.

"Stop her!" The words pounded across this realm, like the rumble of thunder. There was power and command in those words.

I couldn't resist looking over my shoulder. And then I wished I hadn't. Ten wraiths had surrounded us, their long cloaks rippling behind them as they charged.

"Keep cutting. Don't stop." Gareth and a group of souls broke apart and went for the wraiths.

"Come on, Rowyn!" I told myself. I struggled with the blade. Sudden fear made my hand slip, and I nearly dropped it through to whatever existed on the other side.

Not cool. Panicked. I struggled to keep it together. I couldn't fail now. I couldn't. People were depending upon me. I had to fight. I had to do this.

Using both hands, I pressed as hard as I could, slicing my way downward through our containment wall. After a few hits, I cursed. I'd only managed to make a small gap the size of my arm. Maybe it was enough for the souls but not for me.

I peeked over my shoulder. Gareth stood with his back to me in a protective stance, and the souls hit the wraiths like a swarm of bees on steroids. It was helping. But when I glanced over Gareth's shoulder, Derrigor was almost upon us.

I had ten seconds left. Tops.

"Hurry Rowyn. He's almost here!"

"I know," I shouted. Shaking, I put all my weight into it. I cried out as I cut as hard as I could.

Finally, a gap that could fit a person.

"There." I stepped back, the necromancer blade in my hand. "It's open."

I barely had the words out of my mouth before a trail of brilliant globes zipped past me and disappeared through the opening. I watched as the last of the souls swarmed away like a troop of overgrown fireflies and vanished from view. They were free.

"Okay. They've all gone," I said, turning to Gareth just as the last soul disappeared through the gap. The wraiths were gone or had been vanquished by the souls. I didn't know and I didn't care right now.

The ground shook beneath my feet. Strange black and white lightning flashed along the realm, outlining the walls and top of the massive cage that was the realm. The ground all around us lit with a sudden angry blue fire that rose from giant crevices.

"What's happening?" I asked Gareth.

"The souls." He turned, his eyes wide. "The souls must have been powering this place. Without them…"

"It's going to collapse." Great. The realm of Death was crumbling around us, and the looming darkness that was Derrigor was vastly approaching. I loved my life.

"What about Derrigor?" the elf was watching the advancing god.

I shook my head. "Who cares. I didn't come here for him. I came here for you and the souls. Let's go."

"He's going to get his hands on more souls. The necromancers won't just stop at us."

"That's why we need to get out of here and stop them."

Gareth lifted his hand toward my face. I couldn't feel his touch, but I could imagine it.

"Gareth. Go."

The elf dropped his hand and shook his head stubbornly. "No. I'm not going until I know you can go through it too."

I gritted my teeth. "Seriously? We don't have time to argue. I came here to get you back. You don't get a say in this."

Gareth planted himself. "Ladies first."

He was stubborn. I was worse. And he knew it.

"I'm not a lady." I gave him a wicked smile. "In you go," I ordered. "I'll be right behind you."

The elf flashed me a goofy grin, and then his body collapsed into a brilliant white ball, his soul, and with a blur of light, he disappeared into the gap.

The moment he was gone, I felt an enormous sense of relief, but the feeling didn't last.

I whirled around at the other more dominating feeling. Fear.

Derrigor was so close now I could appreciate what he looked like. And it wasn't good. He was huge, and equally powerful, a dark tower of twisting, whirling energies. I didn't think mortal eyes were meant to look upon him. Good thing I was in my astral projection vessel.

The pulsing of power coming from him intensified, nearly sending me to my knees. I stood staring against my own mind, telling me to run, to flee. But I wanted to look at him, just one last time. This guy, this god, was powerful enough to create all of this. A new reality. A new realm. To him, I was just a grasshopper. Go figure.

"You might have found a way to set them free, little grasshopper," said Derrigor, as he slowed his pace into a confident gait. "But my souls will soon replenish. This was nothing. I'll have more than ever before until all of your world will bend to my will. Until every last mortal soul… will be mine."

"You're very full of yourself."

Derrigor's mouth spread into a wide grin. "*I* am a *god.*"

"Tell me about it."

The god's face twisted in a manic glee. "I think I will eat your soul now."

And *that* was my cue to split.

I stared at the gap in this world, wondering if it would work for me or if it would actually kill me. I had a split-second thought of leaving the necromancer dagger but changed my mind. It had saved us. It might come in handy.

"Grasshopper! I will come for you, little grasshopper!"

That last claim was all I heard as I threw myself, headfirst, through the hole in Death.

CHAPTER
31

The trip back wasn't as fun and exciting as the trip into Death had been.

It was like my body was an elastic band, my limbs stretched to impossible lengths, my body squeezed into an impossibly thin size. I mean, we all want to lose a few extra pounds, but having my body crushed and yanked into a spaghetti noodle wasn't the way I wanted to do it.

When I felt pain on my cheek, I knew I was back.

I took a deep breath. Then another. Next, I blinked into the blue eyes of a Siamese cat and felt a weight on my chest and his warm paw on my face. His eyes were dilated and had the focused look of a cat about to pounce.

"She's back! She's back!" shrilled Tyrius. And then he hit me across the face with his paw. "Don't. You. Ever. Do. That. Again!"

Being slapped across the face by a cat when just returning from a journey in Death was not the welcome committee I'd expected. But he was so damn cute when he was worried, with his tiny mouth pouting and his nose scrunched up, I just wanted to squeeze him.

So I did.

I sat up in my bed and grabbed my furry friend, squeezing him tightly against my chest. "I missed you too, Tyrius," I said as I kissed the top of his head. "But why are you here? I thought you were with Kora and the kids."

The cat squirmed out of my arms and gave me the stink eye. "Lance came to get me because they thought you were dead."

I looked around the room. Lance sat on the floor, panting with his tongue hanging out and wagging his tail like a real dog. Layla stood with her mouth hanging open yet still managed to look sexy. Shane still sat in the chair next to my bed where I'd last seen him. He looked the same, apart from the tiny smile that quirked his lips.

"How so?" I asked Tyrius. I was glad to feel my beating heart, and having saliva back in my mouth was golden.

The cat lowered his ears. "You stopped breathing, that's how."

I shrugged. "Well. I'm not dead."

"No shit." Tyrius shook his head.

"Your skin was so cold, Rowyn," said Layla coming forward. "Like a corpse."

"You even *looked* like a corpse by the time I got here," added Tyrius. "You went all pale… clammy… totally freaked us out. You were gone a long time, Rowyn. Too long. I didn't think you'd make it back."

My heart clenched at the worry in his voice. "How long was I gone?" To me it felt like hours, but knowing how time is different in other worlds like Horizon, it could have been days for all I knew.

"An hour and twenty-six minutes," answered the cat.

"Really? That's not that long."

"That's an hour and twenty-six minutes of hell!" Tyrius sighed. "My delicate heart can't take that again. Look." He lifted his paw with something long and thin clutched between his toes. "I lost two whiskers."

I rubbed under his chin. "You big baby. They'll grow back. I'm fine. See?" I swung my legs off the bed and stood. "I feel awesome. Like I just took a big nap."

The cat made a face and flicked the whiskers from his paw. "Yeah, well, you nearly took the nap of the century."

True, if Derrigor had his way. But he didn't.

Shane stood up. "Did it work? Did you free the souls?" he asked, his voice low with a little tension in it.

291

I glanced at the angel, feeling the smile on my face. "It did. I did. Wait—I think I did…" I needed to check on Gareth to be sure.

Tyrius smacked his forehead. "I think she left her brain in Death."

I made to move out of the room and halted. "No. I mean yes." Jeez. I did sound a little loony. "Start over—I mean, *yes*, I managed to free the souls. All of them."

"Including Gareth?" asked the cat.

"Him too." The thought of the elf made my heart patter faster. "It was an odd place." A tingle of apprehension curled around my neck at the memory of the god, as though his hands grabbed ahold of my neck. "Derrigor is mad."

Tyrius snorted. "I'd be mad too if you took away all my catnip."

Lance laughed. "Bet you would."

I shook my head. "No. I mean, the god *is* crazy. He's not well in the head. The world he created, his Death, it's all *wrong*. Chaotic. It was like stepping into his mind, his crazy-ass mind."

Shane rubbed his chin. "I've heard of other gods having a hard time differentiating between reality and fantasy after thousands of years spent alone."

"Well," I sighed. "He can stay there forever, alone again, for all I care." Thoughts and plans came rushing back into my head. My heart slammed in my chest with a vengeance, as though it had been waiting for hours to do so.

I checked my weapons belt. My soul bade hung at my hip, and so did the necromancer blade. "We don't have much time until Derrigor figures out what we're doing."

The cat jumped off the bed. "And what are we doing, exactly?"

"I'll explain on the way," I said and rushed out of my bedroom.

I ran to the living room. Danto jumped up from his chair, which was next to Gareth's.

He looked up at me surprised. "Rowyn? You're back. Did it work?"

Ignoring him I rushed over to Gareth. With trembling fingers, I pulled off the blindfold. Beautiful dark eyes blinked up at me.

"What do you remember?" I asked, my heart pounding, not knowing if our trip into Death would be erased from his memory.

The elf smiled. "Everything."

"You damn sexy elf," I said and crushed my lips against his so I wouldn't start bawling my eyes out. I had a reputation to keep. I pulled away. "Glad to have you back."

The elf grinned. "Nothing like the kiss from a pretty lady to wake a man from a coma. I'd be even happier if you got this rope off of me."

"I got it." Danto moved behind Gareth's chair and began to loosen the knots around the elf's wrists, chest, and then feet until Gareth was free.

As soon as he was, I jumped into his arms. I couldn't help myself. I buried my face into his neck

293

and shoulders, letting the warmth of his body soak into mine, just for a few seconds. Regretfully, I pulled back. There'd be lots of hugging and other stuff later.

Layla was grinning from ear to ear. "I'm so excited... I could... I could just..." she reached out, grabbed Danto, and kissed him fiercely, her hands moving all over him in a way that would have had Father Thomas blushing if he were here.

"Damn," muttered Tyrius. "I'd hate to see what she does when she's *over*excited. Keep the chocolate away. She might explode."

I laughed, long and hard. It felt good. I felt good. Unfortunately, I knew I couldn't enjoy the moment any longer. I still had a job to do. And yup, it was going to suck.

"Necromancers." I turned on the spot. "What's the news on them?"

"The Voldemort wannabes are still here," said Tyrius. He padded over to Gareth. "Nice to have you back again, wizard elf." Then he added in a low voice. "I didn't want to have to think about eating Rowyn's cooking."

"I heard that," I growled, making Gareth laugh. It was no secret I couldn't cook, though I loved Gareth's cooking. Especially when he wore nothing but an apron.

Layla pulled away from Danto, holding her phone in her hand. "I got a text from Alan earlier," she informed me. "He said they were spotted entering the cemetery in Fairview. Looks like they still have ties there."

"Good." It was better than good. It was a freaking miracle.

Alan was another angel-born Operative the Council appointed to the necromancer case after what happened in Times Square. Though I'd never worked directly with him, from his reputation, he was a team lead and a seasoned warrior for the Council. We were lucky to have him.

"How many are there?" If my gut feeling was right, they'd be all there.

"Just a sec." Layla's fingers blurred on the screen of her phone as she typed. A beep came through a moment later. She looked up from her phone and grinned at me, the kind of excited smile like a kid who got a new puppy, make that two new puppies. "Twelve."

"That's all of them." I beamed at her and tapped my weapons at my waist. "This is our lucky day."

"Best day *ever*." Layla mimicked my movement and tapped the whip at her right hip.

"Tell Alan we're on our way," I told her. "We should be there in under thirty minutes. And once we get there, we need to move fast," I said. "If we're lucky, the necromancers won't know about me breaking out the souls."

"But once they try to use their Death magic," said Tyrius, his eyes swiveling. "They'll know."

I clenched my jaw. "Right now, they're running on empty, or close to it." I didn't know if they had residual power from the souls or not. "I don't know if they can still do magic or not. So watch out for their

Death spells. If you feel one coming… you bring that necromancer down. Can't risk any of that magic getting through. We can't allow them to steal more souls—ours included. And don't let them raise the dead. They're going to try."

"Seeing as they're in a friggin' cemetery," muttered the cat.

"Can't let that happen." I watched as all heads bobbed in agreement.

"I'll get my truck ready," said Gareth as he started for the hallway.

I grabbed him. "Are you sure you're up for this?" I didn't know how he felt, but I knew he wasn't back to his normal self. Not yet. "If you wanted to wait this one out, it wouldn't be a big deal."

Gareth's dark eyes were intense. "I'm not letting you out of my sight. You can forget it."

I knew this wasn't a battle I could win. "Fine. You drive then."

The elf gave me a look. "Of course, *I'm* driving." And with that, he grabbed his black fedora hat and disappeared out the front door.

"I have room in my car," informed Danto, looking at the angels. "You can come with us if you like."

"Great idea, vampire," said Tyrius, his blue eyes luminous with his gaze focused on Lance. "The mutt can go with the vampire. I don't think half-breeds mind about fleas."

Lance curled up his lips. "No, they prefer projectile furball vomit."

Tyrius's tail twitched as he thought about it. "Projectile vomit's pretty awesome."

"It is," agreed the dog.

I frowned, looking from cat to dog. What the hell had just happened? Had they secretly bonded while I was in Death?

I grinned. "It's so nice to be back." Excitement rushed through my chest. "Let's do this. I've got a date with Lord Krull." Then I made a face. "But first… I *really* need to pee."

CHAPTER
32

Bladder empty and fully charged with three protein bars, I crouched next to a massive wrought-iron gate that led into a large graveyard with hundreds of silent headstones and memorials. The sky was a deep navy with rolling waves of flame, cherry red, the sun barely visible over the horizon. Only a few minutes of sunlight were left.

It was exhilarating to be in my old body again, feeling the rush of the Hunt—the soaring of sweet adrenaline accompanied by the satisfying push of all my thigh muscles. Granted, having spent some time in an angel body, well, that was something else. An angel body had been the uber of all bodies, equipped with supernatural strength, heightened senses, and let's not forget the never dying thing. Because, if the angel body died, I could always get a replacement.

Perhaps one day I could drive one of those babies again. Perhaps.

A cold, restless energy pressed against me, close to the blood pulsing beneath my skin. Ghouls. Lots of them. I wasn't surprised. There was always a ghoul in a cemetery. They were drawn to them like rats in a granary.

But I wasn't here for them.

I peered over the gray marble headstone with the engraved bold letters: JOHN REID. Underneath it read: DON'T LAUGH. YOU'RE NEXT. Nice. But my attention was pulled elsewhere—to the ring of necromancers beyond the headstones.

The necromancers were in plain sight. I counted twelve of them. They were all here, except for Rath, who'd kissed the sharp end of Father Thomas's sword. They were dressed in identical long black robes with big black hoods that showed nothing of the faces inside. One stood apart from the others. His hood rested on his shoulders, the last of the light casting deep shadows on his face and giving him a more severe, gaunt look like the living dead. Lord Krull. I was sure of it.

The old bastard was mine.

Whispers rolled over the wind, voices in a ghostly cadence. The unnatural, guttural sound could only be one thing—Death magic. They were getting ready to do another ritual. Once they did, they'd know right away something was amiss—their dumbass magic, that's what. Which was fine until they decided to replenish their well of power with more souls.

I would never let that happen.

We'd agreed not to kill the necromancers unless they struck first. I was counting on the hope that they would. I might even give them a little nudge in that direction.

Something moved to my far right, and I spotted Father Thomas kneeling next to a large gravestone with an angel statue on top. Behind him, a bustle of his cavalry, six Knights of Heaven.

"Do the priests know the plan?" whispered Gareth. He was next to me, his musky scent pleasant and comforting.

I nodded. "They'll stay behind with the other angel-borns. If any of the necromancers slip through our hands, they'll get them."

My eyes moved to my far left, to the big black man who was having trouble hiding his large frame behind one of the headstones. Alan. Next to him and hidden behind more gravestones was his army of ten angel-born, armed to the teeth and ready for a chance to show off their skills.

It was strange to think about how far I'd come. Only a few months ago, I would have never trusted the angel-born to work a job with me. But look at us now, both wanting the same thing, both working together. That, was a pretty awesome feeling.

I was so giddy with delight at the prospect of kicking those bony necromancers' asses I could barely contain myself.

Tyrius moved along my shoulders, his tail whipping in my face restlessly. "I'm getting the 'before a fight' tingles. It's going to be damn beautiful."

I smiled. "I know the feeling."

"You ready?" asked Gareth, his hot breath brushing against my cheek.

"You've got no idea." I shifted on the balls of my feet, adrenaline coursing through me. If I didn't hit a necromancer's face soon, I might explode. I yanked out my soul blade and saw the elf's hands dripping with green elf dust.

I looked behind me and gave Layla, Danto, Shane, and Lance the signal, which was just a nod of my head. Not exactly original, but you get the picture. Layla's eyes widened with barely contained excitement, looking more thrilled at the chance of kicking some necromancer butt than I was. I loved my little sis.

The vampire next to her gave me a wink—not the sultry wink of a man who's into me, but a wink to tell me not to worry about my sister, that he would protect her with his life. Behind him was the angel Shane, who'd surprised me when he told me he wanted to come with us.

"The more the merrier," I'd told him, and then I'd punched his shoulder, just to see how he'd react. The angel had laughed. Good enough for me.

Obviously, Lance wouldn't be left behind. The white German Shepard was a skilled fighter and Scout, and having with us was a no-brainer.

Lance's golden eyes gleamed with eagerness and a dangerous light. He was looking at Tyrius on my shoulder. And I swear the dog was smiling.

I grinned. I couldn't ask for a better team.

This was going to be fun.

I turned back around. "Dibs on Lord Krull," I breathed, and Tyrius laughed.

"Go, team," muttered the cat as he leaped off of my shoulders and disappeared through the graveyard.

Following Tyrius's lead, I rushed forward. I knew the others were right behind me, their footsteps silent as we separated. Gareth and I went straight while the others crossed to the other side of the cemetery.

It took a total of ten seconds and we had the necromancers surrounded.

Their unified cries of shock and outrage were music to my ears, a dark melody. I almost broke into a dance.

Lord Krull's eyes found me, and his face twisted in a kind of ugly fury. "You," he hissed.

"Me," I answered brightly, pointing my soul blade at my chest. I smiled at him. "Glad we got that out of the way," I laughed. "You. Me. Me. You. I'm not really good with names."

A light flashed in the cemetery across from me, and I saw a shadow shift and waver. A second later, an enormous black panther paced around the necromancers, muscled and solid, a growl lifting from his throat. Joining him was a large white dog. I could have been mistaken, but I swear Lance looked mildly impressed.

"You think your mongrels are going to save you?" asked Lord Krull, his voice dripping with disdain. "You are a fool," he laughed. "The priest was a fool. He thought he could stop The Passage, change the prophecy. And when he threatened to expose our work, I killed him. He thought his faith would save him. He was wrong. And I took his life because it was mine to take."

A slip of anger fluttered through me. "So, you're the one. You killed Father Martin."

Lord Krull smiled wickedly. "You are weak. Just like him. Just a useless sack of meat contains you," said the necromancer, his voice unchanged by our threat. "This," he lifted his skeletal arms, gesturing toward us, "is entirely inconsequential. It means nothing. Your existence means nothing. But I'll give you certainty, Hunter. This time, I *will* kill you."

I cocked my hip. "Yeah. Not going to happen."

When Gareth stepped out from behind me, Lord Krull's face paled, which was weird since he was already as pale as paper. Now he looked somewhat transparent.

The High necromancer's lips moved, like he was trying to form the words of his utter disbelief, but none would come. I could see the questions racing behind his eyes—the distrust of what he was seeing, the fear, and then the rage. The other necromancers shifted from confident to nervous, not understanding what they saw on their leader's face. But I did.

My grin widened. "Surprise! I come with gifts."

Gareth snorted a few feet away. "You are crazy."

"I know."

Lord Krull didn't seem pleased with my performance. I didn't care. He stepped closer, probably to try and scare me. The size of his nose would do the job.

He raised his voice to a dangerous tempo. "I will destroy you this night, Hunter. You and all of your friends."

I laughed in his face. "You might with your stink. Damnit, man. Do you not believe in bathing?" I told him, and I pinched my face at the rolls of what I could only describe as misty sewer cologne. "Thank god I had my shots this month."

Lord Krull blinked. When he opened his eyes again, they were completely white. "Cilerg Enitz," snarled the necromancer, the scent of rot and sulfur filling my nose until my eyes watered.

Here we go.

"Now!" I shouted as I leaped forward and landed a sidekick in the old man's gut. He let out a grunt and stumbled back.

And then we were moving.

All of us. Like a rehearsed dance of death, we struck. And we struck hard and fast. We weren't going to give the necromancers the chance to invoke their Death magic. Even with Death being empty of souls, I had a feeling they could still draw some of their power. Best not to let them.

Gareth exploded into motion. He was truly the wizard elf, his long black trench coat flapping around him as he hit two necromancers at once with his elf dust like a semi-automatic weapon. Both their eyes rolled in the backs of their heads and crumbled to the ground.

A rush of shouts rose, and then Alan and his team of angel-born were there, spinning and lashing out as their soul blades gleamed in the dusk. I caught a glimpse of Shane fighting with the angel-born, his soul blade out as he followed up with a series of heavy blows. His assault was ferocious and well-calculated.

I lost sight of Layla and Danto, but I wasn't worried. Tyrius and Lance fought side by side, plowing through some necromancers and grabbing those who tried to escape by the legs to yank them back.

Me? I stayed exactly where I was. I wasn't finished.

Lord Krull straightened, his face darkened with fury. He placed himself before me, his lips moving fast in whatever Death curse he was trying to invoke. It sounded familiar. Even with the sound of battle all around me, I could hear it clearly as though Lord Krull and I were alone in a room.

He was trying to take my soul.

I know I should have snapped his neck right there and then, but I was curious. Stupid, maybe, but my curiosity got the better of me. I was waiting to see something on his face.

The necromancer leader never stopped moving his lips. Sweat sheened his forehead as his hairless brows came together.

"Igt'ra tatari!" he cried, his hands splayed, outstretched as he did. And then again. "Igt'ra tatari!"

And then, there it was. That flicker in his eyes. That moment of realization that he was out of his necromancer juice.

It was freaking beautiful.

Lord Krull's lips pulled into an ugly, beast-like snarl. "What did you do?" he spat, looking a little mad and very much like his master, Derrigor.

"I did what needed to be done. I freed the souls you stole."

He opened his mouth then closed it. "You think you've won? You haven't. You can't stop Death. You can't stop the prophecy. I am the—"

I slapped him across the face. "Enough with the prophecies. It's really getting old." I pointed a finger at him. "You need new material."

The necromancer raged, and actual spit flew from his mouth. "Hunter bitch. Those souls were mine! You had no right to take them."

"Those souls never belonged to you, you psychotic douche," I said, anger tightening all my muscles. "Look at you. You can't even twist a curse complex enough to save your own ass. You're a hack. A has-been. You're just an old man with nothing but spite and in dire need of a shower."

Fury flashed in his eyes, and he threw himself at me.

I moved instinctively and without fear, blocking and stepping forward to land a sidekick in his middle. He grunted in pain and crumbled to the ground.

"Rowyn! Look!" I heard Layla cry out.

Fear tightened my gut. I spun around, thinking a necromancer was behind me. Instead, I saw Layla, standing with her high heeled boot on the chest of a fallen necromancer, her whip tightly wrapped around his neck. His face was turning blue.

I beamed at her. "Attagirl, Layla."

She giggled, her eyes widening. "I should have brought the blue whip too."

Blue whip? The woman was nuts, but she loved her toys.

The muffled sounds of a large number of feet stomping the ground along with the grinding of joints reached me, followed by the unmistakable stench of rot.

With my weapon in hand I spun around. "Great. Someone managed to summon the dead."

A handful of zombies shambled forward, leaving long trails of dirt and slops of entrails behind them. They moved together in a rhythmic beat, and for a second I felt like I was in Michael Jackson's Thriller video. Too weird.

"They look fresh," shouted Layla. Her smile was infectious as she stepped off the either unconscious or very dead necromancer.

Yeah. They did look fresh.

"Gareth, behind you!" I shouted when one of the zombies, with half its face rotted off, grabbed the elf from behind and he rocked back.

Teeth bared, Gareth took the zombie's arm. A soft pull and a savage twist, and the arm came popping off. Using the arm as a weapon, the elf swung it and ripped the zombie's head right off.

"Wait for me!" howled Layla as she threw herself into the horde of zombies. She licked her lips before sending her whip out with a crack, slicing the head off the nearest zombie.

In a blur of black, Danto appeared. His black eyes intent, he snarled and thrashed at the zombies' heads with his claws, and the headless zombies fell like pins.

In the corner of my eye, a female necromancer ran from the battle, heading toward the exit.

Oh no, you don't.

I charged her. She saw me and drew a knife from the inside of her robe.

"That's not going to save you," I told her as I positioned myself, feet planted, ready to strike.

With her face a mix of fear and anger, she lunged with her knife, her movements clumsy and untrained. Lost in battle fury, she swung at me, her method desperate.

I sprang sideways to avoid being cut and kicked out for a leg sweep. I caught her and she went down. I kicked the knife from her hand and she cried out in pain. Oops. I might have broken her wrist. My bad.

"Need help?" Lance bounded over.

"Yeah. Watch her." I didn't want to have to kill her if I didn't need to.

"I got it." The white dog bared his teeth and sat next to her.

"Good boy." I took the time to look over the scene. Mounds of decapitated and braindead zombies littered the ground around the cemetery. Father Thomas and his priests were busy wrapping zip ties around the surviving necromancers' wrists with the help from Alan and his team of angel-born.

"Best night ever!" sang Layla as she came forward, fastening her whip on her hip. "Not one of us got hurt. Can you believe that? Those necromancers had nothin' on us. You did it, Rowyn."

"No. We did it. *All* of us."

It was true. We did it. We'd transcended all barriers and fought together as a team. With determination, we'd surmounted the greatest threat. Together, we could accomplish anything.

"What happens to the necromancers now?" asked Layla.

I stared at Father Thomas who was now in conversation with Alan. "It's up to the Council. Prison? I don't know. All I care is that they're off the streets for good."

A loud growl pulled my attention to my left. Tyrius the black panther was hunched next to Lord Krull. The old necromancer was dragging his bony ass across the ground with his hands, trying to get away from the big cat.

"I've got one more thing to do," I told her as Danto joined her. I made my way toward Tyrius.

The black panther's lips were an inch away from the necromancer's face, which was wet with sweat and twisted in fear.

"Fear looks good on you," I told him.

"Get your beast off of me!" shouted the old man.

I grinned. "Sucks, doesn't it? To be without power. Being weak. Being afraid. Now you know how those people felt when you stole their souls."

The necromancer grimaced, and his voice took on the edge of a sneer. "I am the Death Walker. I wield the power to Master Life and Death itself."

"Not anymore," I said.

"Death is a part of you too, Rowyn Sinclair," said the necromancer, his mouth twisted in a snarl. "You Hunt and then you kill. You take lives, just as we take lives. There is no difference. A life is a life. You are just like us. You play with death."

I shook my head. "I'd like to think of myself as more of a badass with some sass," I told him. "I could kill you right now, but I choose not to. Maybe it's the wrong choice, but it's still my choice."

"You're going to regret this," spat the necromancer.

I looked into his eyes and smiled. "Not today," I said, and then I punched him hard on his left temple.

Lord Krull's eyes widened, his mouth opened in a moan, and then he collapsed in a jumble of limbs and black cloth.

CHAPTER
33

It was the perfect day for a wedding. The sky was a cloudless periwinkle blue, the sun high above me, and rays of sunlight slipped through the leaves of the giant oak trees that framed my gran's backyard. Their leaves rustled, and a warm August breeze brought forth the smell of rosebushes and freshly cut grass.

The sound of soft jazz music slipped over the happy chatter outside the pavilion tent and I smiled. It was a glorious day. And I couldn't have been happier.

A few hours ago, my gran's backyard had been frantic with last-minute details and rushing about. She'd been red in the face, a glass of white wine in her hand, as she barked out orders.

It had to be perfect.

Forget the idea of a traditional white dress. Layla wore a blood-red gothic gown with a tight corset bodice and layers of lace and silk that swooped around her. Her dark hair was piled atop of her head in an intricate crown braid, a weave of red ribbons woven through it. She looked magical. She looked like a queen.

Danto, well, he had to match of course. He wore a red suit of the finest silk, which glistened in the sun and rippled like water. He'd made the effort to button up his shirt, but his toes peered from under the cuff of his pants. He was true to himself.

Their hands were interlaced, and they hadn't let each other go since the ceremony had ended.

Yup. Layla and Danto had finally tied the knot—in my gran's backyard.

I always thought outdoor weddings were the most beautiful. It was a small wedding, with only family and friends, which was perfect since my gran's backyard could only fit maybe twenty people comfortably. Throw in six baal demons and a white German Shepard, and it was a full house.

Once Layla and Danto had given us the good news, my grandmother had offered to marry the pair and I'd helped her fill out the ordination application online so she could officiate the wedding. A church wedding was out of the question, for obvious reasons—the most obvious being that both had demonic blood in their veins. It hadn't bothered Layla one bit, as she'd much preferred this type of outdoorsy wedding.

Father Thomas was congratulating the happy couple. He'd been invited, of course, and stood handsome as ever in his usual black priest ensemble.

Four weeks had passed since we'd put an end to the necromancer threat. As far as we knew, the soulless, or rather the victims, didn't make mention of their trip into Death or the necromancers. Perhaps, without having demonic blood in their veins like Gareth, the humans didn't remember what had happened to them. Or so it would seem. Or maybe they didn't want to remember and just wanted to put everything behind them.

The National Guard had been called off that same night, as the so-called infected had all miraculously healed. No traces of the virus. Granted, they still had to get checked over at different New York hospitals, but waiting for hours to see a doctor was a hell of a lot better than not having a life at all.

Laughs echoed around the garden and I looked over to see Kaia riding on Lance's back, squealing in delight as she cried, "Yee-haw!" She was just like her dad, this one. I laughed. The baal kids were taking turns riding the poor angel like a horse. But Lance didn't seem to mind. In fact, the dog looked happy and content.

Tyrius and the angel dog had bonded over the past few weeks. They'd fought together, battling the same enemy, and now, truth be told, they looked like besties.

My heart almost broke from happiness, and I blinked fast so I wouldn't tear up.

"So, people," Tyrius sprawled on the grass next to me and Gareth. "When are you two going to tie the knot?"

I nearly spat out my wine. I took a careful swallow, aware that Gareth was smiling. "Um… what?" My heart was racing, and I wished it would stop doing that.

Tyrius snorted, his whiskers twitching in a smile. "You heard me. You two lovebirds are made for each other. The next logical step is… you know…" he angled his head towards Layla and Danto. "That. I mean, I got hitched." He waved a paw at Kora whose white fur seemed to glow in the sun as she waved back. "Best thing that ever happened to me."

"Hmmm." And I remembered the baal not telling me he was married for years. But I thought it best not to bring that up.

Gareth's smile widened, and I wished he'd stop that.

Tyrius gave me a look that said he wasn't done with this conversation. "Well. Gotta go. Lance promised the kids a two-legged race later."

"How're you going to manage that?" I laughed. "You all have four legs."

The cat beamed. "It's a secret. If you wanna know, you'll just have to watch." And with that, the Siamese cat bounded away across the yard to his family.

I felt eyes on me and knew my face was probably the color of Layla's dress. "What?"

The elf's smile was radiant, the kind that made my stomach do serious flip-flops. "I've never seen you in a dress before. You're beautiful."

Oh… demon balls. Why did he have to say that? Now I was all mushy and I knew I had a goofy smile plastered on my face.

I looked down at the new dress I'd bought for the wedding. It was a pale pink chiffon halter dress that fit snuggly over my curves and flowed to my ankles. I'd picked it out with Layla's help. I never thought I'd be caught dead in a dress. But as soon as I'd slipped it on, I knew this was the one for me.

Now the only one who could get me out of it was Gareth.

I looked into the elf's eyes and opened my mouth to say something sexy—

"Gareth! I need you!" came my grandmother's wail from across the backyard.

Gareth never stopped smiling as he got up. "I'll get you some more wine," he said and took my empty glass from my hand. Then, when I thought he was about to leave, he bent down and kissed me.

It wasn't a fierce kiss with a fiery passion or a hurried one. No, this kiss was full of love, compassion, and a promise. And when he pulled away, I thought I was going to burst into tears. Thank the souls I could control myself.

I watched the sexy elf waltz over to my gran who was in charge of the wine. I didn't know who put her in charge. Probably her.

I'd never really given any thought to marrying Gareth. Okay, yes, that was a total lie. I *had* thought about it a few times. Still, I didn't need a ring or a piece of paper to justify or recognize what I felt in my heart.

Who knew? Maybe one day, it'd be me in a dress in my gran's backyard, saying yes to the very best of men.

One day.

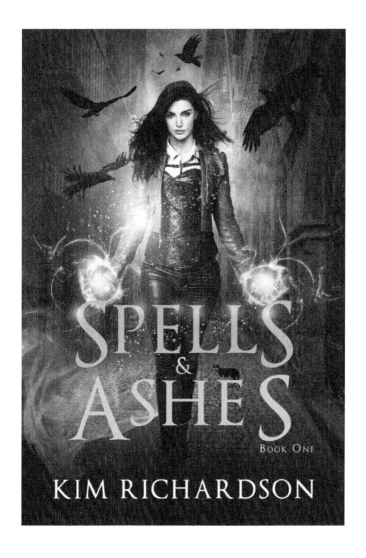

CHAPTER

1

The demon was fast. Damn fast.

It had dragged me all through the streets of Upper East Side Manhattan, snaking through the backwoods of Central Park to finally arrive in Hell's Kitchen.

Groaning, I forced my legs to keep working, my lungs starving for air as I tried to ignore the cramp pinching at my side.

I didn't get paid enough for this crap.

This would be my tenth exorcism this month. No, I'm not talking about heads spinning while spewing out fountains of pea soup. That's Hollywood. This is real life, and demonic possession is very real.

It happened when a demon hitched a ride inside a person's body, making them do obscene things and act out of character, all the while sucking on their lifeforce until they eventually dropped dead.

There had been a sudden influx of demons the past two weeks in New York City. Rumors had it that an unusually large Rift—a tear in the Veil, the dividing line between humans and the Netherworld demons—had opened, and thousands of demons had escaped through it.

It had been a busy month for the city of New York in terms of demon parasites, but that didn't mean the city was free of other demons. Hell no. There were a lot of creepier crawlers and things far worse than your average body-snatching demon bastards. Still, tonight I was graced with the presence of yet another demon.

There was no way in hell a fourteen-year-old human girl could run that fast for so long without having to stop and catch her breath. The demon inside her was running her down, pushing her body to an extreme no human could endure. It had stolen her body and now ran it like a puppet on strings, feeding on her lifeforce. If I didn't get to her soon, the girl's body would collapse and she would die, leaving the demon to consume her soul and then human-hop into another poor bastard. Typically possessions happened when humans were stupid enough to play at summoning demons in exchange for the usual crap—money, fame, sex. Still, I couldn't let her die.

Unlike demons or other half-breeds blessed with supernatural speed and endurance, I had to rely on my bursts of sweet adrenaline and my profound hatred for body-snatching demons to fuel my legs. I was fit, but I wasn't an athlete. My mortal body could only endure so much, and if I didn't banish the demon soon, I was going to drop dead of exhaustion.

I'd been hired by the dark witch court to keep tabs on the Veil, mostly on hunting and banishing whatever demon or supernatural baddy came through. The pay wasn't great, but it took care of the bills and helped me keep my family home, which was all I needed.

Demons were always tampering with the Veil. They'd pierce it and manage to cross over to our world to feast on a few human souls. Days like the solstice or full moons, when the Veil was at its thinnest, resulted in a larger outpour of demons.

That's where I came in.

I'd blast them back to the Netherworld. Fire usually did the trick. A couple of fireballs later and the demons were back in their world, leaving the mortal world a little safer.

I hated nothing more than a body-snatching demon. Okay, maybe *two* body-snatching demons. The fact remained, I loathed them. There was something utterly disturbing about being trapped in your own body while someone else piloted it around and you couldn't do a damn thing about it. I wouldn't stand for it. I would rip that demon out of her through her throat if I had to.

I caught a flicker of movement across the darkened street and turned to see a shadow retreat. Julia, the girl, disappeared through a door at the bottom of a six-story apartment building on West 46th street. Good. I couldn't exorcise a demon openly in the streets of New York City, not without getting my ass arrested and my face splattered all over social media.

I took a deep breath and followed her.

A few humans blurred past me as I ran up the street. Humans—blissfully ignorant of the paranormal dangers and horrors that surrounded them. The Veil acted like a glamour, changing the way things looked to human eyes and preventing them from seeing the paranormal world and its inhabitants. Must be nice to wake up each morning with only your bills and mortgage and kids to worry about. Not the giant winged ugnur demon that slipped through a Rift and decided to feast on your brain because, well, that's what they do.

Exhaust fumes, hot pavement and the stench of garbage displaced the night air as I ran across the street. The gathering dark rushed in to fill the spaces where the streetlights couldn't reach. There were no lights in the windows, which was the perfect breeding grounds for demons who thrived in darkness. In turn, the darkness fed them with power. But that didn't stop me.

By the time I reached the apartment building, my heart wanted to explode through my chest to say hello to the concrete slab at my feet. Damn.

You'd think by now I would have made a charm for endurance and speed. I made a mental note to look into that when I got home. A pair of super-legs would have been golden right about now.

Pinching the cramp at my side, I gulped down buckets of air, feeling slightly dizzy, and pulled open the door. I stepped into the darkened lobby and stopped to listen. The faint whisper of water running through pipes answered back. Then nothing. The dim scent of sulfur lay on the air. I smiled. My demon.

The lobby led into an equally dark hallway—a recipe for more trouble. But I never followed recipes.

With my heart pounding in my ears, I stepped forward, and the sound of glass crunching under my boots stopped me dead in my tracks. I looked to the side wall, and as my eyes adjusted to the darkness, I could make out the two adjacent light fixtures, their glass bulbs shattered.

Not knowing which apartment door the demon had slipped through, I ran to the first door on the first floor and checked the knob. Locked. I hissed in frustration. It would take me hours to check all the doors in this place. Julia didn't have that long.

I made my way forward again and then hesitated for a moment at the corner of the hall. The soft click of a metal door opening and then closing reached me.

Bingo.

I was running. As I rounded the corner, I saw a door with a faded sticker denoting 6A. Soft yellow light shone from the gap between the floor and the door. I went to the door and tried the knob. It rolled freely.

"Gotcha," I whispered.

My pulse pounded and I opened the door as quietly as I could to step inside. The air was filled with the stench of blood. The apartment was of moderate size by New York City standards, lit with nothing more than a few candles on the wood floor. The burning candles lit the walls with dark, vague and creepy shadows. Great.

The ceilings were at least ten feet high, and the walls were covered with wallpaper straight out of the eighties. Chairs, tables, and a desk were strewn against the walls, as though to make a larger space in the middle of the apartment. And then I saw why.

A large stone circle lay in the middle of the room. The stones were small, the size of my thumb, and bone white. Six black chicken heads were spread evenly around the circle, and in the middle was a black lamb's head above a blood-drawn triangle. Strange runes I'd never seen before were written in fresh blood inside the circle, suggesting more of pagan ritual than your modern demon summoning. Creepy.

I took another step forward for a better look.

A girl stepped into my line of sight. Gone was the healthy, happy girl I'd seen in the photo. Her hair hung limp and greasy over her dirty face. Her body was thin, almost gaunt, and her limbs, what I could see of them through her clothes, were stained and dirty. Her jeans and t-shirt were speckled in blood, but I couldn't tell if it was her own or someone else's. The flesh on her face was sunken and the bones sharp, leaving her black eyes feral and unsettling. They watched me with unrelenting rage. She was pissed.

That made two of us.

I knew if I didn't move I was dead. I didn't have time for small talk. Moving on instinct, I dropped to my knees, pulled out my chalk and began to draw a circle with a seven-point star in the middle—the exorcism sigil.

Exorcisms were the highest level of hard magic. Deadly, if you didn't do it right. With an inexperienced priest or witch, more times than not the human died in a rivulet mess of blood and guts.

But I'd been doing this for more than a decade now, and I knew my craft. And I was going to kick this demon's ass back to the Netherworld where it belonged.

There was power in words, magic words, just like there was power in sigils and seals. If you knew how to use them. Not many witches did, though. You needed to be precise in your drawing of them. One little squiggle out of place could send you to the Netherworld or cause you to end up with your head on backwards. Yeah, that happened to a witch down the block before I was born. Since then, witches had grown frightened of the power of sigils. They didn't trust them, but I trusted them more than I trusted blood magic. Sigils were like math and art. You did your calculations and then you did your drawing.

I'd screwed up a few times in the beginning, but I wasn't stupid enough to try complicated sigils at first. No, I started with the typical easy sigil, like a hovering teacup sigil or paint your toenails blue sigil. My toenails had disappeared completely the first time I'd tried. Oops. Thank God it had been winter so no one had to know or see me, Sam the toenail-less idiot.

I was now so good at my sigils that I'd scanned them into the computer and printed out copies. Yes. They worked just as well and saved me the time to draw them up when I was in a hurry.

But I had an advantage over the other witches. My grandpa always said I had a knack for them. I was an artist. I loved to draw and paint, so images came naturally to me just like breathing. My sigils were each a piece of art, and I'd put my energy and time into create them. They were beautiful. And powerful.

But I was also lazy.

When I realized that one sigil was the equivalent in power to hours and hours of spell reciting and reading and then some more conjuring, I opted for the sigils. Why spend hours on a transmutation spell when I could draw the transmutation sigil in thirty seconds flat.

Hence came my passion for Goetia. I'd already mastered the sigils—the drawing and the energy that came from them—so it was time to turn things up a notch.

Sweat beaded on my forehead as I drew quickly as I could without making a mistake. I couldn't screw up now because a mistake could cost me my life, and Julia's.

I brought the chalk up and around, adding three smaller stars inside the circle and making the connections. My pulse quickened, and I strained with effort to keep my hand from shaking from the shots of adrenaline.

Next, I spelled out the word exilium, the Latin word for banishment in each of the three stars. Where I should have put the demon's name, I left it blank. It would have been easier with its name, but I'd done countless exorcisms before successfully without a name. I knew it would work.

The air cracked with electricity. The hairs on my arms rose.

I looked up. Demon-Julia's lips were moving.

Ah. Hell.

A blast of energy hit me in the chest and I shot backwards, hitting the wall at thirty miles an hour. I heard something crack, possibly my skull, as I slid to the ground.

"Ow."

I'd yet to meet a slobbering demon polite enough to wait for me to finish setting my banishment sigils.

The girl giggled. No. Not the girl, but the demon that was riding in her body.

"You need to be quicker with your scribbles, you half-breed bitch," said the demon, its voice harsh and guttural. It sounded disturbingly like a serpentine whisper and had the hairs on the back on my neck rising. That was not a teenage girl's voice, but I was glad it was using English. My Enochian—the angel and demon language—was a little rusty.

"Thanks for the tip." I pitched forward on my stomach, sliding to my circle. With my chalk, I wrote exilium in the last triangle, finishing the sigil.

With my heart pounding in my ears, I glanced back at demon-Julia. She stood in the same spot, grinning at me like I'd just finished doing her laundry. The demon hadn't tried to stop me a second time. That wasn't a good sign.

I shook my head. "You could at least pretend I'm scary. You know, for the overall dramatical effect that I'm about to kick your ass back to the Netherworld. A little shaking would be nice. Tears are best."

The demon-Julia crossed her arms over her chest and showed me her teeth. "I'm going to take my time with you," she sneered. "I'm in a good mood, see. I'm going to start with your arms and rip them off one at a time." She showed me more teeth. "I'll let you watch while I eat your arms and your legs. Then, I'm going to suck your brain out through your eyes, witch bitch."

Nice. Okay then.

I scrambled to my feet and drew upon the energy gathered in the sigil. It grew along with a buzzing in my ears and a prickling along the back of my neck. I was going to fry that demon.

"In the name of our Lord creator," I chanted, bringing forth the energy and molding it. I shaped it into the effect I was looking for with my thoughts, fiercely picturing the exorcism sigil. "I exorcise you, demon," I added fiercely, my stance strong. "Every impure spirit, every demonic power, every incursion of the infernal adversary. I command you." I raised my right palm and said firmly, "Flee this place! Flee this body! May your power issue forth from her. Be not and be gone!"

At the words, the energy poured out of me in a rush. There were no lights, no glowing energy or anything else that would cost a special effects company a crap load of money, just a tingling in the air like tiny electrical currents and a burst of wind.

I staggered as the sigil's energy roared out of me and almost lost my balance.

It hit demon-Julia.

She stumbled back, shock replacing her smile and her features growing distant. She thrashed, her head shaking as she kept muttering the same word, over and over again—*no*. She froze with a frightening suddenness, and her body eased into relaxation. Then her shoulders shook as she began to laugh.

"Told you so," said demon-Julia, a smile in her voice. "Your witch tricks won't work on me."

Damn. This was really not my night. I flicked my gaze back at my sigil. It was fine. Perfect, even drawn under duress. So why hadn't it worked?

Breathing hard, I sagged with a bit of tiredness. Channeling so much energy through me was like running a marathon, and a sudden weakness in my limbs made me sway.

But I wasn't giving up. Not today. Not ever. And not when a young girl's life was at stake.

Jaw clenched, I took a step towards the demon until we were but ten feet apart, focusing on the energy I was still channeling through the sigil.

I took a shaking breath and said, "In the name of our Lord—"

A hard burst of energy hit me, sending me across the room. I landed sprawled on my butt with my legs in the air. Not pretty. My head smashed against the ground a moment later, complete with a burst of black spots in my vision and very real pain. My palms curled into claws as I panted through the pain and tasted blood in my mouth. My concentration vanished, and with it, some of my nerve.

Did I mention this was seriously *not* my night?

"You have no power over me, half-breed," laughed the demon, a sneer to her voice.

My magic didn't work. The exorcism that should have released the girl did absolutely nothing. Head pounding like I'd hit it with a sledgehammer, I blinked and rolled over to my side.

Demon-Julia walked over to me and snarled, "I'm going to feast on your flesh, little witch."

Oh. Shit.

ABOUT THE AUTHOR

KIM RICHARDSON is the award-winning author of the bestselling SOUL GUARDIANS series. She lives in the eastern part of Canada with her husband, two dogs and a very old cat. She is the author of the SOUL GUARDIANS series, the MYSTICS series, and the DIVIDED REALMS series. Kim's books are available in print editions, and translations are available in over seven languages.

To learn more about the author, please visit:
www.kimrichardsonbooks.com

Printed in Great Britain
by Amazon

21399098R00195